Dead Set

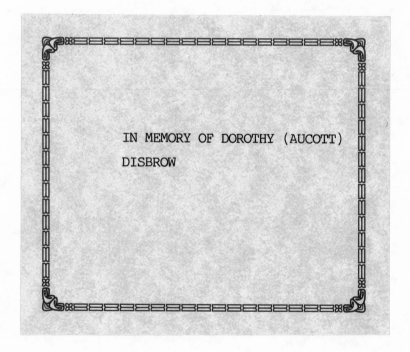

IN MEMORY OF DOROTHY (AUCOTT)

DISBROW

K

Dead Set

Jennie Melville

St. Martin's Press
New York

Library of Congress Cataloging-in-Publication Data

Melville, Jennie.
    Dead set : a Charmian Daniels mystery / Jennie Melville.
      p.   cm.
    "A Thomas Dunne book."
    ISBN 0-312-08757-8
    I. Title.
  PR6065.E44D43   1993
  823'.914—dc20   92-33851
                                                CIP

First Published in Great Britain by MACMILLAN LONDON LIMITED.

First U.S. Edition: January 1993
10 9 8 7 6 5 4 3 2 1

Dead Set

FILOFACE

In the Diary on the police computer which dealt with the Farmer murder was a file called FILOFACE. This was a compilation, made up to date as necessary, which extracted all the details relevant to the character of the murderer from which the computer put together a picture. Sometimes days might pass without much addition.

At the beginning there was little in FILOFACE except for the date of the killing and the suggestion that the killer might be local. Or someone who knew Windsor well.

No literary skill was employed and the comments were brief.

Later events added more material and showed that there were several things right with this picture and several wrong.

1

1 Patches of oil on the stretch of grass behind the trees and bushes which circled the Crimean War Memorial.
2 Suggest the killer might have used a car parked there, either to transport the body or to kill her in it.
3 Faint indications of tyre marks confirm this.
4 Traces of footsteps, possibly of victim and or killer. Overlaid by footprints of Edward Gray. Deliberately?
5 Traces of mud and leaf mould on victim's knees. Fell? Knelt? Or pushed down.
   Killer: a local man who owned and drove a car.

CHAPTER ONE

Early April and a cold season

Charmian Daniels said that any case involving a child was a beast, but in this case there were sixteen, one of them seeing visions.

All the children were at the one school, St Catherine's, Temple Grove, Merrywick, near Windsor.

Mary Erskine walked down the road where she lived in the famous town which nestled beneath the great castle of Windsor. She had lived here all her life, inheriting the family home. Her parents were not dead, but had removed themselves to the warmer climate of Corfu, where they cultivated their famous gardens. They came home occasionally for the winter which was apparently easier to bear in London where you expected to be cold than in Greece where you did not.

Mary walked slowly because she was weighed down with shopping after a visit to her favourite supermarket (Bunji's Cave, run by a charming man from Pakistan, who stocked all the rich indigestible foods she loved, but she never put on an ounce of weight), and because she was thoughtful.

It was unusual for any inhabitant of this pleasant world to have murder on the mind, but at this moment, several people had. In fact, more than was understood or guessed at.

'Oh yes,' a fellow guest (Prudence Damiani, batting her gossip-bright eyes) had said to Mary Erskine at the last drinks party in the Castle precincts, 'of course, Mary darling, you live in Chapel Close, that's where the body was, isn't it? What's it like, having the police on the doorstep?'

'The body was just around the corner, not in the road,' Mary had explained, carefully, defensively. 'And they haven't been on the doorstep. Rather nice men, actually.' Attractive in their way. Mary regarded herself as a good judge of that quality.

The spring afternoon was wet and windy, so that Mary quickened her step, eager to get home.

A florist's van was delivering an arrangement of flowers at Colonel Dalrymple's. That was interesting and the reason did not seem obvious. Jamie Dalrymple was not ill or about to be married as far as she knew and had last been seen playing polo in the Great Park, at which game he was known as a high-scoring player. Something to think about there.

Mary knew all of the people who lived in Chapel Close, and took a kindly if dispassionate interest in their lives, she could usually guess what was going on. Sometimes before they knew themselves, she thought. As for example the way she had known before her parents that Delphine Gillot was on drugs because she had met her in the bank cashing a large (and as it turned out illegal and forged on her mother's account) cheque. Delphine had been sent to a clinic for a cure. Not much hope there, she thought, she had been at school with Delphine, who was distantly related to her, and one way and another Delph had been hooked on something since kindergarten. Take away the drugs and she would be on something else. The Gillots were about to go on tour in a Rattigan revival: they acted. On stage and off. They were not worrying about Delphine, but Mary was, she had a strong guilt feeling to contend with there.

There was scaffolding up at Mrs Curzon's, the roof this time, she observed. Last time it had been the garden wall. Poor Mrs Curzon. Good job she was rich. Curzons Teas, it had been. And the odd coal-mine or two, in the days when people had owned coal-mines, now the money was comfortably invested all round the world. No, she wasn't sorry for Mrs Curzon, it gave her something to think about, other than checking her entry in *Debrett*. An awful lot of scaffolding, Mary noticed, and a builder from London plus an architect, must be more than the roof, but of course houses of this age were bound to need attention. Chapel Close had been built before Queen Victoria was born and when her wicked old uncles were still shocking London society so it had seen a lot of life one way and another.

She passed along the road with her easy, athletic tread; she was a tall girl. There was Mrs Arbuthnot, dead-heading her daffodils. Pity about the granddaughter, but babies were babies when all was said and done, and a good thing. No one bothered these days whether they were born in wedlock or out of it. Mary Erskine herself had several friends who used to be called unmarried mothers and were now called single parents. She even knew a single father and admired him for his skills. She thought Mrs Arbuthnot ought to be grateful to be a great-grandmother at her age. And in any case, hadn't Zelia Arbuthnot herself let something out after two strong cocktails at a party in the Castle about the state of her virginity (or absence of) on her wedding night. 'The gin talking there,' a Canon of the Chapel had whispered in Mary's ear with a sly eccleciastical giggle.

A small group of children, boys and girls, wearing the wasp-coloured striped blazers of St Cath's School, passed round the Circus on their way home and Mary waved. She knew most of them.

It was the top class in the junior department, all six of them, going home a bit early because their class teacher was off sick. All friends, walking together. Pix, Peter Xavier Prescott, lagged behind.

'He's thinking.' He had the reputation of being a thinker.

'It's his baby sister . . . He doesn't like her very much.'

But Pix was not thinking about his infant sister, although she was at the bottom of his darker thoughts; he was thinking about grown-ups and what liars and disappearers they were. His parents, Phyllida and Ian, were both of those things, constantly telling him slight untruths and going off without saying where. It was unsettling.

He had spoken to his mother: 'Can a person split into two and be in two places at once?'

Pix's mother, an economist working for a top firm of bankers, had laughed, she believed in being straight with her children: 'Oh, the *doppelgänger* effect? Yes, it's an interesting idea. I shouldn't worry, my darling, it may be just an intellectual concept. You're not likely to come across one.'

11

Pix had not been pleased. It was very nice not to be talked down to, but sometimes a chap wanted a simple, reassuring statement, such as No, dear, no one can be in two places at once.

The whole group of them saw and gave a wave to Mary Erskine, who waved back without breaking her walk down Chapel Close.

Sir Humphrey Kent (knighted in the last Birthday Honours List) lived in the next house Mary passed, but he was away in Washington on one of those interesting trips he was so secretive about, and his house was let. To nice tenants though, Americans, but Mary knew disappointingly little of their lives. They kept their house clean themselves, so they were not done for by Mrs Templeman who sped up and down the road on her cycle, doing an hour here and a half a day here and passing the gossip round with the dust. Nor did they employ Joe, the jobbing gardener who jobbed where he willed and sometimes where his employers wished he would not: he had a steady, firm hand with pruning shears and a strong desire to subdue the roses. He and Mary had had many a tussle over the bushes, not all of which she had won. So she moved her thoughts on two doors to where Una Gray lived with her husband and two dogs. No children. Pity, Mary thought. Like many unmarried people, she was in the habit of thinking of children as a cure, although all her married friends assured her it was quite otherwise.

Trouble there, oh there was trouble.

Mary Erskine paused at her garden in Chapel Close and looked back along the road to where she could see her neighbour slowly and greyly making for her own house. She was at the gate, but standing still and not trying to lift the hatch.

Mary set down her heavy basket while she waited. 'Never carry a shopping basket,' her mother had said to her child just before fleeing the country. 'Not what People Like Us do. You can be laden down with parcels, darling, have them dangling from your little finger – that's rather chic, actually, dearest, but never a shopping-bag or basket.'

Mary Erskine had long since abandoned this upper class advice, along with such motherly dictums as, 'Always wait for the man to open the door for you.' (Only they never did.) Or, 'Always let the man make the first move.' (Not likely, why be a shy virgin?) Try carrying a piece of cod for the cat on your little finger, mamma, she thought, or half a pound of soft butter. Thus déclassé but happy and perfectly adjusted to her world, Mary conducted her life according to rules which suited her.

She tucked her shopping into the shelter of her garden hedge, praying that the local wandering cat would not steal her supper, and turned back to Una.

I'll talk to Oonie, Mary Erskine told herself. I'll talk to her and make her talk back. Tell me what it's all about. She trusts me. I think she trusts me.

Una did trust Mary Erskine, she didn't trust many people but she did trust her.

Everyone liked Mary Stuart Dalmeny Erskine: the monarch and her court, the Dean and his chapter, the General and the foot-soldier, and all her neighbours, they all liked her. The very policeman on duty at the Castle knew her and liked her and that was something because although he remembered all faces, he kept emotion well out of it.

'No luck, Oonie?'

Una Gray shook her head. 'He wasn't there.' She dragged her grey raincoat round her more closely. The gate still seemed to be defeating her.

If only Una would wear some brighter clothes sometimes, thought Mary. She's in perpetual half-mourning. She could be so pretty, with those lovely big blue eyes, she is pretty, but she seems to have given up trying lately. You had to try, even beauties had to try.

No wonder Teddy went away. If he had gone, she had once or twice had the unnerving feeling that he was still there, tucked away in the Gray house, not coming out. 'Let me open the gate for you.'

'I'm so cold, you see.' Una held out her hand for sympathy. 'My fingers won't work.'

She was huddled in her grey coat like a little mouse. Mrs Mouse, thought Mary, as she dealt briskly with the gate. 'It's not that cold.' And not raining either, no need for the raincoat.

'Come on, inside with you.' The house was cold too. Would be, of course, didn't look as if Una had been in it all day. Not much housework done either. A pity because she had lovely things. Mary had good pieces of furniture, pictures and china herself (all inherited) and knew quality when she saw it. 'What have you been doing to get as cold as that?'

'Waiting.'

'Where this time?'

'At the railway station.'

'What, again? I thought you'd decided not to wait around any more.'

'He said he might be there.'

'Again? And you believed it? How many times has he had you waiting at the station because he might be there? Three times.'

'This is the third time,' said Una mildly. She was putting on the kettle. 'Before that it was only twice.'

'I can count. Twice was enough.' Once would have been enough for that game. 'Why do you go?'

'I want him back.'

'What's it all about, Oonie? Tell me. There's more than you're saying.'

All she knew was that Ted Gray had left his home and not come back. Husbands did not go missing in this quiet street. If the news got about, it would cause a sensation.

Una got some cups out. 'Tea?' she said.

'Oonie!'

Mary had known Una Gray almost all her adult life, she had been Una Dalmeny, a kind of remote cousin of Mary's, and she had known Ted since their marriage some six years ago. Una was a teacher in a distinguished private preparatory school and Ted was a historical researcher, checking facts for busy biographers. Ghost writing, he called it; he too taught in the school occasionally, giving talks on history to the top class. The money helped, although both of the Grays had small private incomes. Ted and Una were in their late thirties, some ten years older than Mary Dalmeny Erskine herself.

'I've told you. Ted went off, didn't say why, and we hadn't quarrelled. And since then he has sent messages telling me to meet him at the station off the train from Waterloo.'

'And he has never turned up. How does he send these messages? That's something you've never been very clear about. And why. Come on, Oonie, there has to be a reason. Why don't you talk about it. You can trust me.'

14

'I do trust you. And I've told you, just told you.'

'Oh come on,' said Mary. 'There's got to be more.' I could shake her, she thought.

Both ladies lived in Chapel Close, the small half-circle of houses that nestles at the foot of the Castle Hill, looked down upon by the great Norman tower of the royal castle in Windsor. The houses curve round a grass centre which is called the Circus and in the middle of which is a bronze statue of a small Greek god holding a bow, but no arrows, he lost them some time ago, in the early nineteenth century to a group of Dr Keating's scholars from Eton, in the old days before disciplines were tightened.

Mary Erskine was the only one to hold the freehold of her dwelling in Chapel Close. Una Gray rented her house from the Royal Estates. It was something of a mystery how the Erskines came to have this valuable freehold, but tradition had it that long ago a royal lover and royal mistress came into it. They had had their place in the register of Royal Bastards tucked away in the royal archives. Not on the Erskine side of the family, not their style but possibly a Stuart Dalmeny daughter, they were known to be a free and easy lot. Mad, some of them.

Mary stirred her tea. Marriage, she thought, husbands. Unpredictable. So far no one had tempted her into the state of matrimony although many had tried. She had her own hopes, however, of someone she could love; you have to try.

I'm a romantic, she told herself, have been ever since I saw *Cinderella* when I was six. I'm waiting for the Transformation Scene. I'm waiting for my Prince. A duke would do. English preferably, but a French duke would be acceptable. She could think of someone, but he didn't seem to fancy her. Work on it, Mary, she told herself, all is fair in love and war.

She sipped her tea. Una had offered her weak Earl Grey in a porcelain cup. Just like Una to produce such a well-bred cup. Yes, she would settle for a French duke. Duc et pair de France. It had a nice ring.

She watched Una holding her cup in both hands, her face miserable. Marriage hadn't done much for her. Rather the reverse.

'He sends a postcard,' Una said suddenly. 'Second-class post. Always posted in London. Can't work out where he is from that.'

'May not even be in London,' said Mary.

'Absolutely.'

'So what does he say on the card?'

'Just meet me off the train. And he gives the time. Never been the same train.'

'And he's never been on it either.'

'No.'

'You must be getting well known at Windsor station.'

'There are two stations,' said Una humbly.

'Don't tell me you run between the two.' Uphill work it would be.

'No, Ted indicates which it's to be.'

Mary shook her head. 'There's no doing anything with you.'

'I love him. Ted's a good man . . . But he hasn't been himself for some time, not since he found the girl's body.'

Ted Gray was a quite, meditative man, the last person you'd think would stumble over a murder victim. But one who would mind if he did. Yes, she conceded that much.

Ted, walking home at night from the lower of the two Windsor railway stations – the one with the initials of Victoria and her Consort proudly displayed on the outside – had found a girl's body lying on the patch of grass near a memorial to a dead prince. She had been strangled.

'He can't get over it. He has dreams. Sees things.'

Mary put down her cup. 'He ought to see a doctor, that's who he ought to see.' Not run away from home and keep sending messages to his poor and puzzled wife. Good job she had some money of her own or she would be hard-up as well as worried. Errant husbands never thought of that practicality.

Una went to the window to look out. Lady Darbyshire's cat was stalking a tiny fledgling bird, which sat there, motionless, transfixed with terror. She knew how the bird felt. If that baby bird did not learn to fly away, it would soon be a dead bird. She turned round to face Mary.

'He thinks the police suspect him of killing her.'

'Oh surely not.'

'They probably do. He found her, that's always suspicious.'

We must tell him not to do that again, thought Mary, suppressing an unhelpful desire to giggle. She considered the situation.

16

'I don't think they can do. If they do suspect you, seriously that is, then I think they ask you to hang around. They didn't ask Ted to do that?'

'No.'

Almost a pity, Mary thought, it might have stopped all this going on. But she kept this thought to herself.

Instead, she said: 'I still think he ought to get some help. Professional help, a psychologist or something. It was a bad experience, he had a shock, but it was a week or so ago now.'

'Shock takes time to wear off,' said Una. She went to a bureau and got out two photographs and held them out to Mary.

'Ted had his camera with him, the sort that takes instant photographs . . . He took pictures of her.'

'Wasn't that strange?' The photograph showed a huddled figure on the ground, the face was not visible. Just as well, Mary thought.

'He said you had to have pictures, just for the record.'

'The police do that.'

Una fell silent.

After a while she said: 'He must be distressed. Said he felt split into two. Like being two people.'

'Sounds a bit schizo to me.'

'He's not mad,' said Una. 'But I think I might be if this goes on.' She started to wander restlessly round the room. 'I haven't done anything lately but worry about Ted and wait for him to get in touch.'

'What about the school?'

'Haven't been in. Said I was ill.'

'Won't the boss mind?'

St Catherine's School, where Una taught maths and art to the most junior forms, was a well-known private establishment owned by the headmaster, Luke Mallet. The school had a distinguished history and was now both fashionable and successful. Mary had observed Luke recently at a party in the Castle and decided he had the best profile of any man she had ever seen. He had been a good-looking boy and now he was a handsome man. Said to be good at his job, too.

Una shook her head. 'Luke's very understanding.'

Need to be with you, thought Mary. She changed the subject. 'Do they know who the girl is?'

Una shook her head. 'I expect so, but they haven't advertised it. Not yet. I telephoned the police to ask, and they said inquiries were still going on.'

'She may not have been local,' said Mary. 'Could have come from London. Or almost anywhere. Slough, Reading, Oxford, there are a lot of buses.'

'I don't think the police liked me asking.'

'Don't worry about that,' said Mary with the stout confidence of one whom the police always saluted and said, 'Good-day, m'lady.'

Una gave a sigh. 'She was so young. Only a kid. Seventeen or eighteen. And looked younger.' A sad look crossed her face. 'So Ted said.'

'Any idea where he might be staying?'

'I don't know, but I think I could guess. He's always had a little office off Bond Street. He's probably there. You aren't supposed to sleep there, but he could do.'

'Why don't you go and have a look?'

'I have thought of it . . . but he'd never let me in if he was there. I reckon if he wanted to see me, he'd be where he said when he said . . . Besides I'm proud.'

'You haven't got a key?'

'No.'

'But he's got one to here?'

'Of course.'

'Doesn't seem fair.'

'He lives here, he only works there. I work in the school. Or I did. I suppose I still do. I have a key there. But this is our home.'

It didn't feel very homelike, Mary thought. All these houses were exactly the same with three large rooms on each floor. Three floors and a basement. Mary's house was filled with furniture, inherited from several generations. She didn't think Una and Ted used more than two floors in their house, leaving the top floor empty. It felt that way. 'It's very cold in here,' said Mary, 'you need comfort. Why don't you light a fire and sit by it, with a good book. I've got a new Dick Francis I could lend you.'

Since she knew her friend was not penniless, it seemed strange to her that the house was so cold and cheerless. Not much cleaning done in the kitchen either, judging by the sour smell. Still, if you were always out looking for your husband, then you couldn't get much done, she supposed. But Una was probably rich enough to afford a housekeeper. 'Or come back with me.'

She gave a hurried thought to the food she had bought and what food she had in the house. There had been a chicken casserole, although Delphine had eaten a lot of that claiming her parents had turned her out to starve, but with salad and hot bread that might do. The Chapel Close families mucked in with each other in a genteel kind of way, feeding each other casually as needed, walking each other's animals as required, and watering the gardens. Taking in the milk, they called it.

Mary realised she was hungry herself. It had been a long day.

Una frowned. 'No. I don't want to leave the house. He might come back. Or telephone. I must be here.'

But you're not here, the whole house reeks of your absence, thought Mary. 'You ought to have a housekeeper,' she said, speaking her thoughts aloud.

'Ted and I like to be alone with each other. Or we did.'

'You don't think he's hiding from someone?'

'But from whom?' said Una.

'You two haven't got an enemy, have you?'

'Only each other.'

'Now, now.'

They sat in silence for a moment, while Una got her burst of anger under control.

Mary considered. 'Has he got a lover, do you think?'

'No,' said Una angrily. 'No, of course not. I won't believe that for a minute.'

'All right, don't.'

Una set down her cup of tea and began to cry. 'I don't understand. It's all so strange. What's going on?' Blindly she turned towards Mary.

Mary put her arms round her friend. 'Bit of a puzzle, isn't it, dear?' she said over Una's weeping head.

She felt a small shiver start inside Una. Oh God, she thought, something terrible is brewing up here and it has to do with that dead girl. She had got a whiff of the horrors to come.

Far away and long ago, a remote Dalmeny ancestress had passed on the gift of second sight to some descendants. The deeply sceptical Mary Erskine had always rejected the idea. But now she could smell blood. Yet there had been no blood on the girl. Her arms tightened around Una.

'Help me.'

'I will if I can.'

So she went to talk to her friend Charmian Daniels, who was a high-ranking policewoman and who also lived in Windsor. Sir Humphrey Kent had introduced them at a party in the Chapel Close.

'You see, there is this friend of mine, and her husband has gone off.'

Charmian started to ask questions, but there were some things Mary was not going to say.

'All I know is, he's missing. That's all I know.'

Which was not absolutely true.

CHAPTER TWO

April 10

When she spoke to Charmian, Mary Dalmeny Erskine had not told her all she knew. She knew something which she had witnessed herself; she knew something about Ted.

She had seen him in prayer.

On occasion, Mary Dalmeny Erskine acted as a guide for visitors in the Chapel of St George in Windsor, showing them around the Close and the Chapel precincts. She recalled the afternoon when, standing in for an absentee, she had been showing a group of Americans who belonged to the 'Friends of St George', and who were therefore both knowledgeable and serious viewers, some of the recent restoration work (a building the age of the fifteenth-century chapel was always in need of repairs somewhere).

Outside it had been sunny and warm, but inside the chapel it was always cool and dark. The choir had been practising an anthem that day, she remembered, and the voices had floated out from the choir-stalls by the high altar.

Ted Gray had been on his knees, tucked away behind a pillar, almost invisible in the gloom. Mary had noticed him because she knew him. A stranger might have passed by, just aware of a bent dark head.

She had found the sight of Ted the agnostic in prayer vaguely disquieting. But she had said nothing when they met later, never mentioned it to anyone.

As a matter of fact, she had never seen him since, now she came to think about it. Una yes, Ted no.

In Mary Dalmeny Erskine's simple ethics you only prayed like that if you were asking for something or if you had done something for which you wanted to be forgiven.

She wouldn't tell Charmian now. Prayer was a private matter, wasn't it?

And Charmian had such a way of seeing through an outer statement to what was unsaid inside.

She looked at Charmian Daniels, as tall as Mary herself but a good deal more slender, and, let's face it, Mary thought, rather better dressed, who was standing in her own sitting-room in Maid of Honour Row offering a drink to her visitor. 'Sherry? Gin or whisky?'

Mary caught a side view of herself in the looking-glass over the fire and smoothed her hair.

'You're tidy.'

'It's been a busy day. I should have changed out of jeans.'

'You look fine. What do you want to drink? Down, Muff.' Muff was the cat who was taking an interest in the sherry bottle. 'I think she's turning into an alcoholic.' Charmian was part-owner of a pedigree dog as well, but he only appeared on occasion, since he passed most of his day with friends of hers. As a police officer, Charmian found she did not have regular enough hours to look after a dog. Benjy, therefore, boarded out with two retired white witches who had gone into faith healing and mystic meditation.

'Whisky, I think. I feel the need of my national drink.'

'Of course, you are a Scot,' said Charmian pouring out the whisky. As she was herself, only not out of the same social drawer. But she knew what to do about whisky. She always kept a good supply of both blended and single-malt whisky: it was the favourite tipple of most of her colleagues in the Force.

'Only by inheritance.'

'What other way is there?'

'Well, living there, having a place there . . . All I've got is an old ancestor who picked up an earldom for winning a few battles against Napoleon. Or not losing them, which was more the way of it, I think.' Mary had never admired her ancestor, seen from his portrait he had a cross old face, he had married three times, and produced a large, impecunious brood of offspring. That might have accounted for the cross face, of course. 'Not much money came with the title and what there was we have more or less lost.' Mary flopped into a chair. 'I've always been poor,' she said comfortably. 'Come here, Muff, and let me stroke you.'

It was all relative, really, thought Charmian, observing Mary Erskine's confidence. What she calls poverty, I would have called riches once. Certainly, Mary, with pearl and diamond earrings just glinting through her glossy hair, her expensive jeans worn with a white silk shirt, had not the air of someone that life had rubbed.

Charmian took a quick look at herself in the glass over the fire. She appeared fit and well. This time last year, she had been in turmoil about her health and career, but she had worked all through that and come out the other side.

And Humphrey Kent was away on one of his trips which made life easier. It put off a decision about what he and what she was and what they were together. If they were together. But she knew he would soon want an answer.

Charmian was six months now into her new position. She was head of SRADIC (Southern Register, Documentation and Index of Crime) in the whole southern police area, coordinating all documentation of crime for all southern Forces, not including London, but the Met was obliged to liaise. Her unit was based in Windsor with a sub-office in Slough. She was a powerful lady, she who knows all, commands all.

That was what she told herself. There had been an attempt, secret but worked at, to put her in as Deputy Head (doing all the work, as she had commented, but getting none of the prestige), and appointing a man as Head, but she had fought that off. All or nothing, she had said.

But the truth was she missed the detection side of life. She was an executive now, an administrator, if an all-knowing one, but she had liked the active, hunting side.

Which was perhaps why she was being helpful to Mary. It amused her that Mary seemed to think that Charmian could simply shake a finger and somehow sort Ted and Una out.

Mary was worried, that was apparent, seriously worried and Mary Dalmeny Erskine was not a girl easily worried.

Charmian sipped her drink and considered. She had listened carefully because it was an interesting little human problem.

23

'There doesn't seem much in it, really. Husbands walk away all the time. The police can't do anything. She could try a private detective.'

'Would you advise that?'

Charmian shrugged. 'Depends. You say she knows where he is staying. Why doesn't she just go there? Have it out with him. You would, I would.'

We aren't like Una, thought Mary.

'She seems frightened.'

'Go over it again. Tell me what Una Gray told you.'

Mary did so. 'Una seems to think it started when Ted found the dead girl. He kept brooding about it, she says, well, it was a shock, he's such a quiet man.'

'Is he?'

'Yes, very. But they both are. Una is a kind of cousin of mine but I don't know her very well. No one does. She keeps things to herself.' Too much so, perhaps. 'Anyway, Ted went off one day, about a week after he found the body, and didn't come home that evening. She said the next day she got a postcard asking her to meet him off the train at Windsor station. He told her which train. She turned up but he didn't.'

'She got the time right? Met the right train?'

'Oh, yes, Una would.'

'And then this happened again?'

Mary nodded. 'Twice again. By which time the poor girl was getting quite wound up, which you can understand.'

'Do you think he's having a love affair?'

'I did ask Una and she said no very loudly. But I'm not sure if she really believes it.'

'Sounds to me as if she knows a whole lot about it already.'

Mary stroked Muff. 'I thought she was hiding something, I must say.' Muff disengaged herself and stalked off. 'She's very, very edgy. Never known her so bad.' And goodness knows Una had her moods. For which one could not blame her. Perhaps it was time to tell Charmian about Una's background. Mary debated the point: family loyalty and honesty at war inside her.

Charmian stood up and went to the window to let Muff out. She considered. 'Has she reason to be afraid of him?' she said at last.

24

'I don't know.' Mary shook her head. 'Surely not.'

Charmian said slowly: 'He might be better kept away from her.'

'You mean he might hurt her?'

'It bears thinking about.'

Mary took the plunge. 'It wouldn't be surprising if Una invented things. I mean, she's a case. There's something I should tell you about her.'

Charmian waited.

'It reflects on the family. Not on all of it, just that bit of the Dalmenys' outfit that stayed tucked away in the north-east of Scotland. What you might call the kailyard lot.' She looked at Charmian.

'I get the literary allusion.'

'It was so cruel, such archaic behaviour, the rest of the family were horrified, only of course no one knew. Not at the time.'

'Get to it.'

'Well, Una's grandparents lived in this very remote spot with their only daughter who somehow managed to get pregnant. She had the child there, Una, and they kept her hidden. Kept in the back of the house, locked up for all I know. No one was allowed to see her and they never admitted she was there.'

'I'm surprised she learnt how to speak,' said Charmian, thinking of the children incarcerated by the Emperor Frederick, and of Peter of Hanover and Kaspar Hauser.

'Sometimes, I think that when she did learn, she learnt a different language from the rest of us.'

'So what happened?' There were a lot of holes to be picked in this story, thought Charmian, children have to be registered, health visitors call, illnesses happen, but this was not the time to pick them.

'Oh they let her out. Or you could say she burst out. Did it herself. When she was about fourteen.'

'Onset of puberty, I suppose,' Charmian nodded.

'TV really. They bought a set. Later than anyone else, of course.' Late even for their neck of the woods. 'And then there was no keeping Una from realising there was a big world out there.'

'So?'

'Oh, they sent her away to school. Where they thought she was

25

very backward in some ways and very advanced in others.' Mary said: 'That's when the family got to know about her. And she decided that she would make her career teaching children. Really little ones. Old Mrs Turveydrop gave her a job. Knew the family, you see.'

'Mrs Turveydrop? Another literary allusion.'

'Mrs Mallet. Luke Mallet's mother. It's what I called her. She was an old Tartar. She ran the school before Luke took over. She's retired now, of course.'

'I know her,' said Charmian. 'She's a neighbour. Lives in Maid of Honour Row.'

'I must say I was surprised when Una married. But Ted too had grown up under similar conditions, oh not exactly the same, but he was an orphan and so on.' Mary Erskine shook her head. 'Wasn't happy as a child. Took it out in dreams. Out of the body fantasies, thought he could fly, that sort of thing. Of course, he outgrew it, but he still thought about it. Told Una. I suppose she guessed she'd found a match. But of course she could never have children: said she couldn't risk it.'

'What was the risk?'

'I don't know. She never said. Just frightened, I think.'

'Some people might have made up for it by having about six.'

'Not Una.'

'You're not making it sound any easier to understand, but I do begin to see why Ted might have walked out.'

Mary nodded, glad she had done her job, she was looking for help now.

'What you are telling me is that they are a pair of difficult people who might do anything to each other.'

Mary looked her friend in the face. She really means it. But it's right what she says. She drank some whisky and let Charmian fill her glass again.

'Let's get drunk,' she said. Cheered up by the whisky, Mary got round to something that interested her, the answer to which she somewhat feared.

'Is anything known about the identity of the girl?'

'She was a perfectly respectable teenager called Loulou Farmer from Merrywick. Nice family, father is a banker, mother runs an art gallery, never been in trouble,' said Charmian briefly.

26

Merrywick was the smart village just beyond Eton, lying between Windsor and Slough. It was a badge of respectability and credit-worthiness if you lived in Merrywick. Merrywick was a village that was resolute to remain one in spite of the increasing wealth and status of its inhabitants. You would have to search to find a farm labourer, but you would easily find a successful accountant, a well-known author and several rich businessmen. Most of the former agricultural cottages had been modified and upgraded into charming and expensive houses. But Merrywick had a church, a village school and a genuine village green with pond on which a few sad ducks swam up and down. If you lived in Merrywick, you were someone. 'Her parents identified her.'

She said no more. The subject moved on to the friends they had in common, Mary being careful not to mention Humphrey Kent, because were they or were they not a couple?

Shortly afterwards, Mary walked home.

On the way she fell into one of her favourite daydreams.

She was in London with a tall, good-looking man. Their exact relationship varied. Sometimes they were married, sometimes they were about to be married, sometimes they were just ships that passed in the night. In certain moods they were caught in a tragic love affair (he was married, his wife mad, or he was dying, or Mary was) in which she was revelling in every doomed moment. They were staying at the Savoy, or Browns or the dear Stafford, and he was just going out to buy a diamond bracelet. Meanwhile, he thrust a large roll of notes in her hand. Amuse yourself, he says. Oh shan't need all that, she answers. Oh by the time you have taken the odd cab and had your hair done, there won't be much left. Buy yourself one of those nifty little skirts that Arabella Pollen is doing: I love your knees. But use the American Express card for that.

Hang on a minute, said the voice of reason, you haven't got an American Express card . . .

The dream began to evaporate. Besides, he knew a little too much about fashion to be totally trustworthy. He ought not to know about Arabella Pollen and the expense of hairdressers.

All right about her knees, though, they were good. She strode on, turning the corner into Chapel Close.

A man was walking down it, pausing to look at the houses.

27

He seemed to linger outside the Gray house. For a moment, she wondered if it was Ted. But no, too short. As she passed, she saw he was too old as well.

She looked back as she turned the key in her lock. He was still there. The fact that she was studying him – and she thought he was well aware of it – seemed not to worry him. He moved on, but slowly.

When she went upstairs in her house to get a view from her bedroom window, she saw that he was making a slow circuit of the central garde᷉ In fact, now she could see that there were two men, and the other man was waiting further down the road.

Presently the man nearest to her walked away, without looking up at her, leaving Chapel Close to the wind and the rain.

At the entrance to Chapel Close he joined the other man and the two walked away together.

She closed her curtains, shutting out the early night. Saw me though. She wondered what Charmian would make of it, wondered if she ought to tell her.

She wondered what Ted had been praying about. Had it been before the girl was found or after? She wished she could remember.

Something else she hadn't told Charmian.

The adrenalin was pumping around. Oh God, it was going to be one of those nights.

She rang up a doctor friend, he with whom she had had more than one romantic passage. 'I've had a large drink of whisky and now I mean to take a sleeping tablet. Will it kill me?'

On being told that it would not but he could think of a much better way of giving her a good night's sleep, she downed one quickly, having first agreed to have dinner with him at the earliest opportunity.

Devil, she thought affectionately as she sank into a deep sleep – he was no prince but he had virtues. Then she wondered what Charmian had really made of the puzzle offered her; she hadn't said much.

The two men made their way in silence to a coffee shop in Peascod Street that stayed open late, where they sat at a table, not saying much but conversing in odd snatches.

Mary Erskine had been right, they were not policemen, but the policewoman would have been interested in their meeting.

One man was called Rivers and the other Farmer, both parents of dead children.

'I'll kill that man Gray, if I get my hands on him,' said one of them. Rivers, as it happened; he was a violent man, but it seemed a mutter that came from both men.

As is always the case with the police, Charmian knew a little more than she had let on.

She knew that although the girl, Louise Farmer, lived with her family in Merrywick, she had had a boyfriend who came from the district lying between Merrywick, Eton and Slough which was called Cheasey.

You had to understand about Cheasey to work out the implications of that one. Merrywick gave you a badge of character, and so did Cheasey, but not a good one.

Cheasey was a place with a bad reputation all to itself. Whenever anything criminous or bad happened in Windsor, Eton or Merrywick, you said: 'Oh, they must have come from Cheasey.'

You kept out of Cheasey if you could and avoided its inhabitants. Cheasey was reputed to have the highest proportion of criminals per hundred of population outside of certain London boroughs. Several families, variously called Fisher, Waters, Seamen or Rivers (they were intermarried and used any of these names as it suited them) dominated the district.

In addition, Cheasey had its family of small men, short of leg but huge of frame, all surnamed Tipper, known as the Cheasey dwarfs. The Tippers were amongst the most hard-working, decent families there, although they sometimes fell into trouble, like almost everyone else in Cheasey.

Of course, there were other respectable and hard-working inhabitants of Cheasey but they tended to say they lived in North Merrywick or Lower Slough or that they only lived where they did because of their job, and intended to move away as soon as they could. The intelligentsia of Cheasey, such as there was, was either very left-wing or violently right-wing.

Cheasey was a population walking round waiting for a war

to happen. Needless to say, in all wars, great and small, the Cheaseyites had performed with courage and skill.

The police hated Cheasey, it was too much for them, usually got the better of them and they knew it. Charmian herself had no reason to love Cheasey, but that is another story.

Louise Farmer had lived with her parents in a pretty cottage facing the village green of Merrywick. The house looked small from the front but had massive additions tucked away at the back, providing extra kitchens and bathrooms for the Farmer family. Mrs Farmer had a studio containing a loom in the garden where she wove beautiful tweeds and woollens, some of which she sold in her gallery, while others were retailed, expensively, in Knightsbridge. Brian Farmer was a banker, working in London, comfortably off now and well on the way to becoming rich.

Such as these do not expect their only daughter to end up strangled.

But between the world of Merrywick and the world of Cheasey, there had been a link.

The link had been a lad called Rob Rivers. Rob had been the boyfriend of Loulou Farmer. They had met at a disco in Windsor and been going strong ever since.

Mr and Mrs Farmer had not known about Rob then, although Brian Farmer knew now, and would have disapproved if they had. Violently disapproved, which was why Loulou kept his existence quiet.

'Dad would lock me in my bedroom if he knew I was meeting you,' she had said jokingly to Rob once.

'And what would you do?'

'I'd climb out,' she had answered, with a kiss.

Ahead of her was that terrible moment when she turned towards a face she had trusted and saw the eyes and mouth turn into a mask of killing.

But you could not suspect Rob of killing Louise, because he was dead. Dead for her, dead and buried and she had gone, weeping, to his funeral.

CHAPTER THREE

April 11, a day later

Could Ted become violent towards Una? Given the peculiar upbringing of them both, wasn't there scope for tension between them? Was that why he had gone away? In case he harmed her? He was a good man, Mary hung on to that conviction, he wouldn't want to hurt his Una. So what? Where was he? Mary Erskine worried away at the problem.

Perhaps that was why he was praying, thought Mary Erskine. Prayer as an occupation had no place in her life, you had to be praying for something: so his prayer was not to harm Una.

Keep an eye on her, Charmian had recommended, a difficult piece of advice to follow with someone as reclusive as Una had become.

She walked past the Gray house the next morning, giving it a quick appraising stare.

It looked closed-up and dead to the world, but she guessed that Una was behind the drawn shutters. Someone had removed the milk from the doorstep and taken in the newspaper which had been there earlier.

'I'll drop in, after my spell in the library.' Mary's neat, willing fingers were due to anoint several leather volumes with lanoline that morning, restoring them to a pristine gleam like rich amber. She enjoyed the task which she performed with one of the junior assistants who was taking a Fine Art degree at the Warburg and liked to earn a little extra money. Precious little it was, truly, but it was done in the best possible surroundings in a room where Elizabeth Tudor had once held state. For Mary it was a labour of love, and she suspected it was so for the girl, Miranda, although as with all her contemporaries she liked to appear hard and of a businesslike frame of mind. Only do it for the money, she had said, giving an angelic smile. She was a pretty girl.

The Gray house did not look welcoming and Una might refuse to open the door, she had done so once or twice, but Mary would try.

On the top floor a curtain moved, although she could not see by whose hand.

Could only be Una. Unless Ted was hidden there, forcing Una to lie about his movements. She had considered that possibility and she felt sure that so had Charmian. Or was possibly now considering it.

On her way home from her morning in the library, her hands soft and greasy from the lanoline, Mary stopped at the market being held on the porch of the old Town Hall.

It was run by and in aid of the local Women's Institute, of which the Queen was confidently believed to be a member. Mary herself belonged but had never made a pot of jam or embroidered a pillow case in her life. 'Of course, you must join, it is expected of one, but never go, they wouldn't like it.'

How little her mother really knew of life, mused Mary as she walked towards the produce stall. There has been a revolution and she hasn't noticed it. Mary had given several talks, one recently to the W.I. here.

'Hello, dear,' said Mrs Fanaly, from behind her row of jams, chutney and cakes. 'Come shopping?'

'A jar of chutney, I thought. For a present, give it to Una.'

Mrs Fanaly was one of those too tactful to comment on the dead body found by Ted so close to where Mary lived, but she was certainly thinking of it. That poor man, finding the girl. What connection could Ted Gray have with a body? Still, one asked oneself, he had found it.

'It's a bit late for a really good chutney, they're so autumny, we're into the marmalade season now . . . ' She was sorting through her jars. 'We did enjoy your talk on horse racing. I've had several little flutters since. I feel I understand the odds better.'

'I'll take some marmalade then . . . Did you win anything?'

'I did,' said Mrs Fanaly with a modest smile. 'Enough to have a little spend-up. The marmalade is mine, dear, made it myself. I chop the peel a bit coarse but it's a lovely jelly, not cloudy like some.' From underneath her lashes she looked across to her friend and rival Jean Mistle, whose marmalade was not crystal clear. 'She lost a tenner on the Grand National, dear,' she whispered. 'But don't tell her I said so.'

'Wouldn't dream of it,' said Mary, paying for her jar. What have I been responsible for, she thought as she walked away.

She gave Jean Mistle a friendly wave, feeling guilty. Mrs Mistle had several children, all being expensively educated, a new baby too, and it would have been so much nicer if she had won.

The shutters were back in the house in Chapel Close and Una opened the door at the first knock.

'Glad you've stopped the house looking so much like a prison.' Mary advanced into the hall.

Una gave her a startled look.

'I know you must feel like a prisoner, but you shouldn't.' She held out the jar. 'Here, I've brought you some marmalade. I still can't think how to help you and Ted but I'm trying.'

Una walked ahead of her into the kitchen. 'Thanks for the marmalade. I shouldn't have been so upset yesterday. It was silly of me.'

'Not silly at all.' Mary sat down at the big scrubbed table which looked to her as though no meal had been prepared on it for some days, and made a policy decision not to tell Una that she had consulted her friend Charmian. 'Got any coffee, I could do with a cup.'

The house was warmer than yesterday and the big oil-burning Aga stove was roaring away comfortably, but Una was wearing a tweed skirt and a pale, oatmeal-coloured jersey. It was a loose and baggy garment, concealing much but far from attractive. And still no colour, thought her friend sadly.

'Any news of Ted?'

Una shook her head. 'Nothing . . . I'm ready to give him up for dead.'

'Don't say that.' Dead Ted, but what a terrible joke to make, and she mustn't, she was picking up the tension from Una.

Una went across to the stove. 'I made a pot of coffee earlier, it's all I seem to want.' She began to fill a mug. 'Black?'

'I should want whisky and strong in your position, I think.'
Mary stretched out a hand for the mug.

The sleeve slipped back on Una's arm as she held out the mug.
On her forearm was a jagged tear, not yet healed but held together
by strips of plaster, surrounded by a yellowing bruise.

'Una, your arm!'

Una drew the sleeve back over her arm. 'Oh, I slipped, hurt
myself in the garden.'

'It looks nasty.' And not much like the result of a fall. Much
much more like an injury resulting from an attack. 'Have you had
it looked at?'

'It's perfectly all right. I always heal well.'

Except inside, thought Mary. Inside you don't seem to heal at
all. 'Una, has Ted been violent to you?'

'Of course not. How could you think it?'

Easily, thought Mary Dalmeny Erskine, I've had the idea
suggested to me by a professional.

She finished her coffee, took up her bags and departed, giving
her cousin a consoling kiss. 'Buck up, Una. And look after that
arm.' After all, she had got what she had come for: an inspection of
Una, arousing the strong suspicion that she had been damaged.

'I'm home all the afternoon,' she said. 'Call me if you want
me.'

She would get in touch with Charmian, tell her that she might
be right in what she said about Ted showing violence to Una. It
was hardly believable, but it could have happened.

She knew that Una would not call. Nor did she.

Charmian had put aside all thoughts of the Ted and Una Gray
puzzle. She had plenty of work to do of her own. Paper work,
committee work, as well as liaising with various senior police
officers. She was not seeing much of the local CID men she
knew. Chief Inspector Father, Inspector Fred Elman and their
juniors Sergeant Dolly Barstow and Sergeant George Rewley.
Rewley to her mind was the best of the lot, better even than
Dolly, and would go right to the top.

The two sergeants were dealing with the Louise Farmer case,
and their reports were the source of her information.

Her interest so far could be called non-official and academic.

34

But that afternoon, her official business took her to a discreet office high in a building to the west of Regent Street. This was her first visit and she was just beginning to understand what part of her work involved. She had been recruited, almost without her knowing it, into a name and place trace system. Was her conscience troubled?

She emerged from her initiation into the sunlight, breathing in fresh air (or as fresh as inner London allowed) and decided to take a short walk towards Bond Street. Her car had an official parking space, so why not use it?

She studied Ferrangamo's window with more than her usual attention. They had some very desirable mock-croc shoes and bags (must be mock, no one wore real crocodile now, did they?), and was just turning towards the Burlington Arcade when she realised that not far away was Ted Gray's office.

She turned back from the delights of window shopping, walked along Bond Street almost to the bottom where a narrow right-hand passage led to the building in which Ted had a room.

Not a smart building for this rather opulent area but a quiet workmanlike one. There was a restaurant on the ground floor, but a side door led upwards.

Ted occupied the topmost floor above a button importer and a silk designer; the rag trade district was not too far away. From behind one closed door she could hear laughter and behind the next a dog barked.

Directly beneath Ted was a plain white door which said: Lisa Nettle, Aromatherapy, and Charmian paused for a little while outside it. Something was reminding her of her childhood, and then she realised it was the smell of lavender, and that her mother had always used lavender water. It was what 'ladies' wore and although her mother hadn't thought of herself as a 'lady', she wouldn't have minded being one.

No, it wasn't only my mother, thought Charmian, as she mounted the next flight, but the French teacher at school who always smelt of lavender, and I had completely forgotten her until now. Memory is a curious thing: I can remember her smell but not her face.

She remembered her name, however, Miss Batty.

She got her breath back on the top floor. Down below, laughter and noise and scents, but up here on the top floor, silence, nothing.

She tapped on the door, there was no bell or knocker, just a letterbox with a circular sticking out of it, and above, a card tacked with Ted's name on it.

EDWARD GRAY, MA.

It made Ted sound grander than he was, her picture of him was of a neat, quiet, unobtrusive man.

He might be there, listening to her and deliberately not answering the door.

She pushed the circular letter through and bent down to look through the box. Only she couldn't. The reason the circular was stuck was because the box was full.

Either Ted never emptied his letterbox or he had not been there for some time.

She stood up. In any case, she would not have been able to see into the room because the letterbox was one of those that had a kind of brush inside against which you forced your fingers at their peril. The box itself closed on you with a nasty snap.

She nursed her fingers. Ted obviously valued his security.

Well, that was an exercise in non-detection, nothing gained. She wasn't as good at this game as she had been once.

She moved down the stairs. She had passed Miss Nettle's door and was hurrying on down when the silk-designer's door swung open and a large man came out with a dog.

'Hello,' he said jovially. 'Looking for Mr Gray? You're not the only one, feet up and down stairs all the day. You won't find him. Hasn't been there all day. Might have been there the day before yesterday, not sure about that.'

'Yes, I was looking for him.' And who else had been?

'I don't know who's been after him or why,' said the man, answering the unasked question. 'But he never has callers as a rule. Never known him have any in all my time here. Don't know what he does up there.'

'Writes, I think.'

'Oh that explains it.' He started down the stairs with the dog, talking to Charmian over his shoulder. 'Quiet chap, but I think he was there this week sometime.'

'You heard something?'

'Well, not two floors down but the postman left him a parcel. He leaves them on the stairs and we all carry them up, taking our own out on the way. I left his parcel on the stair there. And it went.' His voice was fading away round a bend in the stairs. 'Gone . . . gone.' And just before the front door banged, 'It could have been nicked.'

A door had opened above and the aromatherapist stood there, revealing herself as a large, sturdy lady in a pale blue overall.

'Stop shouting, please, I need quiet.' She was not shouting herself but her well-muscled voice projected itself down the stairs without effort. 'I could hear every word. And the poor chap's gone off golfing, if you ask me. Saw him carry his bag. Looked like that. Try St Andrews. Or Wentworth.'

Charmian let herself out of the building, collected her car, and drove home.

As she negotiated the traffic over the Hammersmith flyover, she thought: it isn't just a teasing little puzzle about Ted and Una Gray, and where he is and what he is, there is a dead girl in the case.

This is what you ought to be thinking about, she told herself soberly.

Think about the obvious facts, state them coldly: Louise Farmer who is dead, and who had a boyfriend who died before her, was found by Ted Gray who is now absent from home.

It is possible he has shown violence towards his wife? There's a hint of it.

Does it all link up, or are all these facts unconnected?

At that point she had to take smart action to avoid a large Jaguar which was itself trying to avoid a lorry. She moved into the slow lane and relaxed.

Time for consideration: she could call in to her office and check what had come in while she was away, always too much to absorb comfortably, or she could go straight home and ignore crime for the night.

If it would let her. Crime had a way of walking in when you least expected it.

Her house was still and quiet, even the cat was out. She changed her clothes, took a shower and made some coffee, all the time carefully leaving unopened both her letters (one from her mother, one with a French postmark from an unknown correspondent) and her telephone answering machine with its stored-up voices.

Afterwards, when she looked, she found a message on her answering machine requesting that she telephone Sergeant Rewley.

Well, what did Rewley want?

'I hear you are taking an interest in the Farmer case.' Privately and personally, he meant. Professionally, she was informed and obliged to take an interest in every crime.

'How did you hear that?'

'Word gets around.'

It evidently did, and speedily too. But she knew from experience that George Rewley was always first with the reliable news.

'As a matter of fact, I met Lady Mary at a party.'

'What party was that?' asked Charmian curiously. It seemed unlikely that the paths of Sergeant George Rewley and Mary Dalmeny Erskine would cross.

'In a school, I was there as a public relations exercise. Let all see that the local police are human, that sort of thing.' He had probably enjoyed going, Rewley took a lively interest in all sorts and conditions of men. 'Funny sort of do to find her at, but the head's her friend. She tried to pump me about Ted Gray.'

Yes, that sounded like Mary, she could have gone to the party on purpose.

'As you know Gray found the body of Louise Farmer. We checked up on him naturally, but he seemed just what he said he was: the unlucky bugger who found the body . . . She'd been strangled, you know that, I suppose.' There was an aspect about this strangulation with a looped cord that was provoking thought inside him, but these thoughts were inchoate, so that at this moment he did not wish to talk it over with her. She might not see it his way. It was a mad idea, anyway. But there had been mud on the girl's knees, that was it. A dwarf killer, maybe? No, better not pursue that thought.

He left a pause which she could fill in for herself: Edward Gray had been under suspicion even if not seriously.

'We told him he was in the clear, but we sniffed around. We found nothing, he didn't seem to know the girl. I expect you saw the reports.'

'I did.'

'But then we found an entry in her diary with his address in it. No name but the right house. You won't know about that yet, but it'll be coming through. So that did make us think again.'

'And?' She could tell by his voice that there was some more to come.

'We got information that a man who answered his description had been trying to buy a gun. He didn't succeed but if he keeps at it and offers enough money, sooner or later, he'll get what he wants.'

'Was this before the death of the girl or after?'

'After. Of course, he may have been trying before and escaped our attention . . . And now, it seems, he is not going home to bed.'

'Not answering the door in his office either,' said Charmian. 'I was round there today.'

'Were you, ma'am?' Rewley kept his voice neutral but in the circumstances of their friendship it was not a friendly observation: he was not pleased. 'Well, there you are then, you see. He's gone Walkies and now we are worried.'

'Does he play golf?'

Rewley took it in his stride. 'Not that I've heard.' He was satisfied with himself. Inspector Elman was going through the motions on this case, but he was not deeply involved: the girl had been strangled by some slob whom they might find or they might not. Probably not, and he could take that. Rewley could not; he had seen the dead girl's face, he had seen her parents and thought they deserved more. He tightened his grip on the phone. The entry in the diary had shaken Fred Elman up a bit, he would get a move on with that inside him. And now he had Charmian Daniels interested, although she should not be poking around on her own. That was his job, hers to sit and think. 'No golf that I know of.'

'I think he might have a gun,' said Charmian, remembering the story of his departure from his office with a big bag. 'Not a revolver, nothing small but possibly a shotgun.'

She tried to remember what she knew of Ted Gray, she thought she had been in the same room with him once at a party, but he

39

was slipping away from the edges of her memory. She couldn't even see his face, just the impression of a quiet, gentle-mannered man who somehow gave the impression in turn of not fitting in anywhere.

Not poor, Mary Erskine had said, but not rich either, just a modest inheritance.

She opened the file on Louise Farmer, and studied it over a cup of coffee.

These days she did not usually bring work home, some of the material she was obliged to see would have defiled her house, but this packet she had brought home.

Louise Farmer, born 20.12.1975, very nearly a Christmas baby, had been found dead on April 2, 1990.

Late on the evening of that day, 10.40, to be exact, she had been discovered by a passer-by, Edward Gray, her legs protruding from the bushes around the Crimean War Memorial. He knew the time because he had just got off a train from Waterloo and remembered thinking that for once it was on time. He had seen the shoes first, and then walked across the grass to find the body.

Thought she was drunk or sick, he had said, not dead, not hidden.

— Not really hidden, Charmian thought, placed there to be found. A determined murderer with time could have found a better hiding place. Either this one had no time or did not care.

Or desired the body to be found.

Louise Farmer had been dead a short time so decided the police surgeon who had certified her dead before handing her body over to the pathologist and the forensic experts.

Death had come by strangulation, a thin, looped cord had been pulled round her throat and tightened, cutting into the flesh.

She had probably not been killed where she was found. Her shoulder-bag had been deposited beside her, she had not been robbed. Neither had she been sexually assaulted.

The body was that of a healthy adolescent, she showed no signs of taking drugs and she was still a virgin.

Charmian put the papers down and stroked the cat who had jumped on her lap. 'Hello, Muff, you smell of the garden, so I know where you have been.' Muff purred obligingly, she was a good performer, tactful and willing.

Charmian went back to her reading.

Louise had had a boyfriend, and not one from the smart side of town, either, but from Cheasey, and by all accounts she had been very fond of him.

This too had been flushed out by the investigating team. Together with the fact that although he had no record he came from one of the more criminous Cheasey clans. The Rivers were reputed to have a finger in every crime that took place in Cheasey, Merrywick, Slough and Windsor.

There was a photograph of the boy in the folder which they had found in the girl's handbag. Charmian studied it. An ordinary looking boy, a weak face perhaps but pleasant enough. Loulou Farmer was pretty, this boy was not handsome.

But she had liked him and when he was dying, she had sat by him to the end.

A nurse on the ward was quoted as saying: 'She saw him through to the end. He knew he was dying, and she knew too.'

Charmian put the file of papers down and removed Muff from her lap. She stood up and looked out of her window on the spring garden. Her house in Maid of Honour Row, part of a terrace of early nineteenth-century houses built to provide dwellings for those who worked in the Court at Windsor, had a tiny front garden where the daffodils and narcissi now waved in a strong breeze. The wind was getting stronger, she could hear it blowing in the chimney. No wonder Muff had come in, prudent animal.

It was not so far away from Chapel Close where the Grays and Mary Erskine lived, and near to where Loulou Farmer's dead body had been laid.

I could have found her myself, thought Charmian, but I didn't, Ted Gray did her that service.

She turned back into the room and dialled George Rewley's office number. No answer.

With a smile, she redialled, this time trying the number of her goddaughter Kate.

Kate answered quickly, as she always did. She was a girl for whom life ticked over fast, and to leave a telephone ringing for long would have been impossible for her. 'George? Yes, he's here, we were just starting dinner.'

'Could you hand him over. It won't take a minute.' Charmian

41

waited, thinking that Rewley and Kate seemed well suited, although it was a relationship that had its on and off moments. Of course, they were married, that must make a difference.

'A question, did the Farmer parents know Ted Gray?'

'I asked them. Nice people,' said George Rewley, 'but not the sort that know anything about anything as far as their children are concerned. Too interested in their own affairs. The girl could have been leading a double, a triple life. No, they said they did not know Ted Gray and did not recognise the address.'

'And her friends?'

'I asked around, but the answer was no.'

'What about the boyfriend in Cheasey? Who knew about him?'

'Some of the school friends did and others didn't. She was a discreet little soul, was Louise.'

The records showed no trace of Ted Gray or anyone like him in Louise Farmer's life, her parents had never heard his name, nor any of her friends, and yet his address was in her diary.

Explain that if you can, Ted.

There was one last call to make before she stopped thinking about Louise Farmer for the day.

She dialled Mary Erskine's number.

'Hello.' She was there and breathless. 'I'm late home today and I've got to change . . . going out to dinner but I would have got in touch. Charmian, you were right about Una and Ted, at least, I think so, she has a nasty cut and bruise on her arm. She said it was an accident, she fell or something, but I don't believe her.'

'Has she heard from him again?'

'She says not, but I'm not sure if she's telling the truth.'

Charmian considered whether to tell Mary about the possibility that Ted Gray now had a weapon. 'Keep an eye on her, will you?' Mary made a noise that was a mixture of assent and reluctance, something about 'dinner tonight' came across. 'And I'd like to meet her. Casually, if you can fix it.'

'I'll do what I can. It's not that easy for anyone to meet Una at the moment. She's kind of shut up in that house.'

'Do your best. And Mary, you know all about the Prince Consort Hospital, don't you?'

'Hardly all, but I arrange the library trolley once a week. With others.'

'I want to talk to one of the sisters there.'

'Again casually, I suppose.'

'I'm not sure about it being so casual.'

'You're taking this seriously, aren't you?'

'Yes.'

'Thank you. When I started talking to you about Una, I thought you might think I was imagining things.'

'No, I take the situation very seriously. It's possible Ted Gray has a gun. For what purpose is not clear, it may be for self-defence. He will have to be found.'

'This gets worse by the minute. I started with Una missing Ted and now I have this picture of Ted roaming the streets of Windsor with a gun. What a good job I'm having dinner with a soldier.'

Mary considered cancelling her date with the bright spark from the Scots Guards whose outfit was currently on duty in Windsor.

'I shall cry if you do,' he said promptly, when she spoke to him on the telephone. 'And what is more, I will come and cry outside your house. Loud cries too.'

'We must at least go and call on Una, and we might take her out to dinner, Alex. She's one of my Dalmeny cousins, you know, and therefore a sort of relation, remotely, of yours too. Wasn't your grandmother a Dalmeny?'

'The Dotty Dalmenys,' he said with pride, 'my grandma was the only sane one for generations. Yes, your cousin, I know the school she teaches at, St Cath's, my kid brother is at it. Poor little blighter's seeing visions, in fact they're all at it. Stepma doesn't like it at all.'

Soldiers are so young, thought Mary, they even have brothers still at prep school, still there were several marriages involved and a couple of stepmothers.

'Can't blame Una for that.'

'All right, we'll go and have a look at her, if she's in trouble.'

But Una, when they got there, opened the door no more than a crack and said how kind of Alex and Mary, but no, she didn't want to come out to dinner and she was going to have a hot bath and a tot of whisky and go to bed. No, she hadn't heard from Ted and at the moment, she thought to hell with him.

She closed the door smartly.

Mary went back to the car. 'Well, what did you make of that?'

Alex shrugged.

'Come on, now, get out of the car and take a look at the house. You're a soldier, tell me what you make of it.'

Alex uncoiled his length from his car and walked over to survey the house, with its shuttered front windows. 'Looks a thoroughly well-locked-up house to me. Shut up tight as a drum, I'd say.' He came back to the car and held the door open. 'Come on, m'lady, dinner calls. She can't come to any harm in there.'

'No.' Mary got back into the car.

She found the solid size and warmth of Alex comforting. He was even more of a comfort than her doctor friend. He might not be a prince, and he hadn't a penny to his name, but he was an undoubted support.

From the car she looked up at the firmly locked-up house. You could shut harm out, but you could shut yourself in with harm too.

CHAPTER FOUR

April 12

St Catherine's School, Merrywick, where Una Gray taught and Ted Gray had occasionally helped out and where the children of many of Mary Erskine's friends were scrambling themselves into an education, was in some confusion. It was not usual for this well-ordered if liberal establishment to suffer in this way. Not that discipline was strict or formal; far from it. Ordered disorder was what they aimed at.

'We let our kids go at their pace, we let them have a bit of responsibility for themselves early on, our Trust system, we call it,' Luke said tolerantly. This masked the fact that they headed their pupils pretty firmly in the direction of their chosen schools: Eton and Winchester for the lads, and Heathfield and St Mary's for the girls.

The heart of the school was a large Victorian house where Luke had his offices and his own living quarters. Built in the 1860s for a city businessman, it was of solid red brick and grey stone, with many rooms and several staircases; it had been well suited to house the school for infants and small children that had been the beginnings of St Catherine's. Mrs Mallet had inherited this establishment from her aunt and had converted it into a first-class preparatory school and pre-prep for little boys on the way to their public school. From the first, it had been for day boys with a handful of weekly boarders. Mrs Mallet, ahead of her generation, did not think it good for small children to be away from their family for too long.

The school had prospered and achieved a mild fame, as its

45

pupils grew up and began to make their mark in the world (a Lord Chancellor, a distinguished doctor, a rich industrialist), and to send their own children to St Cath's in their turn.

Mrs Mallet had always allowed sisters and cousins of boys to attend, and even these rules were soon relaxed so that St Catherine's became an equal mix.

Mary Erskine had toddled off to St Catherine's herself when it had been under the stricter rule of Mrs Mallet, who believed in children knowing their place and keeping to it.

As numbers grew, a new teaching annexe was built, and a swimming pool and a gymnasium erected across the playing fields. But still at the heart of it was the old school building where only the youngest were now taught in Victorian comfort. Carriages no longer met the pupils, but there was a school bus, and a parking place for staff cars, well hidden behind shrubberies so as not to spoil the view.

So it was a smart, sensible, orderly school. But it had not taken long for Pix's conviction that people, some people, could be in two places at once, to communicate it to his fellows. Fifteen disturbed contemporaries of Pix, aged eight. Starting with Billy Albert and James Bradley, Adam Cannon and his twin brother Robin, Mark Landy, Tony Meredith, Harry Paget, through several others, right down to David Young and Joe Zalay.

Very soon, there was a strong belief among many of them that it was rife. Perhaps it was on all sides of you. Perhaps you could never be sure that the person you were seeing, who might be teaching you to paint a picture or hearing you read a piece of poetry, was really there at all, but was outside doing something quite different.

Once the idea had spread, alarming some small children very much, making others full of tricks and making all of them restless, even the agnostics among them were soon seeing visions.

It was catching, a disease of the spirit, which some were fearful of picking up, others eager, but all of them secretly enjoying it.

Pix, who was a true believer, had not been explicit about whom he had seen in double form, given no details and been reluctant to talk. That was the mark of the convinced, as the headmaster, Luke Mallet, recognised.

He did not grumble at him, or show anger, Pix was, after all, still such a young boy, but he tried to reason with him.

'Tell me whom you saw, and we can deal with it, Pix. Show you it can't be.'

'My mother says the *doppelgänger* story is well established.'

Damn your mother, thought Luke.

'So who did you see?' There has to be a way through this wood.

Pix was reluctant to name names but his headmaster pressed him.

'It was only the cat, the school cat.' The school cat was a strongly marked tabby. 'He was in the kindy art room with us and then I looked at him and he was outside too.'

Luke sat back and let his hands fall away. Anyone could mistake a cat, in or outside the kindergarten art room.

'But there are any number of cats that look like Tiger,' he said with relief. 'Genuine mistake, Pix, forget it.'

If that was the root of it, there was nothing to it, the episode was over.

But it wasn't, naturally, he was experienced enough and sensitive enough to know the truth when he heard it, and he wasn't hearing it now.

The boy was lying.

'Let's go and have a look at the room together, Pix,' he said gently. 'Not afraid to go?'

Pix shook his head. No, not afraid.

He took the boy's hand as they went back into the art room, the so-called creative play centre, where the youngest children painted, mixed plaster, made papier-mâché models and generally enjoyed themselves. They had their play stuff there as well: the miniature shop with its tins and jars and packets, most of which they made themselves, and the large toy Play House with its windows and doors, a great favourite. Beyond this house were the glass doors opening on to grass with a view across the playing fields to the parking lot and the road.

The room was empty now as a rehearsal for a school play had absorbed almost everyone.

'No cat,' he said to Pix. 'Don't you think you were imagining it all?' Not the sort of thing he usually said, he respected the imagination of the child.

Pix just drew away his hand and said nothing.

'Cut off to the rehearsal,' Luke said, still gently. 'Got a good part have you?'

'I'm a cat,' said Pix. He sounded gloomy.

'He's afraid of something, though,' Luke said a few minutes later to his assistant, Minette Deligny, a young recruit from France. She was very beautiful, as Luke was beginning to realise, in an unEnglish way with dark hair, pale skin and deep brown eyes. A gentle good girl, he called her. He still missed his wife who had not been dead more than a year, but he was young enough to know that he could love again. It would not be as it was with Netta, but there were different ways of loving. His mother had taken up the duties necessary to a headmaster's wife, a part she played to perfection, having invented it more or less. It had, after all, been her school. But she had enjoyed retirement, by no means an idle one in her case, and would like to get back to it. A respectable female figure was absolutely essential in a school like St Catherine's, and if that figure was married to the headmaster so much the better. Parents liked it. They might be much married and divorced themselves, real sexual wanderers, but they wanted old-fashioned virtue in their headmaster.

Minette and Luke were together in his kitchen. The headmaster had a flat on the top floor of the main house of St Catherine's which also housed the small number of weekly boarders. At the moment, his mother shared this flat with him, but she went back to her own house as much as she could, and was there now, playing bridge and gossiping.

Luke was teaching Minette to make tea; English tea with loose leaves and not tea bags. It was a useful, indeed vital, skill if she was going to be his wife. Suddenly he saw that this was what he wanted for her.

'Boiling water, heat the pot . . . and one teaspoon for each person and one for the pot.' He watched judiciously. 'Pot to the kettle, not kettle to the pot.' He carried the teapot to the table. 'Now we let it infuse for a minute or two.'

She watched him stir the pot.

'Shouldn't do this really,' he said. 'Considered vulgar. I always do it, though.'

'Why do you like tea so much?' He was pouring out with a kind of dedicated skill. 'Not just for the taste?'

'No,' he considered while he sipped his brew. 'I suppose it brings back pleasant memories. Happy times.' Nursery tea, Oxford days. Reading Oscar Wilde and Jane Austen, tea linked everything.

'I might get to like it,' said Minette. 'If I persevere. If I stay.'

'Oh, you must stay,' said Luke in alarm.

'My contract is for two years,' began Minette. 'And I have almost completed the first.'

'Oh, we can soon fix that,' said Luke. 'The children like you so much. And you are so good with them.'

He had a small staff of teachers, all loyal and all good with the children, as Minette knew very well. Miss Smithjohn, Mrs Bissett, Adam Hallows, a student just from college, and Mr Wright who taught games and physical education and Mr Oriel who was an artist but not above teaching how to make simple furniture. Alison Smithjohn and Una Gray had charge of the two youngest classes, in one of which was Pix.

They were all known by their Christian names: Alison, Margaret, Adam and Bill, and Martin.

The headmaster was called Luke, but his mother was always, as she had ever been, Mrs Mallet, that marked the difference between them.

St Catherine's was a happy, relaxed school. It was expensive, you rarely get good things without due payment. If there was any trouble, staff away, hold-ups anywhere, they all, as Luke put it, mucked in. Not his mother though. Mrs Mallet never mucked in, never had and never would.

'You mustn't go, Minette. We need you.'

Minette looked thoughtful; she had a boyfriend back in Lyons who needed her too. 'My mother,' she began tactfully. Luke was a very nice man, she could see one might come to love him. But not just yet. She had a lot of other things to do in her life.

'Oh we'll sort her out.'

Minette gave a polite but sceptical smile: he had not met her mother.

'About the boy, Pix, he's very nice, I don't think he's a liar.'

'Well, he is and he isn't.' Pix had been known to be a bit fanciful, a story-teller, and Luke did not think the worse of him for that.

'Boys see truth differently from us,' said Minette seriously.

'Don't they just,' said Luke, 'but you learn to read them.'

'It is this murdered girl,' said Minette. 'It has upset them. Murder is so terrible.' She went pale.

'I don't think the boys know about it.' Luke was surprised.

'Of course they do. These things cannot be forgotten. At home, in Toulouse we had a string of murders of young girls. Just like this.' Minette's pretty face suddenly looked pinched. 'Strangled . . . I found one of those girls.'

'Minette . . . ' Luke moved forward to comfort her.

The telephone rang. 'Oh Mary.' Luke was always glad to speak to Lady Mary. She had such a pleasant voice, and Luke responded to voices. And then, he was the tiniest bit of a snob, he wouldn't pretend otherwise, and Mary did know everyone who mattered in their small world, from the highest (Oh yes, Ma'am, what a nice person Lady Mary is, I do agree) to the lowest. 'No, not busy, oh well, you know, term is roaring on, nearly over but the kids get very nervy . . . Oh, you've heard about that . . . Yes, Pix, dear little chap but full of ideas.' And adept at passing them on to his peers. 'The boy's unhappy.' And his mother isn't helping. She's being reasonable. And the little chap doesn't want reasoning, he needs comfort. 'I'm trying to see what I can do about it . . . No, I haven't heard from Una . . . Yes, I am worried about her and we miss . . . Yes, Mary, I will try to persuade her to come back if she telephones. Well, to be truthful I had heard that Ted had gone off . . . We miss him too.'

Lady Mary seemed to launch into a long passage while Minette drank her tea. 'Oh, love to come round for a drink, Mary, and meet your friend. A parent?' he asked. No point in beating about the bush, he liked to get certain things established. Not as far as Lady Mary knew. 'Charmian Daniels?' His voice dropped a key. He knew *her*, a policewoman. Ted's brush with the police was really as far as he wished to go in meeting the police. Of course, they had had that nice chap, George Rewley, at the school. 'Love to, Mary. Shall I bring Mother?' Mother was a great protection.

He put the telephone down and picked up his cup. The tea was tepid. 'Lady Mary Erskine,' he said to Minette as he put the kettle

50

on again to revive the brew. 'Asked me round for drinks. You must come too. Mary won't mind, endlessly hospitable. Mother will be there.'

The kettle boiled and he had just got the cup to his lips when the telephone rang again. 'Damn.' Minette looked at him with sympathy and took the cup away. 'Una, Una dear, how are you . . . I know. And what about Ted?'

Covering the telephone, he said to Minette, 'She's lost her husband . . . Well, mislaid more.'

Or had Ted mislaid himself? He liked Ted, but he wished, as the headmaster of a good school, he had not found a girl's body. A nice girl too, not at all the sort that was usually found dead in the street.

'Oh, we're managing, Una, don't you worry. Thanks to Minette, she's a marvel, isn't she? We're lucky there.' He threw a smile at Minette. 'Oh yes, do come back, dear, if you feel up to it.'

He listened while Una talked; he knew a little about her past, about her upbringing and always marvelled that she was as balanced as she was. 'Right, I'm delighted. Look after yourself.' He put the telephone down. 'Una's coming on Monday.'

Presently, Minette cycled off to where she lodged in Windsor in a house in the shadow of the castle, carefully selected by old Mrs Mallet as suitable for her. 'I was at college with her grandmother, I am responsible for the gal,' she had said.

Luke watched Minette's departure fondly; then he took his usual after school hours tour through the building, beginning in the old Victorian heartland. It was Friday, the weekly boarders had joyfully sped home, the day pupils had departed an hour or so since. The old Victorian house was empty except for him and his dog.

He shut a few doors, turned off a light carelessly left on. Not even dark, he thought crossly, wasting money.

He passed through the creative play centre, where activities from painting to mime to dance took place for the three youngest sets of pupils. They were called sets, not classes, as being less formal, more free and easy, but they were sets that were carefully steered in the right direction.

He closed a window which had been left open and turned the lock. Careless again.

He paused for a moment by a portrait of himself done by a pupil; he appeared to have three eyes. Colourful papier-mâché masks, some portraits, others imaginary, all done by the children, hung near by.

A good school, he was happy with it. Could do with more working capital though, money was always a problem. He was not thinking about Loulou Farmer nor Lily Paget, her contemporary, although both girls had been at the school, only not in his day.

He passed the Play House and noted it needed repainting.

Then he heard a noise.

He went out into the hall, looked in the cloakrooms and saw a small figure sitting on the floor by his locker. He was probably crying, although he made a noble attempt to cover it up.

'Pix! What are you doing here? You should have been off home ages ago.'

Pix muttered something.

'Well, stand up.' Pix stood up. 'That's better. So what's the story? They went off and left you? I expect you were slow.'

Pix murmured something about losing his coat, he was a notorious loser of his possessions and his mother had issued a stern warning about the new school overcoat.

'Right,' said Luke. 'Come on, follow me.' Pix dutifully followed. 'You could have got shut in, you know.' Boy's in a state, he thought, but better not to probe now. If ever. Some things were best left undisturbed. It was not the case, in his opinion, that truth was the better for an airing. 'I'll drive you home.'

He was striding forward to where the cars hid behind the trees, when he became aware that Pix was lagging behind.

He turned round. 'Not frightened of me, are you, Pix?'

Pix shook his head. 'Could we walk?'

'All right. As you wish.' He took Pix's damp hand in his. 'Forward, friend.'

As they walked, he said quietly: 'Wasn't the cat you saw, was it, Pix? It was a person.'

Charmian, driving home, saw them. A tall man, and a small boy, hand in hand.

She sat there watching, they were in a hurry, but she took her time, driving slowly off.

CHAPTER FIVE

The same day, April 12, Thursday

Charmian had a theory that she had two selves, a working self and private self, and that the two should keep well apart and not get in each other's path. Everyone had their own fantasies and this was hers.

But, of course, life being what it was it did not work out that way.

Last year, she had been in some anxiety, kept well under cover, about her own health. But all the same, the anxiety had coloured her work. There had been nothing to it, or not much, although not something she was happy about, but now she felt fit, strong and confident, and her weight was her only problem. Get fat, get thin, nothing stayed the same, it was always a struggle. Having lost weight last year, she was now gaining it fast, so she had put herself and Muff the cat (also a lady with weight problems) on strict diets.

The bad side was that now she always felt slightly hungry. Perhaps she had been eating to cheer herself up.

Just before taking over her present position she had gone through a potentially humiliating experience, a kind of moral rape, but she had not accepted the humiliation, and kept her head up. In fact, she had turned it to her own advantage so that her colleagues now accorded her the wary respect due to a tough lady.

Her only concession to weakness was to let her London doctor (a chirpy female) order an annual check-up. For Charmian's convenience this was done at the local hospital on the Datchet

Road, which she now entered unobtrusively through the side entrance to the private wing. Today was the day.

She was in and out of the consultant's rooms quickly, carrying with her the judgement that she had performed well so that a satisfactory report would be dispatched to London and relayed to her by her doctor there. Protocol had to be observed.

The hospital clinician, Dr Barlow, smiled cheerfully. 'Be sending the test results to Dr Evans.' Marian Evans was her London doctor, a powerful if diminutive figure, well known to Dr Barlow who had trained with her and always been somewhat in awe of her. 'But I don't anticipate any trouble.'

'Good.' Charmian let herself be ushered out with a politely opened door. The corridor outside was empty, and she leaned against the wall, taking a deep breath.

More tension there inside her than she had been prepared for, you always expected the worst right deep down inside you. This time all right, but next time? Well, that was a comfortable way off and not worth thinking about yet.

But hospitals are intimidating even to the brave and fit. Something to do with the smell and the general air of detached efficiency. You were just a body, no not even that, a set of responses to certain stimuli.

She took another deep breath, and momentarily, just momentarily, closed her eyes.

A blue-aproned nurse appeared in front of her, asking anxiously, 'Are you all right?'

Charmian opened her eyes. 'Yes, fine.'

'Sure?' She was a very young girl with bright red hair and a square pleasant face, and was pushing a drug trolley.

Charmian smiled and nodded.

'Well, go and have a cup of coffee . . . The canteen's that way.' She gestured to the middle distance where a large yellow signpost gave directions.

'Thank you.' She hadn't been considering it, hospital coffee was not famous for flavour, but it was a good idea. Coffee, yes.

The nurse gave a grin and trundled off. 'See our new canteen,' she said over her shoulder. 'Worth a look.' The idea seemed to amuse her. 'Just look for the signs.'

Charmian followed the arrows to the large new building which

54

housed a shopping area, a bank and the canteen. It was carpeted in blue and was bright with white paint, contriving to look more like the entrance to a major airport than a place of healing, but the smell of disinfectant had already invaded it, driving out cosiness and any suggestion that life was a ball.

The canteen was fiercely democratic so that patients, their visitors, and doctors and nurses all queued up and ate together, although Charmian noted with some amusement that the senior consultants seemed to have carved a little enclave out for themselves behind a plastic barrier. Democracy can go only so far.

She got herself a cup of coffee which she took to a table in the corner of the room. Automatically, from long training she always took up a position where her back was protected and from which she could survey the room and all the exits.

To her pleasure and mild surprise, the cup of coffee was hot and strong. At the table to her right, a staff nurse in her lavender uniform and stiff white cap was reading a newspaper while she poured a cup of tea. Charmian could see the headline: LATEST ON THE WINDSOR MURDER. A picture of Louise Farmer was clearly visible. The couple seen leaving a wisteria-covered house must be her parents.

Suddenly she put the newspaper down with a muttered exclamation. She turned her head to meet Charmian's interested eyes. 'It's a tragic case,' she said. 'That pretty little thing. I hope they get whoever did it.' She threw the paper aside as if she was angry.

'You knew her?'

'Not really knew. But I had met her. I nursed a friend of hers.' She fell silent for a moment.

So this is the woman I wanted to meet, thought Charmian. I won't need to invoke Lady Mary and her library trolley. She gave a sympathetic smile while saying absolutely nothing. There were times when it was best to keep quiet, and this was one of them. In her job it was what you had to learn.

'She was such a good kid. They both were. He was a nice boy, he didn't deserve to die.'

Charmian moved nearer to take up the paper. 'May I look?' She ran her eyes over the story. Nothing there that she did not know, of course. 'How sad,' she murmured. 'What happened to the boy?'

'Oh he died. He never had much of a chance, the damage he had, but he might just have pulled through. He put up a fight, I can testify to that. And she sat with him all the time, held his hand, till he went. Don't know where her parents thought she was. Not that he took long to go. "I've got to tell you, I want to confess." He said that, he knew he was going.' She folded up the paper. 'Oh well, there it goes. I'd better get back. You save some, you lose some.'

As she moved away, Charmian heard her murmur, 'What could a boy like that have to confess?'

Charmian shook her head. Confess? A boy from Cheasey? Who knew?

She was remembering this conversation as she accepted a drink from Mary Erskine. Lady Mary had an upstairs sitting-room which commanded a splendid view of Chapel Close to the Circus with its small garden and bronze statue. Daffodils were blowing in the stiff breeze that usually accompanied spring in this part of the Thames Valley.

Charmian took her drink to the window. She envied Mary Erskine her view, it was at once private and dignified. Outside the window, on a short pole and placed at a carefully calculated angle to the street below, was a square of looking-glass.

Charmian smiled and Mary saw her. 'You're looking at my spy glass.'

'Haven't seen one of those since I left Scotland.'

Mary came over to the window to look out. 'Oh, I think you will find one or two still around down here in the south. I saw some in Bruges too. It's the Victorian equivalent of the answerphone on the door: you could sus out who was calling before you answered . . . Or that was its purpose so my grandmother claimed. Really, it gave her and all the other old gossips a chance to survey the whole street.'

'But you've kept yours?'

'Yes, it's a historical monument . . . ' She grinned. 'And I use it, for I too like to take a look at my neighbours.'

'Do you keep a diary?'

'I could do, I know plenty about them. Who's in debt, who's on drugs . . . ' Here Charmian opened her eyes wide, and Mary went on hastily, 'Joke, joke, of course, and who is thinking of

56

marrying again.' That was one for Charmian, because she knew very well that Humphrey Kent had redecorated his whole house in the hopes that Charmian would say yes. Very Victorian, old Humphrey, no modern lover would think a clean drawing-room was prerequisite for a wedding. If Charmian wouldn't say yes, then she could think of someone else who would. 'They know plenty about me as well.'

'Who is on drugs, Mary?'

'Just a silly girl. And I'm only guessing.'

'See what you can do to find out, and then stop her. If you don't, then I will.' Charmian was not joking; it was a matter she felt strongly about. Her closest friend, a distinguished artist, had recently admitted an addiction and Charmian reproached herself bitterly for not having noticed what was wrong with Anny.

Mary shrugged. 'Well, I will if I can, but you know how difficult that can be. Anyway, I could be wrong, it was half a joke.'

You're protesting too much, thought Charmian, you know something, but she left it there, and changed the subject. 'By the way, I have jumped the gun on you about the hospital visit. I saw the very nurse I wanted a word with. It just happened that I did.'

'Just chance?'

'Yes, the opportunity came and I took it.' But had it been just chance? Sometimes, in some cases, she had the feeling that life itself was taking a hand and that there was no true coincidence or chance anywhere. Things fitted in.

Mary said with interest: 'Did you get anything?'

'I might have done . . . ' She was not going into that now. 'And on the way round here, I saw Luke Mallet.'

'Ah, our wandering boy?'

'What do you mean?'

'Well, he loved Netta, of course he did, but even when Netta was alive he wandered a bit. More than a bit. Even made a pass at me once.'

'What did you do?'

'Pretended not to notice. Much the best thing. I was a friend of Netta's. Friend of Luke's for that matter.' There was a charming arrogance in her attitude. Marie Antoinette might have spoken thus.

'When did his wife die?'

'Almost two years ago . . . Yes, it must be.'

'She was ill?'

'No, a hit-and-run accident. She was knocked off her bike. For a time it looked as though she might come round, but she never did. They never caught the driver.'

The second hit-and-run death that Charmian had heard of in a few hours. Separated in time, and in place, and people did drive fast round here, but it was interesting.

'Hard for Luke,' she said.

'Oh, he minded. Desperately, I think. But he stood it well. He's a survivor . . . Of course, they had their ups and downs, Netta took one or two episodes badly, but they would never have divorced, you can't in his job, like being the Prince of Wales.' Mary walked to the window to look out. 'He'll be coming round here. Should be on his way. I asked him in for a drink. Una as well.'

'Why did you do that?'

'I thought you all ought to meet.'

There it was again: chance, or unchance?

'He might be a while yet; he seemed to be taking a pupil home.'

'I don't know who that boy was,' said Mary deliberately. 'But I do know one who is in trouble.'

'What sort of trouble?' Looking at Mary's spy mirror, Charmian saw the reflection of a man, Luke, walking fast down Chapel Close. If she moved her head a fraction, she could see him in the flesh as well, a kind of double man. He had hurried here.

'Not sure,' said Mary, 'tell you more later.'

Some minutes later Luke Mallet came up the stairs with athletic bounds, calling a greeting to Mary so that Charmian got a whiff of his manic energy, and he was no sooner in the room before he was telling her that he knew about her, his mother said what a good neighbour she was, and of course she was going to speak at their Jubilee day, wasn't she?

'Sorry to be late. Vodka, please, Mary. Headmasters mustn't smell of drink.' He had charm, Charmian admitted to herself, a kind of boldness that could be attractive. 'Had to take a lad home. In a bit of a state. Pix. You know him, Mary?'

'Know his brother, half-brother really.' Alex was one of her regular escorts, half an admirer, half a critic. Mary seemed to him too insouciant, so well-born and confident as if the world could not touch her. He found that dangerous.

'Well, you know Pix, then.' Luke downed his vodka. 'Poor lad seems to be seeing double. Claims he saw the double of the school cat, one inside asleep, one outside. A fib that, of course, it's a person he saw . . . Or thought he did.' Luke sipped his vodka. 'Won't say whom.'

'Oh it's imagination,' said Mary easily. 'Poor old Pix, they're so madly rational at home, his imagination has got to have outlet somehow.'

'It's more than that.' Luke swirled his drink around. 'Got some lemon, Mary? Thanks. No, there's something real there . . . And it's catching, all his mates are claiming they see *doppelgängers* too.'

'Playing games.'

'Yes, sure. Some of them. One or two are genuinely frightened. I can deal with it. In the long run it will roll up its skirts and fade away . . . But it doesn't do a school any good.'

Una had crept quietly into the room.

'What doesn't do a school any good? Hello, Mary, I let myself in. No, don't go on, Luke, I heard as I came up the stairs, you have a very carrying voice, you know.'

'You need it in my job.'

Una accepted a drink from Mary; she had dressed for the occasion in a yellow silk shirt and dark kilt, and she had applied a little lipstick. With a charming smile, she acknowledged an introduction to Charmian and said she knew her by sight, and had been to a talk she gave on Women and Crime. 'I never thought of Pix as imaginative, but he is sensitive and easily frightened. His mother frightens him.'

'Poor kid,' said Luke.

'Oh mothers are good at that.'

'You can say that again,' said Luke, thinking of Mrs Mallet.

'You shouldn't let parents frighten you,' said Mary robustly. No one had ever frightened her.

'They terrify me,' said Luke. 'But I have to pretend not.'

He looked round the room cheerfully, admiring the big bowl

59

of narcissi that Mary had blooming. She was good with flowers, good with everything, he thought.

'You know in the Middle Ages people thought children were just miniature adults: we know better now.'

'Of course we do,' said Mary, wondering if they did.

'They're a different tribe altogether. Not like us at all.'

'Should an educationalist say that?'

'I know it, they know it. We both try to hide it.' He took a quick swig of his vodka. 'My job is to turn them into us.' He began to laugh and Una and Mary joined in.

Charmian observed the three of them, laughing with each other. They know each other so well, she thought. They can make that sort of joke and understand it. If I did it, I would get it wrong. They'd laugh, politely, but they would know it was wrong. And so would I when I thought it over.

'Don't worry over Ted,' Luke said to Una. 'He'll be back. Why don't you return to work?'

'I'm coming back,' said Una. 'You asked and I'm coming.'

'Bravo, you do that, Una.' He put his arm round her shoulders in his usual friendly style. 'We depend on you, Una. Pix needs cheering up.'

'I'll come back and cheer Pix up.'

'Do that.' He dropped his arm.

'Another drink?' Mary offered.

Luke finished what he had. 'I'd better be off, I've got papers to see to, and it's a bit of a trudge home.'

'You're on foot?'

'The boy didn't want to go in the car, which was strange in itself. They're a lazy lot, lads. Anyway, I don't drive as much at night as I did.' He kissed Mary on the cheek. 'Not since Netta . . . I told her not to cycle at night, cyclists can be invisible, can't they?'

'You'd never hit one,' said Una.

He shrugged, then shook his head. 'Supposing . . . Just imagine, I can imagine. Could happen to anyone . . . I'm off. I'll let myself out.' He kissed Mary on the cheek. 'Bye, Una, goodbye Miss Daniels.' He touched hands lightly with Una. Charmian saw that on his right hand and her left there was a gold ring with the same crest on it. Looked like dragon rampant.

60

Mary saw her looking and smiled. 'The school ring. I've got one somewhere. Anyone can have one.'

'Anyone?'

'Perhaps not anyone.'

Never say class is dead in England, thought Charmian, seeing them as somehow apart from herself, but having everything in common with each other. That's what it is: the right to wear the correct ring, the proper tie, and to know where to get your hair cut.

They heard Luke go bounding down the stairs, two at a time.

'He'll fall one day,' said Mary.

Una said: 'It was very dark that corner where she was hit, just about where the dead girl was lying.'

'The same reason in both cases.' Mary was dismissive. 'As you say, it was dark.'

Una waited for the sound of the front door closing before she spoke. 'I've got something to show you. If you wait here, I'll get it.'

CHAPTER SIX

On that same April evening, April 12

Left alone, Charmian and Mary Erskine sat for a moment in silence. Mary stretched out a hand towards the drinks tray and raised an eyebrow.

Charmian shook her head. 'No, thank you. I'm driving.' Her house was not far away, but in her position she had to be careful. All police officers can expect scrutiny and criticism, a high-ranking policewoman needs to be specially careful.

'I'll make some coffee.'

'Good idea.' Charmian followed her downstairs to the kitchen. Mary's kitchen reflected her own view of life, since it was both an interesting mixture of the antique and the starkly functional up-to-date. Charmian stared with respect at the gas range which looked a museum piece, but noted that its very cleanness and neatness suggested that Mary Erskine's cooking, such as it was, took place in the large microwave oven. The kitchen table was clearly an antique, around which generations of servants could have worked, but the sink unit was modern and equipped with all the rubbish disposal and automatic built-in dishwasher units that anyone could desire.

'I only wash up once a week,' said Mary, following her gaze. 'Unless I've had guests, of course.'

The coffee started to filter through, filling the kitchen with its pleasant rich smell. Mary used a good blend, bought in a famous Piccadilly shop and called Sandringham. It was supposed that King Edward VII had chosen it.

'What do you suppose she's up to?'

'Una? Who knows with Una? Something she wants to show so she said.'

Charmian took her cup of coffee over to the small boiler that was singing away quietly to itself. It was warmer over there.

'She's quite a character, your cousin.'

'You're saying she's a nut?'

'No, certainly not . . . but she has a different quality.' Partly the clothes, partly a kind of nun-like, gentle manner, not often met with in secular life.

Mary sighed. 'I told you about her past. It marked her. She's never been quite the same as other people.'

The clock, on the wall, round of face and old, with a ship painted on its dial, chimed the hour, in a thin silvery voice. Charmian looked at her watch, the old clock was an accurate performer. 'Wonder how long she will be?'

'Any minute now.'

'Why is she being such a time?'

Mary shrugged. 'She says she's gone to get something so I suppose she has and she's looking for it . . . She nearly always tells the truth. Wraps it up a bit sometimes, but it's there if you look. Must be something to do with Ted. Disappearing old Ted.'

'It's a strange business, the way the husband is behaving.'

'Well, didn't I say so?' Mary had produced a tin of oatmeal biscuits. 'Have a biscuit, I get them specially from a lovely old shop in Perth.'

Charmian crumbled a biscuit, Mary was right; they were delicious, friable without being dry. But how did she get them from Perth?

'I suppose it's all true, these stories about Ted Gray?' As it happened, Charmian supposed nothing of the sort. Some truth there but not all of it, was her view. Truth was lying at the bottom of a deep and murky well here.

'What I told you is true, and it's what Una told me; I can't go deeper than that. And I've already said she's a truthful person.'

Charmian meditated. So Una might be, but equally she could be lying, yet that in itself might tell you something. A person's lie could be very revealing of some truth about them.

'Was it the way you would expect Ted to behave?'

Mary gave a shrug. 'No, not really, not in the normal run of things.' She gave a short laugh. 'But people never do what you expect of them. You must know that.'

'Summoning her to meet him and then not turning up. Strange thing to do.'

'That's what's worrying Una. I suppose she thinks he's having some sort of emotional breakdown.'

'There could be a very practical reason for doing it.'

Mary stared. 'So, what?'

'There could be a purpose. To put something in the house. Or to take something out.'

There was a pause.

'Why would he do that?' Mary spoke slowly. 'It's kind of a long way round for something he could do easily if he chose; it *is* where he lives.'

Nothing was ordinary at the moment as she knew well enough.

'Let's make a picture,' said Charmian. 'Say he wants to take something away, and for some reason does not want Una to know.'

'But three times?'

'He can't find it.'

Mary had a vision of Ted Gray going through the house in Chapel Close, going from floor to floor, seeking and never finding. Oh poor little Ted. Suddenly he had shrunk in her mind's eyes to something small and anxious, a tiny hunted creature like a mouse. Oh poor wee Ted, what had he got caught up in? She felt guilty.

She poured Charmian some more coffee, her hand shaking slightly. 'Excuse me a moment. Take your coffee back to the sitting-room.'

She moved across the landing to her bedroom, where she opened a drawer and fumbled around for a moment in the soft silken underclothes.

Still there. Goodness knows what she was going to do with it.

Charmian would kill me, she thought.

I could flush it down the lavatory . . . But they can tell by the traces . . . But they wouldn't look, no reason to . . . There again you couldn't be sure.

Silence could be bought. But it meant going into Cheasey.

But I don't want to go into Cheasey. Cheasey could dirty those who touched it. She turned her head, she could hear footsteps on the stairs. Damn.

Charmian appeared at her bedroom door. 'Lost something?'

Mary closed the drawer. 'Just getting a hanky out. Got the sniffles.' Wrong thing to say, she told herself, sniffles were a danger sign, sniffles were not the thing to have, and in fact, her nose was perfectly clear and dry.

Then to her fury, she sneezed. Nerves and a tricky conscience.

The front door was drawn to with a thud. 'Una's back.' She took a deep breath of relief.

'How did she get in?'

'Oh, we all run in and out, she slipped the catch, I expect. Anyway, she has a key.'

I am getting some insight into how they live in Chapel Close, though Charmian, every community has its own rules. She herself did not hand out keys to her house to anyone.

Una came up the staircase, under her arm was a bundle wrapped in newspaper. She was carrying it as if she would rather it was not seen and if it was seen then you could assume it was nothing important.

Charmian looked at her. Why, she's trembling.

Una marched into Mary's sitting-room, and turned towards them, her face bleak and tight. 'I want to show you something.'

'Wait a minute.' Mary Erskine bent down to put a match to the log fire already laid. 'Let me light the fire. I feel cold.'

The wood caught at once and blazed up, the flames reflected in the brass fire irons. Across the room the image of the marble fireplace, curving and elegant, could be seen in the gilt mirror on the wall opposite the window.

Between the two long windows at the front of the house, Mary Erskine had placed a small round table on which stood a bowl of white narcissi. Una went over, moved the flowers aside and put her parcel on it. From the disturbed flowers came a breath of sweetness.

The newspaper fell away to reveal a plastic carrier bag underneath. Dark green, it bore the name of a famous shop. Charmian felt a flash of amusement: how like Chapel Close to wrap its secrets up in a Harrods bag.

Una drew a garment out of the bag and laid it on the table. It was a jacket in soft blue wool, crumpled and mud-stained.

Charmian stared at it: the night on which Louise Farmer had died had been rainy.

Una read her face. 'Yes, it's hers. No name or anything but I think it's hers. The girl's.'

Charmian advanced towards the table. 'Where did you get it?' Mary walked over and reached out a hand. 'No, don't touch it?' Mary drew back quickly. 'If it's evidence, there are certain rules and not touching is one. If it is evidence. Where did you find it?' she said again.

Una had controlled her shaking and her voice was steady, but it was so low that it could hardly be heard. 'Found it tucked away in the old kitchen scullery. Not in this bag. I put it in that. Wrapped in paper, newspaper.'

'What newspaper? This newspaper?'

'No. A London evening paper,' Una said quickly. 'But that doesn't mean anything . . . I collect them from everyone, I use them for the children, papier-mâché stuff which we make at school, everyone gives them to me. Mary has, haven't you, Mary?' Mary Erskine, appealed to, nodded, but with reluctance, she would rather be out of this.

'Where is it now?' Information had to be extracted from Una like squeezing a lemon.

'Burnt it.'

'Did you see the date on it?' Charmian had to repeat the question before Una answered.

Una turned her face away. 'I didn't notice.'

'Sure? I think you did. Why did you bring this jacket to me, if you are not going to be open about it?'

'It might have been the day the girl was found,' said Una reluctantly.

'And when did you find it?'

'Might have been a day or two afterwards.'

'And your husband, what did he say? Did he know?'

'Well, he wasn't around,' said Una evasively.

'Where has it been all this time?' asked Mary. Her eyes met Charmian's who gave a small nod. It would have been her next question.

Una gave a little shake of her head, like a dog brushing away something uncomfortable. 'I took it and hid it. Locked it away.'

'Where it could not be found easily?'

'I suppose so.'

'And has Ted been looking for it, do you think?'

'Well, he could have been . . . I considered it.'

I bet you did, thought Charmian.

'Why have you brought it out to me now?'

Una raised her voice a degree: 'I wanted it to come into the open. It's making me feel sick.'

She put out a hand. 'I've touched it before, so I might as well do so again.' She opened the jacket, gently shaking out the folds.

Inside the jacket was creased and a bit grubby. Might be minute traces there, she thought. Invisible evidence to be found by the scientists.

'Tell me again where you found the jacket.'

'In the old scullery, tucked away behind some pipes.' Una looked towards Mary who came forward and put an arm round her shoulders.

'You went looking? Why did you do that?'

Una shrugged. 'Don't know.'

'It's the question you will be asked. Did you suspect something was hidden there? What made you suspect?'

'Just felt like looking,' said Una doggedly.

Charmian and Mary Erskine exchanged looks. Una had suspected Ted of something.

Charmian left that question hanging in the air. In a way, Una had answered it: she had reason to suspect Ted of some close knowledge about the death of the girl. Had she seen him hide the garment?

'So what did you do with the jacket when you found it?'

Reluctantly, Una said: 'I hid it again. In a place of my own.'

'Which was?'

'I have a place,' said Una. She took a deep breath. 'Behind the book shelves.'

The secrets of Chapel Close are coming tumbling out of the cupboard, thought Charmian. Here is Una more or less accusing her husband of murder, and there is dear Mary Erskine who is certainly up to something and thinks she has got away with it. What was she doing in that drawer?

She gave them both a bleak smile. Two conspirators, she thought, but perhaps not in the same plot. 'I shall have to take this jacket away, you understand that?' Una nodded. 'And you will be questioned.' Una looked frightened.

'And Ted?' She moved a step away from Mary Erskine, and seemed to brace herself.

Charmian said: 'We shall have to find him.'

She meant her voice to sound gentle, but in spite of herself, it came out grimly.

The room felt cold, although the fire leapt and crackled: there was a cold wind blowing through the room and round the three women.

Before she left Mary Erskine's house, Charmian had the jacket and its bag neatly stowed away inside a plastic sack which Mary produced. It looked like the thick plastic bags that line rubbish bins, grey and sulky looking, but it would do.

Then she had Una sign a note saying how she had found it and when, and how she had handed it over to Charmian.

She drove to her office, dark and fastened up for the night, disturbing the security guard, who appeared with his dog and his thermos flask, and locked it away in her safe.

Lights showed here and there in the darkness in the small secluded building which housed her department, it was never quite asleep. Even when the human staff slept the computer and the electronic equipment went on working. It had been part of her task to oversee the installation of the new computer which was linked with the mainframe at headquarters which was itself locked into a national network. Her office was only yards away from the Force's Regional HQ but no one walked across with messages nor always spoke on the telephone but poured out words across the fax.

She must encourage terseness in the people she worked with, it was too easy to be verbose these days what with word processors and fax machines. Recruiting the right staff had been another of her responsibilities. And a difficult job it had been too. Her second in command, Bernard Jaysmith, had been wished on her, being the man who would have got her position if she hadn't, never a very good beginning to a relationship, and he had been pesky ever since.

She would like to have recruited Sergeant George Rewley, but his feet were set on another path and what she could offer might not have led to the promotion he deserved. She kept in close touch with him nevertheless.

There were advantages after all to this electronic talking, she reflected as she left him a message to telephone her in the morning.

She drove home to Maid of Honour Row in good spirits. Her life was going well: she was enjoying her new position. But intellectually it was a desert.

So now she had sought out for herself a puzzle. She had never seen the dead girl, Louise Farmer, so for the moment she could keep emotion out of it. At a distance, anyway. Pity, dislike of the killer, even fear would creep in closer and closer as she learned more about the case and how Louise had died and why. Towards the end you always wanted to kick someone, if not kill them, then at the absolute end there was very often despair. But for now it was a puzzle, and no more.

The puzzle of Ted, the disappearing husband, where was he and what lay behind his strange behaviour. Not just shock at finding Louise Farmer's dead body, of this she was convinced.

She found herself thinking about the circle of children at St Catherine's who seemed infected with visions. Sixteen of them had Luke Mallet said? Now that was a pretty puzzle in itself.

Luke himself was an interesting character. Too fond of young girls? She thought she had picked up a hint of that. Had he had a fancy for Louise? No evidence on that score but it was something to think about.

Nor was this all, there was Mary Dalmeny Erskine, so delightful, a genuine friend, with her own genuine little problem unless Charmian was much mistaken.

And what about Una, an enigma inside a problem inside a puzzle? Her strange upbringing might have produced eccentric behaviour but why had she produced the jacket which made a tacitly damning accusation of her husband? Lady Mary said she loved him.

Wish I could see Ted Gray, thought Charmian, I'd ask him a few pointed questions.

Such as: Have you indeed got a shotgun, and what are you planning to do with it and why? Also: Have you been looking for the jacket while Una was got out of the house under the pretext of meeting you at the railway station? Una herself seemed to think this might be so.

Ted Gray and Una, his wife, the way they went on, they were part of the puzzle indeed; but the heart of it was the dead girl, Louise Farmer. Never forget that, she told herself.

Charmian sat up in her bed, propped up by pillows, and jotted down a few notes, with her cat, Muff, leaning on her feet.

Her house was warm and quiet. She looked around her bedroom with pleasure. Nicer here than in Chapel Close. Not so grand but more comfortable.

Muff yawned and turned over, her tail giving a lazy flick which said Do Not Disturb, Cat Sleeping. Charmian turned off the radio by her bed; she had been listening to the local late-night news.

Nothing of interest, which was how she liked it. No blazing fires which might be arson, no explosions, no robberies and no dead bodies, in or out of cars, on the roadside or hidden among the bushes. Windsor, Eton, Merrywick, Cheasey and Slough seemed to be at peace.

But she was not deceived, she knew that violence and crimes were taking place in that dark world outside her windows. Someone, somewhere would be up to something.

She was surprised to be disturbed by a telephone call from George Rewley while she was still sitting over her breakfast cup of coffee at the kitchen table.

The first cup too, she thought, vaguely irritated, I'm not awake yet.

It had to be Rewley, the phone seemed to ring with special vibrancy for him, she could feel his energy pulsing over the line. So early, too.

But it meant Rewley was anxious, and an anxious Rewley was not someone to keep waiting. She reached out for the portable telephone.

Her kitchen was a small friendly, comfortable place, very unlike

70

the one in Chapel Close. Charmian was not much of a cook, and certainly not a natural homemaker, but she was pleased with what she had made of this room which was the original Victorian kitchen and scullery knocked into one with a big window looking out on the garden. The walls had recently been painted a bright buttercup yellow, and she had a few kelim rugs chosen for their warm, strong colours on the waxed wooden floor. On the wall opposite the window was a large crayon drawing of a bitch with puppies. She kept it there because the price she had paid for it had gone to an animal charity, but also because once the bitch had saved her life and she wanted to be reminded of it and be grateful as well. She liked this life she had, and you didn't get too many second chances in it.

'Rewley?'

'Understand you've got something for me, ma'am?' It was a work conversation, so although married to Charmian's god-daughter, they were to be formal. She bestirred herself from her morning sleepiness, dislodged the cat from her lap and dragged her dressing-gown closer around her.

'Yes, a jacket that may have belonged to the girl, Louise Farmer.' She recounted how it had come into her hands.

Rewley was silent for such a long time that she thought he might have gone away.

'George?'

'Here. Sorry to be slow. I was thinking. It's really interesting what you're telling me. The fact is there was a jacket of the girl's that she was thought to have had with her and which was missing. Not on her body, not on the ground where she was lying. But we haven't advertised this missing piece . . . Looks as though you've struck gold there, ma'am.'

Muff appeared through the cat-flap in the kitchen door, leapt on the table and thrust her cold nose into Charmian's face. She liked the telephone and usually appeared if you were talking on it.

Charmian pushed her away. 'It may not be the right one, probably is though, it feels right.'

'Ted Gray will have some explaining to do when we find him.'

'He's around somewhere, I think. I had a feeling there was someone lurking around Chapel Close last night, but I may be

71

wrong.' She hadn't actually seen anyone, just had the impression of movement. 'You'll want to confirm it did belong to the girl, and also have forensics run over it.'

'And we'll need to have a look at the place where it was hidden. And talk to Una Gray.'

'I don't know if you'll get anything out of her. She didn't say much to me, except it made her feel ill. The jacket's a bit dirty, you might get something of use, blood maybe.' Unseen by the naked eye.

Another pause followed. Then, 'No blood on the girl,' Rewley said. 'None, not a trace, and not much dirt.'

'Blood is always useful,' said Charmian drily. 'You can analyse it and hopefully match it.'

'Hope is the word.' Rewley did not sound cheerful. 'Someone's blood, yes, sure, but you have to locate that someone.'

Charmian recognised the mood. 'No progress?' Every case stalled at some point and sometimes they never took off again.

'Finding the jacket opens things up, yes, I admit it, but I just have that feeling in the pit of my stomach that says it's going to turn out to be one of those opportunist crimes that you can never get a handle on.' Rewley was definitely gloomy now. 'Some chancer, Ted Gray, maybe someone else, just took what the devil gave him.'

'No rape or robbery, though, that's odd, isn't it?'

'Interrupted perhaps,' said Rewley even more gloomily. 'Or he gets his kicks some other way.'

'You won't get anywhere thinking that way. You must take a positive line. Why was she killed?'

'I don't think we are going to get anywhere, I have that feeling . . . But there's one thing: she wasn't killed where she was found.'

'That's your way forward then.'

'If we can find out where, yes . . . Forensics may come up with something. There was a hint of something pink on the back of her neck and on the blouse . . . Seems to be powder of some sort. Chalky and tinted. Could be face powder but it's a bit red for that.'

'Rouge?'

'Perhaps she was killed in a chemist's shop or a beauty salon, or by someone who worked in one,' said Rewley. 'But somehow I don't think so. Any suggestions are welcome.'

'Well, the jacket may help there.'

'Agreed, and thanks. I mean I really am grateful, even if I don't sound it. It does seem to point to Ted Gray.'

'Yes, he'll have to be found.'

'It may not be left to us . . . Two other people are in the field, and they may find him first. It's been noticed that Brian Farmer, Louise's father, has been meeting with Ginger Rivers, the dad of her boyfriend, the one who was killed by a hit-and-run driver. Remember him?'

'Oh yes.' The hit and run motif again.

'It's not clear what they are up to, but if they've elected Ted Gray as the killer and get to him first, then I wouldn't say much for his chances. Rivers is a real tough operator and quite capable of doing a number on Gray if he finds him.' There was a pause, and Charmian could hear the rustle of paper as if he was consulting notes. 'They've been seen hanging around together. Constable on the beat identified them. It could have been one of them, or both, that you sensed in Chapel Close. I wish you'd got a proper look.'

'Rivers is in it for money, I take it?'

'That would come into it, but there might be something personal as well. The two kids loved each other. I'd say it was more straight revenge, but I expect Farmer will be paying him expenses.'

'I knew there was someone hanging about Chapel Close last night,' said Charmian. 'I wish I had trusted my instinct and taken a look.'

'Can't be helped, ma'am. I think I'll have to take a look round there myself.'

'What you want is someone to walk in off the street, and give you something new to start you off again.' The jacket might be that fresh start.

'A gift from the gods? An answer to a prayer.'

'I've known it happen.'

That was it for the moment. Charmian finished her breakfast, gave Muff some warm milk and went upstairs to dress.

No need to make the bed or do any tidying up, her delightful daily help, young Minnie Beadle, was due to arrive soon. But

Charmian was giving a small dinner party soon so there were a few notes about food and shopping to leave for Minnie, and that would mean consulting the recipe in a cookery book.

She would be cooking the meal herself, something simple but she was beginning to read cookery books even if not to learn much from them. Was cooking a substitute for sex?

Mrs Mallet was going to be one of the dinner guests. A local couple with whom she had become friendly and possibly Lady Mary. On the table in the kitchen was her large diary which told her which day she would be giving one of the speeches at St Catherine's Jubilee celebrations. Mrs Mallet and her own sense of public relations had got her into that engagement.

I'd like to meet that Pix, she thought, checking the date on which she was due to appear, the boy that sees doubles, and infects a whole circle of seers. It's an interesting phenomenon. You can't say that it's been caused by the girl's murder but it might have been triggered off by it. A child psychologist might have some pertinent observations to make, possibly about Pix's home life and how happy he was in it. Did he have siblings and how he did he feel about her or him?

The telephone rang as she was getting into her car. She fielded it neatly on the angle of her arm.

Rewley again.

'Have you been doing any praying?'

'No. Why?'

'Well, you've had an answer to the prayer anyway. What you predicted has come about. Enter the stranger.' He sounded excited.

'Go on.'

When Rewley spoke again, there was an odd note in his voice. 'A girl has come forward. School friend of Louise. Came in yesterday afternoon, but I've only just heard about it. Says she knows something.' He paused. 'Cuts across everything I've been saying about a chancer, everything I had felt about this case. I haven't seen the girl yet myself, but I have read her statement. Dolly Barstow took it. She claims that Louise was frightened, knew she might be killed.'

CHAPTER SEVEN

A look at the day previous, April 11, and then on to April 13

In every case, as Charmian knew well, there can be an unexpected someone who walks on the scene and opens it up.

This time it was Lily Paget. She had walked into the Merrywick Road Police Station, after school, unaware that she was an answer to a prayer, well aware that she was something of a goddess, and after a substantial row with her parents. 'Keep out of it, darling,' her mother had said. 'I don't want you part of this,' had been her father's judgement.

She was a goddess, was Lily, because of her looks: tall, fair and with big blue eyes. She also had a high IQ and was considering joining Mensa. Her father had tried and been turned down, which made a good reason for Lily going in to win. She was a natural competitor.

But she was not a girl who went behind people's backs: if she was going to the police to talk about her friend, Louise Farmer, then she had to tell her parents first.

The Paget home was just around the corner from the Merrywick police station, so Lily had had the opportunity to think about what she wanted to do every time she passed it. She had considered walking into Windsor to call in the Headquarters there but had decided upon the local unit, because she knew one of the station sergeants. Jim Macaulay was based there, his daughter was a school mate, although much junior, and he had been very decent to her when her cycle had skidded into a shop window in Merrywick Parade. Which was more than could be said for the shop owner who had been more concerned for his window than her skin. Lily never forgot friends or enemies and ever since had looked after little Emma Macaulay (who had won an open scholarship to the expensive school and was possibly its cleverest pupil), while jilting her own boyfriend whose father was the unlucky owner of the fruit shop and whose strawberries had been squashed by Lily on her bike.

Accordingly she went into the station on her way home from school on the afternoon after the confrontation with her parents. Jim might be on duty or he might not, but she was hopeful; Emma thought he was. He'd be around, anyway, was the word.

'Hello, Jim.' He was there behind the desk, talking to a WPC. Lily turned on the charm. Legitimate occasion, she didn't do it all the time, she had good taste, and knew how to use her assets.

'Hello, Lily. What can I do for you?'

In a few carefully chosen and well-rehearsed sentences (not a Mensa and Oxford hopeful for nothing) she told him.

She saw his face change. The jokey look went, to be replaced by a severe, professional face. Quite frightening, this was not the cosy friend who made you laugh and helped you mend a puncture on your bike.

'If this isn't for real, you're in dead trouble, Lily.'

'I can't prove it, it was said to me privately, but I'm telling the truth.'

Jim Macaulay studied her face. 'I believe you,' he said, turning away. 'Come through here. I'll get someone to talk to you.'

'What about you? Can't I talk to you?' Suddenly, Lily felt more nervous than she had expected.

'Not my case. Besides, there'll be questions. Can you stand up to that, Lily?'

Lily nodded, but she lagged behind, confidence ebbing away fast; she tried to hang on to the charm, but she could feel that slipping too. 'If I'm going to be late, I ought to tell my mother.'

'Do your parents know you are coming here?'

'Yes.' Not an absolute truth, she had not told them exactly when and how.

'Good.' He looked at Lily with something of a kinder look. 'We'll get your mother. She'd better come in.'

Lily looked worried. She knew how her mother would react: badly.

She had recovered her composure by the time Sergeant (CID) Dolly Barstow, in company with her mother, appeared. After a look at Dolly's face, she decided not to try for the charm again. Charm would not work with this one, only truth and honest statements would do.

All at once, what she had to say seemed terribly little, maybe not important after all.

Dolly Barstow had driven over from the Incident Room in Bassecourt Road in Windsor where the group investigating Louise Farmer's death was based. Mrs Paget sat in the corner, after giving Lily a kiss in which affection, anxiety and reproach were nicely blended. Lily could see What is your father going to say? floating in smoking letters over her head.

Sergeant Dolly Barstow was a tall, slender woman, whose gentle manner was deceptive. She was bright, clever and tough. For work she dressed conservatively, but off duty she allowed herself a wilder taste in fashion, and even on duty she sometimes indulged a little. She enjoyed the soft silk underneath her tailored shirt and what she wore there was her own business.

Lily gave her a nervous look.

Dolly took it quietly. She let Lily establish her credentials. How she was Louise's best friend, how they always walked home together, how they were in the same set for French and English, but not for Maths. Lily was too good for Louise in this subject. She got the delicate implication that Lily was the cleverer girl.

'She had a boyfriend?'

Lily nodded. 'Yes, I knew him, that is I'd seen him. Well, I was there when we all met. They took off straight away . . . I liked him too, but it was her he fancied.' She gave a smile and tried to look sophisticated.

'Where was this?'

'In a wine bar on the Cheasey Road.'

Dolly knew the place. 'The White Cavalier?'

Lily nodded. 'We were old enough,' she said defensively. 'And we had something to eat.'

Just old enough, Dolly thought. Just.

77

'Then we went to a disco, he knew people there. He was a really wild boy. Well, Cheasey's like that, isn't it? We knew that.'

Part of the fun, Dolly thought.

'All the same, he was nice. And he and Louise really took off. I didn't see much of her except for school after that.' Lily looked away to the window. They were in a bleak little interview room, but outside it was blustery spring and the trees were waving in the wind. 'That is, until he died. He was hit by a car and died. Louise came and talked to me after that. She told me that he said he'd been run down on purpose. That he thought he knew who did it.'

'Did you believe her?'

'Yes, I did, and she believed him.' It was said in a strong, defiant voice.

'Go on.'

'Can I have a drink of water?'

Dolly gave her one, pouring it herself into a plastic mug. Her own throat was dry.

'And he thought he knew why: he'd been offered a contract and got cold feet and drawn back. Said no.'

'Are you saying what I think you are saying?'

'Yes. Cheasey is like that, you know.' Dolly thought she did know. All the same, what this girl was saying was remarkable. 'Someone wanted someone killed. For money. He'd been approached. At first, he'd said yes. But he couldn't do it, Louise said, and so he'd been done himself. To keep him quiet.'

'Why did she tell you?'

'She had to talk to someone . . . And she was a bit frightened. She had an address and meant to go there, she was going to do something about it.'

'I'll ask again: did you believe her?'

'Yes. And you do too.' Lily was firm. 'I think she told me just in case . . . and she was right.'

'You didn't try and stop her?'

'You couldn't stop Louise.'

'Did she give you any names?'

'No. She knew a name, but she didn't tell me.'

Dolly studied her face. Yes, she believed her. But was there something else behind those large blue eyes.

'Hint at anything?' she asked.

Lily dropped her eyes and shook her head.

Something there, Dolly thought, but for the moment, she left it.

Sex? What about that, Dolly wanted to know, trying to establish the parameters of this relationship. Had Louise and the boy had a close sexual relationship?

'Well, you know . . . '

So they probably had. Or to a limited extent. She recalled that the girl had been a virgin.

'But I don't really know,' said Lily, recovering her spirit. 'I didn't ask and she didn't say. But I would have, so there,' she ended defiantly. 'What I'm trying to say is that they were both nice people and serious about each other.'

Drugs? Dolly inquired.

'We knew where they were to be had . . . but I didn't and I'm sure Louise didn't.'

They probably had then, a little bit, Dolly thought, and she might use that as a handle, a pressure point, or someone else would later, if it had be done.

'Why did you wait before coming in to tell all this?'

'Because of the sort of questions you're asking now,' said Lily with spirit.

Dolly made some careful notes on a pad, or pretended to, she had a tape recorder going for the real business, then said: 'Are you sure she didn't give any hint? Names or places?'

Lily gave her mother a careful look. You aren't going to like this, it said.

'Something else . . . Do you know St Catherine's School?'

'Good Lord,' said her mother.

'I've heard of it,' said Dolly cautiously. She knew of it as an expensive private school. She also knew, since she had excellent local information and liked to know what her superiors were up to (since such knowledge could influence one's own behaviour), that Charmian had an engagement at the school as guest speaker on the occasion of the school's Jubilee. 'So what about it?'

Lily gave her silent mother another cautious look.

'Louise sort of hinted that the school might be involved some-how . . . Just an impression she gave me, I didn't really think

79

much of it until the little boys started seeing things . . . visions. My small brother has been having terrible nightmares . . . ' She looked at her mother. 'Sorry, mum, we didn't tell you. He asked me not to.' She turned to Dolly, 'It's his best friend, Pix, you see.'

At that time, Dolly Barstow did not know anything of Pix and his visions, but she realised she was hearing something quite unique in criminal investigation.

So Dolly reported back to Inspector Elman in the Incident Room who passed on the information to Chief Inspector Father. In the course of nature, Sergeant George Rewley became privy to it, and in his turn told Charmian Daniels, who would have got to hear anyway, but it might have taken time.

'So we have a motive for the killing of the girl,' said George Rewley, 'and a few more questions to ask Ted Gray when we get to him.'

Such as: Whom did you want a contract on?

Charmian heard what he had to say with interest and asked for all notes and reports to be sent at once, and to speed up the forensics on the jacket.

We'll have to shake that Pix and get some information out of him, she thought.

CHAPTER EIGHT

The next day but one, April 15

Inside Charmian was a small observer who watched everything and then told it all back to her. Making a story out of a chain of events. I am telling you, this person would say, listen to me, this is how it is.

Childlike almost, which was why Charmian thought she, of all the police team, would understand Pix and his visions.

Pix and Lily Paget, the jacket and Una Gray, and Louise Farmer seemed part of the same pattern, but it was hard, Charmian thought, to make out the grand design. She felt as though she had conjured up Lily Paget herself out of the air. It was as if a bell had tolled with Lily's entrance.

The formal identification of the jacket by Louise's father was attended by Inspector Fred Elman himself, conscious as he was of the presence of Charmian Daniels in the background.

'This way, sir.' Elman led the man into a small room at the back of the Bassecourt Road premises, an old school taken over by the police. 'Sorry to ask this of you, but you understand that I have to.'

Her father was led to the jacket where it was laid out on a table. He stared at it, nodded, and then turned away, his eyes full of tears. 'It's hers.'

'You're sure. Take another look if you want to.'

'I remember the day she bought it and came home with it. First time she got a proper dress allowance . . . Not much, but it gave her a bit of freedom.' In a thick voice, he said: 'Don't let her mother see it. Never let her mother see it.'

'It won't be necessary. Sorry I had to drag you here.'

'Drag me anywhere and any time you like if it will help catch Louise's killer . . . ' He hesitated, then said in a low voice: 'Is there blood on it?'

Elman hesitated. 'Can't say yet, sir.'

'His blood or Louise's?' There was no mistaking the anger in his voice or who he was accusing.

'We'll be looking, sir. It has to be gone into.'

'Where did you find the jacket?'

'I can't tell you that at the moment, sir.' Perhaps his very refusal said something, revealed more than he thought, because Farmer said something under his breath: it sounded very much like a threat.

'Don't do anything rash, sir.' Elman spoke kindly.

'What did you say?' It was a question but there was total comprehension in the man's eyes, he had heard and knew what Elman meant, yet there was something more, knowledge of himself perhaps, and resolution.

'Just advice.'

Farmer fixed his eyes on Fred Elman's face. You can't stop me doing what I want, his eyes said.

'I'll show you out, sir.' Fred Elman took Farmer to the door and watched him drive away. I wish we could keep tabs on that man, he thought uneasily. But he knew he had no solid justification, except an uneasy feeling that something was brewing. He had no officers to spare anyway, for one reason and another, the Force was stretched.

He sat down heavily and stared at the top of his desk while the thought ran round his mind: I'm looking for Ted Gray, and that man is looking for Ted Gray and perhaps he thinks he has found him. I don't like what I see in his eyes.

It would not have been much good if he had put a watch on Farmer. Farmer and Rivers had worked out a way of communicating that kept them very private, and now Brian Farmer went to the nearest public call box. He dialled a number and the telephone rang in another public call box in Cheasey, and was soon picked up and answered.

The message was simple: same time, same place.

He knew when they would meet and where, it had all been set

up, and what they had in mind to do was better kept as secret as possible.

'I'll keep Grace out of this, but by God, I'll get Gray,' he told himself. How he would keep the truth from his wife, when Grace could see through him straight to the other side, he did not know, but it had better be done: she had enough to bear. This was a man's work.

Una, interviewed as soon as possible by Inspector Elman in company with Sergeant Rewley, dutifully revealed where she had found the blue jacket. She had removed it from underneath the old sink in an unused outbuilding which was a part of the old kitchen premises.

'It was a laundry once, where the washerwoman washed the clothes. Of course, we don't use it now.' She managed a small smile at the notion of a washerwoman. Rewley thought that the ghost of that unlucky Victorian working woman (must have been a whole succession of them in fact, poor things) still hung around the dank little room.

Not a room they ever went into, Una had said.

It was dark and damp and empty, smelling of dry rot and decay. But that was just the potatoes, Una explained, they used to keep root vegetables there. Still a few in the corner. Not a pleasant place all the same.

So wasn't that just the place to hide something unpleasant you didn't want found, Rewley thought, and yet at the same time, just the place you would search?

If you were looking, but Una said she had not been, the jacket had been found by chance, she just happened to go in there. 'And I looked down and saw the flash of blue.'

Rewley didn't believe her for a minute. 'Don't believe you, madam,' he said to himself, but since Elman was doing the questioning, he did not say it aloud. 'You are lying.' He thought she would have had to bend down quite far to see the jacket. She was looking for what she found.

Una confirmed the story of trying to met Ted Gray at the station. Three times, she said. No, she did not know why he was behaving like this, nor where he was. No, she had had no more messages.

Yes, she had thought he might be camping out in his office, but she was beginning to doubt this idea now although he might have been there earlier. He was somewhere, but she didn't know where.

'Can this room be locked, Mrs Gray?' Elman had asked politely. 'We'll have to go over it, you see.'

Una nodded. 'Yes. You can have the key.' There was a large old key in the door. 'So I suppose you'll all be coming back?'

'Some other officers, Mrs Gray,' said Elman. 'They will try not to trouble you.'

Rewley had listened to Fred Elman questioning her and thought his own thoughts. The house was still and quiet. Chill too, as if Una did not mind being cold. He had observed some good furniture and pieces of silver here and there, and a couple of nice pictures, a landscape and a few portraits on the walls. All inherited, he supposed. In a place of honour on a desk was a photograph of a group of small children with Una in the middle and Luke Mallet standing behind. Una was smiling and looked happy. She had looked pretty then as well as cheerful.

She didn't look happy now, nor pretty.

'That woman is scared stiff,' he reported in due course later that day to Charmian Daniels. 'Emotion there all right.'

'Yes, I'm sure,' said Charmian cautiously. She was in her office where all the walls had ears.

'She may think her husband is a killer who is out to kill her next. And he could be, too.'

'Motive? He has to have a reason.'

'They've both got money, haven't they? He may want hers. That may be the primary motive.'

'Possibly,' agreed Charmian. 'What did you make of her? Think she's telling the truth?'

'She's hard to read but I suppose I would say she's holding something back. She may be telling the truth as far as she can . . . I'd like to inspect all that house. It's a house of secrets.' Elman would probably take his chance once he got his men in.

'Isn't it?' agreed Charmian. 'Exactly how I felt.' But she couldn't make out whose secrets and how old they were. They might be very old indeed, it was a house in which a lot might have happened.

'She has a photograph of her with some children. From the

school, I suppose. Didn't seem the same woman in that picture, younger, jollier.' Charmian reflected that it was hard to feel the Una Gray she had met had ever been jolly. 'St Catherine's? The school might be worth taking a look at. Don't know what excuse you could find.'

'I could think of one,' said Rewley confidently. 'Not too hard. Security or some such.'

Charmian thought she could find a better reason: she was going to speak there, she could ask to see the hall, so she would know how to project her voice. In any case, she wanted another sight of Luke Mallet, he seemed the sort of man with whom many women might be in love, and it could be this was the trouble with Mary Dalmeny Erskine.

Mary would not like being in love with someone who was not interested in her. Nor could you blame her.

She would drive round there tonight and take a look at the school. It was a habit of hers, if it was at all possible, to take a look at a building or a site that figured, however remotely, in a murder. You could pick up clues to the puzzle, visually, or out of the air.

Or she could borrow her dog Benjy from his weekday home with the retired witches, Birdie Peacock and Winifred Eagle, and take him for a long walk that way. Dogs always provided a splendid excuse for strolling about. Or come to think of it, Birdie and Winifred were a mine of local information and could provide the newest gossip.

As, for that matter, could old Mrs Beadle, who was coming in to help her daughter-in-law clear up after the dinner party. But Mrs Beadle was inclined to focus on her own neighbourhood and thus was better informed on Merrywick and its affairs than Windsor.

It was probably not the best of times to hold a dinner party with all that she had in her mind of suspicion and doubt, but she was not going to put it off. It would be interesting to see what, if anything, she could get out of Mrs Mallet senior. Her two other friends, a vet and his wife, herself a journalist and the daughter of a local editor, usually knew all the gossip too. And there was Lady Mary who could be prodded to say something about Una and Ted Gray that cleared up some points.

'I'll invite her ladyship, last minute but she might be able

85

to come.' Aloud, she said to her secretary: 'Tess, see if you can get Lady Mary Erskine to my dinner . . . the details are in my diary.'

Tess gave her a startled look and nodded, she looked perpetually anxious these days. 'Wonder if I overwork her?' Charmian asked herself before applying herself to some necessary reports.

She might go on look round tonight. Or tomorrow. Nothing would happen tonight, it was a slow sort of case. It would come to the boil in the end, but not just yet.

That was how she felt then on the spring afternoon.

Pix, that late afternoon on which Charmian was deciding that nothing would come to the boil just yet, was painting a picture. He had drawn the outline of a figure and was now filling it in with colour. He was in a black mood.

He had lost a bit of weight lately and his face was pinched. His little sister was more than ever a trouble to him, keeping him awake when she cried. Teething, his mother said, but he thought she was just bored in the middle of the night and wanted company. You were supposed to love your sister, but so far he did not love her. He hoped he got to like her better but she didn't grow on him. Frankly, he doubted if they'd ever have much in common.

For that matter, his elder half-brother, Alex, was almost as much a trouble to him since he had wished on him a kind of extra aunt, Mary Erskine, who kept hanging over him, asking him how he was. Not what he was doing, the usual question one got asked, but how he was. Pix did not appreciate being dug up every so often and having his roots examined. He *was* in a black mood. His mother was better in that way: she just looked out a book and said read that, dear, it will help you, as if every worry could be solved by reading about it. Sometimes it could. She was clever, his mother. But there were moments when a cuddle would have helped him more. He wished she knew that simple fact.

Pix put his brush around the figure he had drawn and irresistibly his brush painted in a shadow head behind. He stopped, dabbing water on it to get rid of it; there must be no shadow.

Una looked over his shoulder. 'What is it you are painting, Pix?' It looked a thorough mess, Pix was no artist, words were his medium, but she recognised the picture meant something to him. Maybe something important from the look on his face.

'A person.'

Yes, she thought she could see something or someone there, but he was now busily covering the outline with fresh paint, wiping it out. Una had come back to work only that day. Luke had welcomed her, putting a fond protective arm round her shoulders. 'Thanks, Una.' She had been glad to come and let him know it with a smile that was braver and more touching than she guessed. 'Any news of Ted?' he had gone on to ask. 'No news . . . I think he's dead.' Luke had looked shocked. 'Oh, come on now, Una, you mustn't say that.' What Una did not say aloud was: 'And I think he wanted to kill me.' What a thought to come to, what an end to a marriage.

Luke would understand if she had told him, he was a very sympathetic person, and she had wanted Luke's sympathy, but not then and in that place. Sympathy can be very dampening both to the receiver and to the giver if not offered in the right way. The rest of the teaching staff were being very sympathetic, Mary Erskine was being very sympathetic, and Una felt accordingly dampened.

In spite of Pix's efforts to wipe out his two-headed figure it remained there, shadowy but menacing.

'I think I can see what you are getting at,' she said thoughtfully to Pix.

Pix seemed to have imprisoned his creature inside a kind of Punch and Judy booth. Or a cage.

Pix thought she couldn't have understood what he was drawing as he hardly knew himself, his pencil and brush seemed to have taken over. Pix wished ardently that Una would go away. He drew away as far as he could and she saw this move with a frown.

The group of sixteen was changing its nature. Only Pix and his very closest friends still believed in the doubleman as such. The jokers had fallen away while suffering a few dark nights of the spirit, but there were still a few children suffering nightmares, for Pix had been a powerful persuader. Pix was the only one who knew. Knew for sure.

Nor was it a cat he had seen, that had been a stupid lie. He had seen what he had seen, touched what he had touched. There was a body there, he told himself, I felt it, even if it did not move. So what was the other one? The other that walked and got into a car?

Infections of a minor sort abounded that spring; it was a bad time at St Catherine's, with so many absences in the school at the moment, well above the average for this time of the year, that Luke was worried. Many of Pix's set were away sick, troubled with strange illnesses.

There were only six of them in the kindergarten art room whereas usually the number would have been about sixteen, some painting, others modelling in plasticine and one or two quietly engaged in creating messes.

It was late afternoon. Home soon, Pix thought trying to feel safe, he'd walk home with his gang. Toast for tea.

Although it was spring, darkness came early that day, with the low cloud that promised rain. The weather forecast at midday had said 'strong winds and rain'. On account of this prediction, Pix's mother had telephoned that she would meet him in the car. Wait for her by the school car park was the order.

She was late, of course. Pix stood with shoulders hunched in the dim cold spring afternoon and waited in loyal obedience. She would come, she never let you down, she always came in the end as she said she would. But patience was required.

It was lonely where he stood. All his friends had rushed away, melting into the dusk, scuffling and laughing.

Pix withdrew into the shelter of the old cycle shed while keeping his eyes on the road for the car. Would she bring the big car or the little one? The headlights would be on, so he would see her coming in the distance. He knew the way she came round that bend, fast and a bit reckless but really quite safe. He did feel safe with her. A desirable quality in a mother.

He wished she would hurry up, it wasn't even raining, he could very well have walked home, so a slight sense of grievance built up inside him. The old bike shed was not the most cosy place in the world, smelling as it did of damp earth. Rats too, so he had heard.

No headlights yet and it was getting darker with every passing minute. She wouldn't bring the baby, that precious article was not allowed out after dark. Perhaps the baby was ill, dead even, he couldn't resist hoping so. Not likely, however, baby sister seemed strong to his eyes. Too strong. So it was all right to think of her being dead as it was not going to happen, for children didn't die, so it wasn't wicked of him.

Thus thinking his primitive, powerful thoughts Pix stood there. He heard a movement behind him.

He started to turn round, but a hand came over his eyes, while he was grabbed by the neck and at the same time forced down on his knees on the damp ground.

A voice said, muffled and deep: 'Never speak of what you think you saw. You did not see it. Nothing was there. You saw nothing.'

He was dragged backwards. It was no longer the cycle shed, a familiar if unpleasing place. Pix felt as if he was in a dark vault with an earthy smell. Graves smelt like that, must do, he knew it in his bones. A hand lay heavy on his shoulder, pressing him down.

'You must never, ever, talk of what you think you saw again. If you do, then I will come and get you.'

The ancient, terrible fear of childhood: that someone would come and get you.

So far Pix had said nothing.

'I am dead,' said the voice, 'but you do not realise it.'

'People can't be dead and walk around,' said Pix stoutly. But it seemed they could.

'I will take you with me.'

'Children don't die.'

'Oh children can and frequently do.'

Do . . . Do . . . Do.

The words died away in a cavernous echo.

And that was how he passed it on later in his deepest conviction.

There are deaders out there.

Charmian discovered a gap in her working day, one committee ended earlier than expected and another was cancelled. She could have stayed in her office to work on, in certain moods she would have done just that, but on this day she used the time to collect her dog Benjy from her neighbours, the retired witches, and take him for a walk.

In doing so, she tried to pump them about Luke Mallet and the school, where Winifred Eagle had taught for a brief space, but the two ladies were busy chopping oranges for marmalade and not inclined to talk much. 'Luke was a nice little boy, pretty manners, but people grow up in their own way, don't they, dear? Old Margaret Mallet is a bit of a bully,' was all she got from Winifred and Birdie said nothing except, 'Yes, do take Benjy for a walk, the dear boy is panting for it.'

Panting for a run, Benjy was not. Sometimes Benjy liked to walk while at other times he felt lazy. Today he felt lazy. He had his own ways of showing it, such as dragging on the lead, or actually sitting down so that his bottom slid along the ground. But he was not a stupid dog, today he sensed that Charmian was not going to let him get away with anything much. So after ten minutes of sloth, he decided to step out. His mistress, not realising he was the victim of accidie, that vice compounded of sadness and laziness, strode forward, giving an absent-minded tug on the leash if Benjy seemed to be slowing.

She headed in the direction of St Catherine's School, it made a pleasant walk and there was a patch of open ground for Benjy to run in (not that he ever ran, a gentle trot was the utmost he tried for) and in any case, she wanted to look at the school. She might be able to get in and study the school hall where she would talk.

The late afternoon had become very misty. She surveyed the main school building at a careful distance from the road. It was a pleasing huddle of a building which gave a good impression of the school as being a place where appearances had value. It was well cared for, the paintwork was fresh around the newly washed windows. Daffodils brightened up the patch of grass between the school and the pavement.

She walked round the curve of the road towards the parking place. She could see this was empty but there was a car drawn up at the kerb. To her surprise she recognised it as Mary Erskine's.

She halted, and Benjy sat down gratefully. 'Hello Mary, what are you doing here?'

Mary looked troubled. 'It's Pix. His mother was going to pick him up from school but her car wouldn't start. So I said I'd do it. But I can't find him.'

'Probably walking home.'

'Do you think so?' Mary sounded doubtful. 'I didn't see him.'

'Gone home with a friend?'

'Oh I don't know.' She shook her head. 'I don't think so somehow. Not like Pix.'

Mary looked ruffled, her hair was untidy, there was a streak of mud up her sleeve. Not too pleased to see me, either, Charmian decided. Perhaps Lady Mary was one of those who hated to be seen except looking their very best. It struck her suddenly that she had rarely seen Mary other than well groomed and well dressed.

'Let's have a look round the school, he might be there.'

'Oh it's too late, he'd have left.'

You're not really putting your back into this. 'We'd better take a look round all the same.' Charmian dragged Benjy to his feet, he had sagged gratefully on to his bottom. 'Now where have you tried already?'

'Main school, but it's all locked up.'

'Quick work, you'd have expected someone to still be around.' Charmian thought of her own school days when the staff seemed to stay around talking and marking books for ages. But times had changed. 'Anywhere he's likely to be? Can you make an intelligent guess?'

'His mother said she would pick him up by the staff car park.' Mary pointed across the pavement to the pebbled stretch beyond the bushes. 'He's not there. No one is.'

'I'll go that way, you walk across the playing field.' Charmian strode forward. Then she stopped. This was an imaginative, anxious child who was already disturbed, he had to be found. 'What's Pix's mother like?' She had the feeling that she was dragging Mary behind her as well as Benjy.

'Oh a nice girl, second marriage for her too. Got married first when she was seventeen. Too young, really. She's the sister of Jamie Dalrymple. A kind of kin of mine, her grandmother and mine were cousins. And Alex, Billy Prescott's son by his first wife, is a friend . . . We all know each other. Philly's all right. Intellectual and all that but good . . . ' She stopped talking, conscious that Charmian was hardly listening to her.

91

Charmian nodded, taking in what she was told automatically and filing it away with all the other records she kept inside her head. All these people had interlocking relationships, she decided half irritably. There was that class thing again: knowing your cousins to the third degree. 'Are you all related?'

'Sort of. Don't sound so cross about it.'

'Not cross. I'm concerned about the boy.'

'Don't you think I am?'

Charmian pointed: 'What's that place?'

'The old bike shelter. It's never used now, the kids have a better, newer place near the front gate. No one goes there, except the gardener. There was a rat's nest in it last year.'

'All the more reason to look. Come on with me, we've got the dog.' Yes, Benjy might provide a protection against a ratling. He would certainly bark. She would bark herself if it came to that.

She led her little band across the gravel to the shed. It had no door but was a kind of dark hutch with unexpected depth. A vault-like place with a strong earthy smell.

No Pix. No little boy crouching there. But had she expected to find him there? Dead or alive? What a horrible thing to say. She must have said it aloud too because Mary gave a little cry of protest. 'No, not dead, don't say that.'

There was an old sack over in the corner. But it moved. Benjy growled. She dropped his leash and let him go forward. Rats?

And that was how they found Pix.

He was curled up tightly with hands over his face. Stiff, unwilling to be uncurled. Mary knelt by him. 'Pix?' She took his hand and tried to comfort him. 'Pix, what happened?' But he turned his face away and would not talk.

'Let me,' said Charmian. She lifted him from the ground. 'Let's get him home.'

Pix was still rigid, fixed in a curled up position. But 'Deaders,' he seemed to mutter, Charmian thought, as she carried him away, and then again. 'Deaders.'

'Who does he mean?' whispered Mary as they got into her car. 'Louise Farmer?'

Charmian shook her head silently. No, if Louise Farmer's ghost

92

was anywhere it was not frightening a little boy. About Ted Gray she was not so sure. She could think of circumstances in which he might have frightened Pix.

If Ted had killed Louise Farmer, which looked very likely on the evidence of the jacket, and Pix knew something, then he might find it worthwhile to frighten the child.

It was even possible he might take pleasure in it, and that was a horrible thought.

But she was careful this time that she did not say any of this aloud. Not to Mary, who was a friend of Ted's and a cousin of Una, his wife.

'She's the only one who's dead,' said Mary

CHAPTER NINE

That same day, April 15

It was while they were driving Pix to his home, with Benjy whining on the back seat, that Charmian had the thought that if she wanted to get to the bottom of this puzzle (which had started in such a small way with a missing husband and was now swelling with every passing day) then she must hang on to Mary Erskine.

Not literally so, Mary Erskine was not going to run away, but to her picture of Mary. Only by seeing her for what she was, understanding her, if that was not too patronising, would she be able to weave her way through this complex set of relationships to which Mary seemed to have the key.

A bit unrealistic this thought, Charmian decided, watching Mary Erskine's hands on the wheel; she was driving fast, but efficiently. Let's say I need a handle and she is it.

Mary gave her a couple of quick sideways looks, then turned back to the road ahead. 'How's the boy?'

Charmian had Pix in her arms, she looked down at him. Shivery, eyes closed. 'Not well. He's in a state of shock. Something or someone has frightened him.' Terrified him was probably truer.

'We'll have to get him talking.'

'I don't think he wants to talk to either of us.'

Mary drove on without a word. 'Can't blame him,' she said after a bit. 'Nearly back now.'

'Perhaps he'll talk to his mother.'

'Will you, Pix?' said Mary over her shoulder.

Pix did not answer.

It was not far from the school to where Pix lived; he could

walk home, and often did so with his gang of friends, the route was usually quiet, but tonight the Merrywick Road had a traffic diversion in the middle of it with a ROAD UP sign so that Mary had to concentrate on her driving. But as the way turned through the village, past the church and library, past old Mrs Beadle's house (who was looking out of her window as usual), the traffic lessened and she could talk.

'Don't you think sometimes it's better not to talk a thing out, but to keep it quiet inside and let it float away as if it had never happened?'

'Not really.'

'I suppose I couldn't expect you to.'

'I don't believe bad events float away, Mary. Be nice if they did. But they hang around, dirtying everything they touch.'

'I'll think about that.'

A slow tear rolled down Pix's cheeks as if he had heard what they said to his pain. Charmian stroked his hand. 'How much further?'

'Well, we're here now.' Mary drew up outside the pretty house where Pix lived with his mother and new sister. Phyllida Prescott was looking anxiously out of the window, she ran out when she saw them.

Charmian got out of the car, still carrying Pix. His mother held out her arms and Pix went into them stiff and unseeing like a doll upon whose cheek fell a solitary tear.

Charmian drove home, taking Benjy with her. He could stay the night, somehow she felt she wanted his company. He was more soothing and comforting than Muff who knew how to disappear in a cloud of enigmatic cat fur.

She had a strange feeling now about St Catherine's whose Jubilee she was invited to help celebrate. She understood she was not the only speaker, a famous lawyer (St Catherine's 1950) was also going to be present. She knew his name and reputation: he was said to be terrifying both in cross-examination and also in private life, but she would not be terrified because owing to her new position she was privy to certain information about him that revealed some facts he might have preferred hidden. He would never know she knew but it gave her a certain inner confidence:

95

she did not have a phobia about cats, nor did she have his rather strange obsession with dogs.

Just as well, she thought, as she met Muff on the doorstep. She picked up Benjy and carried him in, he too had a phobia about cats but with him it took the form of ardent love, which he was prepared to put into physical action if possible.

Her house was tidy and fresh, having been cleaned that day from top to bottom by Mrs Beadle Junior who came in from Merrywick on her cycle for that purpose, delighted, as she made clear, both to earn the money (Charmian was a generous employer) and to escape from her mother-in-law, Gertrude Beadle, the doyenne of Merrywick's old inhabitants, cleaning ladies, laundresses and general gossips. Young Mrs Beadle, while knowing everything, as she must do living in such close contact with that fountain-head of gossip, never tattled and rarely spoke.

Charmian went into the kitchen where she gave Muff a dish of food on the table and Benjy a bowl on the floor so that neither animal could interfere with the other while feeding. Whether he liked it or not, Benjy ate tinned cat food with Muff, which perhaps accounted for his identification with cats.

For herself she made a pot of tea, which she put in the middle of the table where Muff could not knock it over, while she went to take off her coat.

The tea would help her think. It would clear her mind while soothing her. Without the charming physical presence of Mary Dalmeny Erskine, questions were rising in her mind. Had Lady Mary only just arrived when Charmian had met her? Why had she looked dishevelled and where had the mud on her sleeve come from?

She was certainly lying about something, but what exactly?

Charmian stood in the middle of her bedroom without taking off her coat, and let the cold doubts surface. She didn't like what she had seen tonight, didn't like what she had heard about the terrors of some of the other children. The tough ones would cope, but the others, like Lily Paget's brother, might be bruised for life. Pix was in a different category, he was a special case, somehow the starting point for this infection of fear.

I'll get inside that school and tear it apart if I have to, she told herself. Might talk to Lily Paget, pretty sharp observer that girl, and as central to the whole business as Pix himself might be. Lily Paget knew both Louise Farmer and the school. She didn't know Ted Gray but she had pointed the finger at him.

Had it been Ted Gray who had frightened Pix tonight? Where was the man? So elusive and so much thought about, a tricky combination.

She went down to the kitchen to pour her tea, which had brewed nicely. Queen Anne's blend, which she bought at Fortnum and Mason's, is a delicate mixture which requires time to gather its strength and today she needed its strength.

Mrs Beadle had placed a pile of letters and a heavy manila envelope on the table by the flowers. Work, it could wait. She had already observed that her answerphone had two messages lined up for her. They could wait too. She finished her tea and swirled the cup round. Queen Anne's blend had thick, dark leaves which left a pattern in her cup. You could tell your fortune from the pattern, Mrs Beadle said, she did not want to know her fortune, but she could not help noticing that it looked black and ominous.

The double line going to a point looked like a knife. And there was a hangman's noose. Oh great, said a lot for your past, never mind your future, to see such symbols in your cup.

One way and another, your work did follow you about shaping your life. Or was it that you took on the work that fitted what you had it inside you to become?

Even as she sat there considering another cup of tea, the telephone rang. She ignored it for a moment, then answered. It was George Rewley.

'Oh there you are. I rang earlier. Did you get my message?'

'I've only just come in,' she lied. 'What is it?'

'It's about the blood.'

'Blood, what blood?' Her mind was still full of Pix. No blood there, although she would swear he was bleeding inside.

'The blood on the jacket, Louise Farmer's jacket.' George Rewley had an expressive voice which managed to get surprise, concern and faint reproof across while yet preserving the respect due to Charmian's rank.

Charmian got her mind to work. 'So there were traces? And not hers?' He wouldn't be ringing if it had been. The victim's own blood can tell you what they were, but you know that already,

97

what you want is someone else's blood because that person could be the killer.

'Microscopic traces but enough to group: Louise was group O and this blood is AB.' Just plain old O for Louise but AB was a blood group shared with only about three per cent of the population. 'And the AB blood group person was also possessed of a rhesus factor that is very unusual. That ought to help.' If we lay hands on a suspect, he meant.

'Too much to hope that Ted Gray was a blood donor?' said Charmian.

'He wasn't. I checked.'

'You might get a look at his medical records?'

'I might, but it would have to be strictly unofficial, and he happens to have a very prickly GP who is hot on patients' privacy.'

So he had tried. 'George,' Charmian said, 'see if you can get any information on Gray's mental state . . . Whether there is anything in his past or present life that might make him a torturer of children.'

'Eh?' Rewley was startled.

'We have a group of frightened children. One of whom is very badly frightened indeed. It may have nothing to do with the death of Louise Farmer, nor with Ted Gray.'

'But you think it has?'

'Just a feeling.'

'You mean he is going round terrorising these children? Do they say so?'

'No one is saying anything. Or not nearly enough. But a dead person comes into it somewhere.'

Very briefly, she told him of the events of that afternoon. 'Pix's mother will probably get her doctor to look at him, and she may make a complaint to the police. I recommended it, but I don't think we ought to wait . . . There's something nasty going on out there.' Not too far out there either. Let us say St Catherine's School.

There was a pause before George Rewley spoke again. 'Are you saying that serious child abuse is going on?'

'Not physical. If there is any maltreatment at all, it's emotional and mental.'

'Coming from inside the family?'

'How can I know? But I think not . . . It seems connected with the school, St Catherine's. You really have got to lay hands on Ted Gray.'

Who might be a murderer and a frightener of children. A modern monster prowling through the undergrowth.

At the back of her mind, although she did not want it to surface, was a residue of doubt about Mary Erskine, who had been on the spot where Pix was found and from whom Pix had turned away.

'Look, tomorrow I am having some friends to dinner in the evening. One of them is the former owner and headmistress of the school. Join us. Bring Kate, if you like.' Her god-daughter made a good dinner guest, being lively and cheerful, as well as exceedingly pleasant to look at. Moreover, her clothes were always a matter of interest to Charmian. If you watched what Kate was wearing you were always a step ahead of the fashion game. Also, her presence would provide a smoke screen for Rewley: he would come as her escort and not as a policeman.

Before she went to bed, she had one other telephone call.

'Mary here. I thought you might like to know about the boy.'

'How is he?'

'His mother sent for the family doctor. I stayed until he had been. He gave the boy a sedative. I think Philly could have done with one as well.'

'Did Pix say anything?'

'Didn't say a word.'

'He needs help. Professional help from a child psychologist.'

'Don't you think some episodes are best left to heal their own wounds?'

'No.' Her voice was cold. 'We've had that one out, Mary. No.'

'I don't think there is anything real behind it, you know, not a real happening. I think Pix has been frightening himself. I know him better than you do and he is that sort of little boy. Given to imaginings and fantasy, many children are. It all comes from inside Pix, it's spread all through that group like a kind of infection, some having nightmares, and others just making a joke of it. Luke says as many as sixteen have been involved. But there's nothing behind it, all fantasy.'

99

So she had been discussing it with Luke Mallet.

'Luke's been told about the latest, has he?'

'Of course,' said Mary Erskine. 'He had to be told.'

'I believe something real did happen to Pix, and something pretty nasty too.'

'Oh Charmian,' said Mary, 'you feel like that because it's your job, you're used to seeing into dark places. But it's not like that with this business, it would be better for Pix if we treat it as a bit of his imagination. Luke thinks so too.'

So that was how it was going to be played? Charmian put the receiver down feeling cynical and wary.

I'm not looking for work, she told herself, I was brought into this by you, Mary Erskine, but I am in it and I shall sort it out.

When you are giving a dinner party, a husband is a very useful piece of equipment, almost vital in fact. He can open the door, serve the wine and carve the meat. If he gets time he can also be useful talking to the guests.

Like most women who live alone, Charmian got round this by learning how to manage the wine, serving meat that did not need carving and doing the talking herself.

The social rule about the balance of the sexes she ignored. If she wanted to have three women and one man, she did so. Sometimes she had three men and one woman: herself. Social rules were made to be broken.

Of course, when George Rewley and Kate Cooper came to dinner, Charmian's own house rules were broken. Rewley opened the door to the guests and Kate saw to the wine. Kate had the sophisticated knowledge of good wines of a rich girl who had travelled, so that she sometimes raised an eyebrow at the wine Charmian had chosen.

'Chill it, dear,' she said, studying a Chablis selected to go with the fish. 'Chill it to an inch of its life and then they won't notice.'

Charmian was in the kitchen stirring a sauce when she became aware from the sound of voices that all her guests were arriving at once. When she went into the sitting-room there they all were.

Present were old Mrs Mallet, Luke's mother, whose dress, deportment and style of behaviour to her son fully deserved

100

her Dickensian nickname of Mrs Turveydrop, together with the young vet and his wife, the journalist, and Mary Erskine.

Also present were Luke and a pretty young girl, both of whom were being upbraided by Mrs Mallet for the way Luke drove.

Charmian handed round the drinks. 'Sherry, Luke?' I didn't ask Luke, and as for the girl I never saw her before. If they stay, I wonder if the fish will go round.

Luke hurried to explain. 'We drove mother here, she wished it' – a hundred yards, if that, Charmian thought – 'and George asked us up for a drink.'

So he knew Rewley?

'Play squash together,' said Rewley, answering the unspoken question. 'And this is Minette.'

The girl smiled. She was very pretty, a real femme fatale in the making. Miniature too, she was delicate both of bone and colouring and so young, a combination hard to better. She was making her impact on Rewley, and on Doug Fraser, the young vet. Angela, his wife, was keeping her distance, and Kate too eyed Minette with caution. Luke had brought in a prize, and he seemed aware of it as well. What his mother thought of Minette was not clear, she had her professional smile firmly fixed in place.

Charmian poured the drinks. 'Stay and have a meal, Luke, won't you, there's plenty of food.' She caught Rewley's eye and he gave a slight nod. Yes, a good idea. 'Minette, some more sherry?' The girl accepted it without a word. Presumably she could talk English? 'Excuse me a minute, I must go into the kitchen.'

Kate followed her out. 'Shall I rearrange the table for two more people?'

'Please.' Her hands were busy at the stove.

'That girl is ravishingly pretty, fortunately not Rewley's style, but I shall keep an eye open. Why did you do it?'

'I want to have a better look at Luke Mallet.'

'He's worth looking at,' said Kate appreciatively. 'A lovely man.'

'Hands off, Kate,' warned Charmian. 'You're married now.'

'Don't worry, I'm quite content with Rewley, he has more than good looks.'

'Glad to hear it.' Charmian checked the fish, yes, plenty there if no one was greedy.

'Do you think Mary is in love with Luke?' Kate had chosen the extra knives and forks and was carrying them away.

'No idea,' said Charmian absently, her thoughts elsewhere. Rewley had brought her some news, which she was still thinking about. 'Mary doesn't let you into that sort of secret.'

'I don't think he's rich enough for her,' said Kate from the door. 'She hasn't got much herself and she really needs it, Mary does. He does too.'

'Oh?' Interesting.

'Yes, I've heard that the school needs money.'

'How did you hear that?'

Kate shrugged. Money interested her, her own and other people's. 'Just picked it up.'

'I'll be five minutes,' said Charmian, 'then we will eat.' She put the fish on a big dish, covered it with the sauce, then stood thinking.

Rewley had told her that as well as blood on the blue jacket belonging to Louise Farmer there had been found other traces. 'This is new information that won't come your way just yet, I just happened to be talking to someone in the lab.' He always did 'just happen to be talking to someone'. ' . . . Oil and paint,' he had said, 'blue paint. Could be from a car. She must have been in it. Interesting, isn't it?'

It was the sort of information that helped to solve cases. But first find the car.

'The family car?'

No, apparently not, Rewley had said, that had already been checked. A new and unknown car. It added to the picture formed around Louise Farmer, filling it out with a detail.

While she was handing the fish round and people were making the customary polite noises people make at such times, she managed to say quietly to Rewley: 'Find a chance to get out and look over Luke Mallet's car. Just a check.'

'Any special reason?'

'No, just a feeling . . . The sauce has mushrooms in it,' she said in a louder voice, as if he had asked.

Rewley smiled gravely. 'Love mushrooms,' and then: 'I'll have to oil them all well if they're not to notice me disappearing . . . hope you've got plenty of wine?'

'You're enjoying this,' said Charmian as she passed on with the fish. She could trust Kate to be generous with the wine.

He disappeared while she got the casserole out of the oven and put the roast potatoes under the grill to get that final browned look she never achieved otherwise. She wasn't going to achieve it now, they were burning. She removed them hastily.

When she got back into the dining-room, Rewley had still not come back and Kate was beginning to raise an eyebrow.

He slipped back into the room in time to help her serve. 'Nothing there. A spanking new car, no oil, no paint. And the car is black. Worth a try, though. We might check when he bought it, I suppose.'

Charmian noticed that Minette sat quietly hardly saying a word – but she was having her effect on the party. Afterwards Charmian thought it was her presence that had precipitated the quarrel. It had not proved difficult to persuade the two of them to stay. Perhaps Luke was as interested to observe Charmian as she was to assess him.

And yet it was Angie Fraser who had actually started things off; she always knew all the gossip. Also, she was not above a touch of malice.

'I hear the St Cath's ghost is walking again.'

Luke jerked to attention. 'Certainly not. And there's never been a ghost.'

'Always was supposed to be in my time.' She sneaked a look down the table at Mrs Turveydrop, she had been at St Catherine's herself and was not above baiting her old headmistress. 'We used to give each other the creeps with it.'

'Angela!' said Mrs Mallet heavily.

'I didn't say we believed it . . . '

'You need to keep a tight rein on a school.' Mrs Mallet spoke to the ceiling but was really addressing her son. 'Firm but gentle.'

Luke rose to the criticism. 'I find trusting them very effective. Our Trust system works wonderfully well.'

'No one ever trusted us much,' said Angela in a reminiscent voice 'Mind you, it was just as well, the things we got up to, I remember once . . . '

'Heel, Angela,' murmured her husband. She subsided, drinking her wine with an appreciative smile at Charmian.

103

Until now Mary Erskine had kept quiet, now she put in her word: 'I think children are really better left to themselves, so often they know best.'

Mrs Mallet made a noise that in a less august lady would have been a snort. 'Peace at any price, you mean.'

Minette looked as if they managed things better in France, but before she could say anything Luke joined in.

It was a short bitter interchange between mother and son in which money and discipline were sharply mentioned.

Revealing, Charmian thought.

Then it was over, and by the time the sorbet was going round, voices were quiet and civilised, but now she knew what was underneath.

Later, Charmian saw her guests to their cars, watched them drive away, then went slowly back up the garden path.

She kept a large scented geranium in a pot just inside the front door. She could see a piece of paper between it and the wall as if it had somehow blown there and Mrs Beadle had not tidied it away.

With a frown Charmian picked it up. Then she saw that it was both chewed and claw-marked which looked like the handiwork of dear Muff in one of her paper-catching moods. She liked a piece of paper to tear and scratch and had gravely defaced more than one letter.

But this was only a sheet of paper which had been folded over. Pushed through the front door perhaps and then found by a bored cat.

A pale pencilled message survived, the end and beginning badly chewed.

But she could read: I know what you think but I am innocent.

Nothing else, unless she could make out the word Help under a smear of mud or Muff's dinner. No signature and no address. No date either, of course. If there ever had been any of these usual items they had been dealt with by Muff.

How long had it been in the house? It looked as though it had been knocking around for some time.

From whom and to whom? She accepted the message was meant for her. But who had sent the message?

He who is thought guilty, came the answer.

Whoever that was. There had been plenty of people in Charmian's life whom she had thought guilty, but not one whom she could imagine pushing a note through her door.

Someone who knew her perhaps.

She picked up Muff, stroking the soft fur and feeling the firm muscles underneath. 'Oh Muff, Muff, what have you done?'

CHAPTER TEN

Earlier in April

Ted Gray thought he could feel the wind on his face. And was that a leaf fluttering down on to his hand?

But he could not be sure, because he was out of his body, somewhere on a level with where the ceiling would have been if he had been in a room. He was not in a room, he was in the open air, up among the treetops, out of his body and looking down upon himself.

Not his first experience of this, but his strongest.

Even so it came and went, not a steady vision by any means. Indeed, the universe itself was not steady, he knew that now, but given to great pulsations. Throbs.

Throb.

Yes, that was the word which sprang to mind. If he knew where his mind was exactly, he seemed to have mislaid it. It might be down there with his body, or up here with what was also him.

He was carrying a suitcase of memories around with him and it felt very heavy. He could feel its weight on his body, pressing him down so that he could not lift his chest to breathe. Not that breathing seemed essential, he seemed to be managing without it.

He remembered Louise Farmer, he carried her around with him, the girl was inside the suitcase, he could feel her weight which was tremendous. Strange when she was so small and slight. He could also smell her blood. Blood.

Here were voices speaking. It seemed to him he could hear someone confessing to her murder. He hoped it was not his own voice. I am not a murderer, he reacted. But there was blood in him, he was a killer somehow. He had been told so.

The suitcase was not only heavy, but was both hot and cold by turns. At the moment it was cold.

But of course, it was not a suitcase, it was a golf bag with a shotgun in it. His bag, his gun. Purchased on purpose. Guns were for killing.

Una pervaded his whole body, whether absent or present. He hadn't dared to go home to face Una, had stayed in his office. No communication there and none possible.

Later. Somehow there was a letter. He had written a letter, a statement, and put it through a door to a woman he had heard of but never met. Just a port of call in his wanderings. Not Una's door. That door that must never open again to let man in or let maid out.

Una was with him now. From his vantage point above the trees where he hovered, he could see her standing by his body that was not his body. He could make out her face, all blurred.

He was very cold now. A thought crawled out from the back of his brain: you smell blood, not the girl's blood, she did not bleed.

Whose blood? His blood.

His eyes closed and he was out of the body for ever.

Edward Gray was not found until the next morning. He lay under a group of trees in Windsor Great Park, not far from one of the small roads that run through it, by a parking place, but his position was masked by a thicket of trees and bushes.

He had died from a gunshot wound to the head. A gun lay by his side.

He was not immediately identified as he carried no wallet or papers on him; his features had been considerably damaged. It was early evening before the police could be fairly sure. His waterproof was rolled up like a cushion under his head as if he had made himself comfortable before pulling the trigger.

He had not died at once, but had lingered on for some hours in a state of semi-consciousness.

Was it suicide – it looked like it – or accident, or murder?

FILOFACE

2

This followed the finding of Ted Gray's body.
Tyre marks leading from car park to the area where the victim was found similar to those found near where Louise Farmer was found.

Two cases go together. In which case possible serial murderer. Therefore probably male. But must not overlook that it could be a rare female serial killer.

Suggestions:
Gray driven to the killing ground either alive and then shot.
Gray driven there already dead.
Or he met the killer there.
Slight evidence to suggest he walked.
Coat under his head, neatly folded. As a man would do? Do women fold things differently?
Profile.
If killer of Ted Gray and Louise Farmer is the same person then:
1 Local. Or knows the district well.
2 Probably male.
3 Drives a car.
4 Probably known to both victims. However, could be a voyeur who was then a random killer. Still makes killer local.

Contradiction to duality: Method of killing different.

CHAPTER ELEVEN

Two days have passed: April 17

In the night, a fine, thick blanket of rain came down over Windsor, Eton and Merrywick, blotting out the towers of the castle, hiding the Royal Standard, and bringing down a curtain over the high roof of the Chapel of Eton College, and wreathing with mist the roofs and chimney of all the terraces, crescents and squares of the city.

Una Gray lay in bed, unsleeping. Ahead of her stretched a day she did not want to meet. It was coming relentlessly, as the night swung towards morning and short of killing herself (which she did not intend to do) she had to get up and face what was on the way. She stared up at the ceiling where the street lamp created shadows and patterns. It reminded her of her childhood when she had played games of seeing pictures and stories in the ceiling. The light then had come from a fire in her nursery grate, she had spent most of her young life in that one room so it was just that she should have the comfort of a fire. The fire had been her companion; you could make out whole worlds in the fire as the logs crumbled and the sea-coal burned itself out. Did anyone else but her grandfather (dead now but having outlived almost everyone), talk of sea-coal? What a Victorian he had been. And how he had punished her mother so that she had almost disappeared as a person, turning her into a pallid ghost who hardly spoke, and whose child must never be seen or mentioned.

Una herself had been a prisoner, as secret and hidden as the Man in the Iron Mask. Of course, she had not realised her state at the time. All children believe their lives to be normal, what everyone else has, it takes years to understand that you are different.

And yet he had loved them both, she could swear to that, because she had sensed it even through his anger. There had been plenty of that around. Never voices raised, but quiet tough sounds in voices like steel with a cutting edge. The women in that household had never much to say for themselves, she could hardly remember her grandmother now, although she remembered her death and her mother crying in a soft, sad way for days.

But suddenly, overnight, it seemed, she herself had grown up and found her own voice. To her surprise, it was a voice that could speak loudly and firmly. She must have more of her grandfather in her than anyone guessed. (About her father, she could not speak, since he was never mentioned. A bit of nameless sperm, was all he was in that family.) This voice of hers, which seemed almost a separate entity on its own, so that she was as startled as anyone when it spoke, demanded education.

Looking back, she had to admire the cunning and skill with which this self had got what she wanted. Being a Victorian, Grandpapa could not resist a demand for education.

The joke was that once in the world, she discovered that the village had known all about her all the time. There are no real secrets, it seems, someone always knows.

After her grandfather died, she came across her birth certificate where she learnt her father's name: Andrew Ross. No more, that was all she knew, but she did have an infant memory of her mother whispering that he had been a gentle man. Or had she said gentleman? Subtle difference.

Once out in the world, she had recognised herself as a part of a clan, out there were cousins in plenty, all of whom were willing to recognise 'Allie's girl'. It turned out that they too had long known what there was to know about her. It was hard to feel close to them, however, because she was different.

Naturally, inevitably, her upbringing had marked her. She was not as other people are, she knew the difference even if they did not. After a while, she realised that they did know. She did not quite match the rest of them. Tribes always know their own kind, secret signs pass between them.

She shared some things with her numerous cousins like a name and certain physical characteristics, such as the colour of her eyes and the shape of her hands, but not one of them had a past like hers. She admired Mary Erskine but they had very little in common. Mary too had a secret life no doubt, everyone had, but what it was Una could not guess and it was certainly far from hers.

Daylight was coming, a cold light dulling some shadows on the ceiling while changing others. A new shape was being created every second now as a wind got up. That was a little house with a window and a door. No face at the window. The house was empty. Just for a minute it reminded her of the Play House in the junior art and craft room in St Catherine's and she smiled. She had helped make and paint that little house. It folded away and the roof came off but it had curtains, contained a table and chair, while being large enough for a group of children to play in together. The house on the ceiling faded away, she must have gone to sleep.

Suddenly, she was back in her childhood, in her bedroom there in Perthshire and she was crying. Even in her sleep, even while she knew, as you sometimes do, that it was all a dream, she knew why she was crying. It was because she could never be what other people were. She was marked. Grandpa had said so. The dream went on and on, as it always did, never coming to a proper ending because there was no ending.

When she woke up, her mood was set in deep despair which the day seemed to match with its low clouds and thick rain. She made some breakfast but there was no comfort to be gained from food and drink; she hardly tasted what she ate.

The telephone call last night had not been much of a surprise. There are some experiences that seem to be lying in wait for you. Almost like a guest you have invited, but dread to see.

A polite voice had reminded her that he was Sergeant Rewley. They had met, he had called on her already, once bringing with him a woman police officer. She had no difficulty in remembering either of them. Now he wondered if he could call again tomorrow and drive her . . .

Drive her where? she had asked quickly.

Had he actually said the police mortuary, or had she supplied that word herself? Memory blurred. A place she did not wish to go.

And had he said that he had someone there, he would like her to look at, or had she supplied that too? No, that had come from him: a possible identification.

She had begun by liking the young sergeant, who was personable and good mannered, although he had an unnerving way of studying her face as if he was reading all she wished to keep secret. Someone had told her afterwards that he could lip-read very well since he was the only member of his family who was not deaf. That would explain it, she thought. He was also very clever.

I too am clever, she told herself, going to the sink and rinsing out her cup. The cold water ran down over her hands, chilling them further.

She put on her coat and went to the door. He was going to pick her up and drive her to that place. She heard his car and was on the step waiting for him when he arrived.

He hesitated when he saw her. 'Are you all right, Mrs Gray?'

'Yes. Let's get it over. Don't worry about me.' She wished she could wear a thick veil over her features so he could not read her thoughts, but she must make do with the fact that she was paralysingly cold and might be frozen into immobility. It was amazing how misery chilled one down.

She got into the car. 'Don't let's talk,' she said. 'Not on the way. Afterwards, yes, if we have to, but not now.'

Rewley took her at her word; he nodded and drove the car forward without a word.

Through the town, past the castle, down Slough Road. So this was where the police mortuary was? Well, now she would know. Rewley did not drive fast, perhaps he was being kind.

They were as gentle with her as they could be, showing her a jacket, which she said looked like one of Ted's but she could not be sure, one tweed jacket was like another, and then offering a brief, obligatory look at Ted's face.

The shot had left his face bruised, slightly lopsided, but still recognisable. The face that had rested next to yours on the pillow, the face you had kissed, the face you had loved. No, even battered and torn, you knew it.

'Yes, yes, that is Ted.'

They had the head neatly tied up in a white towel so that Ted looked like an eighteenth-century savant in his library. Only his eyes were closed and he was covered in a sheet.

'How did he die?'

'Gunshot to the head,' said Rewley, briefly. He began to lead Una out of the room, but she stood still.

'Did he shoot himself?'

It was the crucial question, the bad moment.

'It *could* be suicide,' said Rewley.

'And if he killed himself, then you will also believe he murdered Louise Farmer, you will take it as a confession of guilt?'

'I didn't say that, Mrs Gray.'

'No, but it's true.'

Rewley remained silent. Two can play at the silence game, he thought.

Una said, almost without emotion: 'You're keeping something from me.'

'Not really, Mrs Gray.' The gun which had been used, however, was the gun which Ted had managed to provide himself with in London, which made suicide the most likely judgement, but it would be for the pathologist to say.

'It was suicide,' said Una. She swayed slightly, but there were no tears, she suffered from an inability to cry. An inherited trait, she thought, handed down from Grandpapa, also a non-cryer. He in fact was such a bad case that he had to use little phials of artificial tears. She remembered the little bottles.

She took one last look at her husband.

Teddy Bear, she thought, giving him his nickname for the last time; she would not use it again, it belonged to the past. Her mind went back to their first meeting. No one introduced them, they had met in a library, both reaching for the same book: Sir Kenneth Clark's *Landscape in Art*. She knew at that moment they were a pair. Ted's hand had fallen away and she had got the book. He had always been a gentle man.

But gentle people can be terrifying too, they have their own menace.

On that occasion, they had gone out of the library together, Una clutching the book, and gone to drink coffee together. For

113

hours they talked about art and life and art and history, art and themselves.

Almost at once he had admitted to this strange childhood. She had held back about hers for a while longer, but eventually it all came out, too. Like being sick, she thought, she just vomited it out. Spewed it out.

When had she started calling him Teddy Bear? There was a block in her memory. People said there was always a reason for such blocks, here the reason might have been that Ted Gray had not really liked his nickname. She had persevered in using it, though, until he turned on her one day and ordered her to stop.

Was there not then a little irony in the fact that now he was dead, she was using it again?

The floor seemed to tilt and Rewley put his arm forward. 'Don't touch,' said Una, like a child that has been hurt.

'Come and sit down, Mrs Gray,' said Rewley. 'I'll get you a cup of tea before we go back.'

'Not here,' Una spoke quickly. 'Couldn't.'

'No, not here. There's a place across the road . . . I need to talk to you, Mrs Gray. Here and now, or later. As you prefer.' Not too much later, though, was the implication.

Her face had changed since they came into this room, fallen away into little crevices and hollows so that she looked older. How old was she? Forty? He had thought her younger when they first met.

'I don't think I can tell you anything.'

'We won't know till we try.'

Outside in the damp air, it was raining harder than ever, Una said: 'I'll take that drink, but make it coffee.' What she was saying to herself was, I cannot go back to my own house yet. She nodded her head towards the café. 'If we have to talk, let it be over there.'

'Right.' Rewley accepted the arrangement, silently reserving to himself the right to interview her in more official surroundings as and when he thought best. She probably knew as well as he did that it would not end with one talk over a cup of coffee.

To his surprise, the girl behind the serving counter greeted Una. 'Hello, Mrs Gray, nice to see you. I'll bring the coffee over, I know how you like it.'

'I used to teach her.' Una sat down. 'Don't look surprised. What are you doing working here, Molly?'

'My place, my very own,' said the girl cheerily. 'MOLLY'S GARDEN, didn't you see the name, my name? Molly Morris, licensed to sell wines. Would you like something else? Cake, biscuit? A glass of sherry? Or white wine? The claret is good. I'll bring some over just in case. The chocolate cake is fine today.'

Una shrugged. 'I thought she was going on the stage or be a brain surgeon, she had those ambitions.'

It was a smart little place, with white and green furniture and potted plants on the tables.

Molly hung around chattering and bringing cream, hot milk and offering more cakes. Not surprisingly, Rewley did not make much headway in his questioning.

The coffee was as good as promised, MOLLY'S GARDEN might be a find, as might be Molly herself, a chirpy, cheerful girl, but she was getting in his way. He looked at Una, head bent, sipping coffee.

I swear she knew that Molly owns this place, Rewley told himself, and used that knowledge. She's blocking me, I feel the block, I can see it in her face.

No, she did not know why Ted had gone missing, she had said this before, had she not? She did not know why he had killed himself or where he had got the gun. Perhaps they did?

A sharp shot, that, Rewley admitted, because they did know he had bought it in Bermondsey, south London.

And she did not know why he had killed Louise Farmer. If, indeed, he had.

The coffee and cakes sat on the table and with them two glasses of red wine which might be claret. The right colour anyway, thought the sceptical Rewley. A sip convinced him that Molly knew how to choose her wine. Good for her.

'You could say that you and St Catherine's invented me,' said Molly coming up with a burst of exuberance. 'You told me I could do anything.'

'I didn't know I had said that.'

'And I'm so sorry that Mr Gray is dead.'

Una stirred her coffee. 'How do you know about that?'

'Oh everyone knows.' Molly shook her head vigorously. 'I

mean, living across the road,' she hesitated cautiously, not wanting
to use names that might cause pain, 'from that place as we are, we
get to know things. But he couldn't have killed Louise Farmer.
Of course he couldn't. He was such a gentleman. He couldn't
kill a fly.'

'Of course he could, you silly girl.' Una leapt to her feet. 'We
all could, we do it all the time. She was nothing but a fly to him.'
She rushed for the door, knocking over her coffee.

Rewley stood up. 'Thank you, Molly Morris,' he said. He did
not keep the irritation out of his tone.

Molly gave him a baffled smile. What had she done? 'Have it
on me,' she said. 'Molly's treat.'

'It's a motive of a sort,' he said to Charmian over another cup
of coffee, this time in her office where he had called late that
afternoon as darkness fell. The rain had now turned into a low
cloud that hung like a white fog over castle, town and river. 'Louise
Farmer was buzzing around, being a nuisance and a threat and
he brushed her off . . . And then, of course, regretted it . . . It's
what his wife thinks, anyway.'

'Widow,' said Charmian. She was sensitive on this point, her
own past history suggested sensitivity here.

Rewley accepted the implied rebuke. He too knew a little of her
life. She had attended his and Kate's wedding the month before
with the reserved enthusiasm of one who knows that marriages
end as well as begin. His mother-in-law, Anny Cooper, the
friend of Charmian since their youth, had enlightened him to
what lay behind. 'She was really upset when he had his heart
attack. Thought it was her fault. Might have been too,' Anny
had added thoughtfully. 'No angel, our Charmian, especially as a
wife. Bit of guilt there, you know.' A massive amount, she might
have said.

'Widow. I have treated her carefully. She's a difficult woman,
though. Tense, reserved, anxious. You can't get through.'

'She's got plenty to be anxious about . . . Did you get the impression that she knows what Louise Farmer had against him?'

'The contract to kill? I think's she got an idea,' said Rewley. 'I
think she's heard that most murders are domestic and that many
wives get killed by their spouses.'

116

'We don't know for sure that it was Una he wanted killed.'

'But you think it likely.'

Charmian nodded. 'In default of another better victim, yes, it was her . . . What would be a motive?'

'Do husbands need a motive?'

'That's sour for you, so recently married.'

'I was speaking professionally,' said Rewley.

'So the idea is that he killed Louise Farmer and now himself?'

'Yes, I believe that's what his wife thinks.'

'And he might have been the hit-and-run driver who killed the boy Rivers?'

'We have to guess on that one.'

'The Grays have a car?'

'Yes, but no sign of any accident damage on the outside anywhere, I had a sneak look. He could have hired one under a false name. We are checking.'

Charmian thought about it. 'Good.'

Then Rewley said: 'I wonder who her friends are? Or if she's got any? She needs some.' He had been struck by a sense of Una as isolated.

'Mary Erskine,' said Charmian. 'She's everyone's friend. And Una is a cousin of sorts . . . There's Luke Mallet. I think Una would call him a friend.'

She poured herself another cup of coffee. She had recently installed a new coffee-making machine, personal to her in her office, in which she used the blend of coffee favoured by her. No other hands touched the machine, because she had noticed that Tess, her secretary, invariably produced a pale, sepia brew.

The room was warm and comfortable on this cold day. Long and narrow, L-shaped, with an alcove at one end, it had not been easy to decorate, but Charmian had had help from her friend Anny Cooper. Anny, being in her red phase (which came and went, alternating with a white, whiter, and blue phases, but in the eighties had been a very good selling period, seeing some of her best pictures and pottery), had suggested white walls and a red carpet. Darkish red. But Charmian had protested. 'No, I don't want to see myself walking on a carpet of blood, even though I sometimes feel as if I am.'

On her desk at this moment, she had a photograph of a great

117

pool of blood in a surburban street in Slough, the result of a man shooting his wife's lover; a video of a bank robbery in High Wycombe (blood there too, the security guard's), and the preliminary report of a gang rape in a garage in Woking. There was also, which worried her much more, a secret report that drugs were being peddled in this area with a police involvement. There was a hint that the police contact involved was a woman. No blood spilled in that case yet, but easily could be. One way and another she dealt in blood, her own and other people's. 'Blood can be beautiful,' Anny had argued. 'If you see it right. You ought to be a bit more visual, Char'.' She shook her head sadly, her friend Anny needed educating about the toughness of life. Perhaps a sight of some of the evidence Charmian had stored away in the files of her unit might do it.

But Anny had given way, and had advised a grass-green carpet with apricot walls (strong apricot, please Charmian, none of your wishy-washy pastels) and ginger-coloured curtains.

Charmian had accepted most of the advice, only whitening the apricot walls a shade or two as Anny had known she would do, and choosing cinnamon rather than ginger silk for the curtains. Anny had not approved of silk: should have been linen, she said, or thick cotton, but Charmian liked silk to wear and to see; it was one more barrier between this Charmian and her austere hard-up youth.

All was business on her desk here, her private letters she kept at home among the papers which Muff attacked with tooth and claw on occasion, but the Merrywick case was becoming a kind of obsession. She took a sharp personal interest in the murder of Louise Farmer. Was it because of the girl, or Pix and his nightmares? Or was it that Mary Erskine and Una Gray both irritated and fascinated her with their polite ways of hinting that they were above it all, that they could get away with murder?

Charmian looked down at a photograph which Rewley had put before her. On her desk was a small pot of hyacinths, breathing sweetness at her. To the right was a photograph of a body lying on its back. The body was clothed, wearing trousers and shirt and a tweed jacket, tie neatly knotted. The head rested on a rolled-up coat, the exact nature of which she could not make out from the photograph, but she understood it was a raincoat. Except for a small amount of money, there

118

had been nothing much in the pockets, which had held up identification.

In addition she had before her a close-up photograph of Ted's face; it was placed next to that picture of the pool of blood in Slough, which wasn't connected to the Farmer case. She moved away to the sight of blood-stained Slough.

But the close-up interested her. She wondered about the wound.

'Exactly where was he shoot?'

'Side of the head.'

She studied the photograph. 'Could he have done that himself?'

'Yes, apparently. Just about.'

'Don't suicides using shotguns usually shoot themselves through the mouth?'

'Not everyone fancies that. Women don't.'

Charmian could understand, the features are not improved by a blast through the mouth. Even in death a woman likes to look her best. Or so it seemed. She wondered if she would worry; she had been near death once or twice in her life but she couldn't remember worrying about her face; survival had been more sharply on her mind.

But the photograph still teased her.

'And the rolled-up coat on which Gray's head is resting?'

Their eyes met, a question to be read in each.

'Yes, that is worrying,' said Rewley. 'Could a suicide kill himself and then fall back upon a rolled-up coat? Well, again, possibly. But all this is what you might call first judgement. Speculation. Forensics plus the pathologist will give us the real answer and we shan't have those reports for the next day or two . . . ' He paused, he knew he might be able to extract a verbal answer from one of his lab pals before too long, he had been careful to cultivate good contacts. 'But his wife seemed to accept it was suicide and I think she knows more than she's telling.'

'Wives usually do,' said Charmian. But whether what they know is the truth or self-delusion has to be considered.

'She believes he killed the girl, and for her, his suicide confirms it. She went looking for that coat of the girl's, you know, she knew something even then.'

119

'Everything possibly,' said Charmian. 'Right. Well, if suicide is confirmed it looks as though the killer of Louise Farmer is found. We take it as a tacit admission of guilt.'

Una had fled from MOLLY'S GARDEN without looking back, and although Rewley could have followed her, he had decided to let her run. The road was on a bus route into Windsor, there was a taxi rank on the corner, and it was even possible for her to walk home if she wanted. The rain had eased and the day was brighter. He knew where to find her.

Una ran, then becoming breathless she changed to a walk. She walked for some time, aware that the rain had stopped, that the sun was out and that she was surrounded by shoppers. It was early afternoon, so she must have been walking for over an hour. Where had she been? Buried in mystery, her mind did not know. But she must have bought a newspaper because she was clutching one. It was the City Prices edition of the London evening newspaper. Presumably she had paid for it? Yes, she was carrying a few coins in the palm of her hand. But she didn't know why she had bought the newspaper, nor did it show any sign of having been read.

She had been walking without a conscious sense of direction, only the terrible feeling that Teddy Bear was walking with her, but she found she had turned into a shopping complex. She recognised the place now, so she knew where she was. Royal Court, it was called. There was a fountain in the middle of a courtyard with seats around it. A large lady carrying a basket got up, leaving a seat empty into which Una sank gratefully. From the look on the large lady's face she got the idea that it was the sight of Una herself that had driven her away.

She could see herself in a mirror in the furniture shop across the concourse: hair wild, coat open, tears on her face, she knew how to cry now. Yes, a mess, the woman had been right to move. She might even have been talking to herself, Una couldn't be sure about that.

The department store beyond the fountain offered shelter, warmth and a cloakroom. She walked through the bright displays of new spring clothes to that female haven, mercifully empty. She tidied herself up, conscious all the time of the silent, dumpy, sturdy figure of Teddy Bear beside her, so unlike what Ted had been physically but so redolent of what he had been as a person. You trusted Teddy Bear and he trusted you.

Most of the time.

That was what made treachery so terrible.

She cleaned her face with a wadded tissue, combing her hair and applying fresh lipstick, then she took a deep breath and exorcised the figure of Teddy Bear. He must go, otherwise she would be like that poor boy Pix, seeing a person where no person should be.

Danger there, great danger. You must stay within yourself. If you fly out, then you might not get back.

Face clean, she walked out into Peascod Street where a mist was coming up from the river. She would go to see Luke. She was only back at work at St Catherine's on a part-time basis, so he would not be expecting her today, but she would creep into the staffroom where she might find comfort. Have a cigarette (once given up but now a necessity), and warm her hands. Her home in Chapel Close did not make a strong appeal at the moment and never would again; too many memories. One way and another she knew she would move as soon as possible.

As soon as the inquest on Ted was over and done with and the matter of his guilt tidied away, then she would sell the lease on the house. It was only rented from the Crown but she had a long lease. House values were not as high as this time last year, but as a period house in a well-known town it should still bring a good price. And there would be Ted's money.

As she walked down the road that led to the school, she was passed by a small, scurrying figure.

'Pix!'

He ran on, head down, unseeing.

'Well, he's got his legs back again, but what a face.' Pix's features had looked contorted, either with pain or anger. She didn't like what she saw. That was not a face that promised well. Una stood still in a spasm of doubt. Should she go after him? No, better not, find someone in the school and tell them.

She pushed open the big front door. Silence. Of course, school was over for the day.

She turned into the art and creative play room in which poor Pix had seen whatever he had seen, the room stood empty. It looked bigger than when full of active, cheerful children.

The large Play House stood against the window. One of its little windows was broken, the curtains torn and by the look of it someone had kicked the door in. There had obviously been a fight in or around it.

As she stood looking at it, Luke and Mary Erskine walked in.

'Oh Una, I'm so glad to see you, we're so understaffed.' He gave her a hug. 'Three of the staff have flu and Minette's ill too, and now all this.' He waved a hand.

'What's the matter with Minette?'

Luke looked worried. 'Oh, she's away ill . . . . Nerves, I think, poor girl. She's been getting more and more upset about the death of the girl, Louise Farmer. She keeps remembering the string of cases like it near where she lived in Toulouse. Of course they were what the police call serial killings, motiveless apparently, and they never got the killer.' He sounded exasperated. 'And, of course, there's no connection, not that it seems to make any difference to her, she's so distressed.' He was beginning to think that his beautiful Minette was not so stable a character as he had hoped. Not headmaster's wife material, after all. She should not be so upset as she was. She hadn't known the dead girl, had she? 'She said it was one of the reasons she took a job away from France, and now the killing seems to have followed her here.'

Unnecessary emotion, Una thought, hysterical girl beneath that calm, pretty look. Just as well Luke was seeing her as she was, he had been too infatuated. As he so often was alas, he needed a wife, poor love.

But there were other things to concern her. She pointed to the signs of mayhem. 'But what's happened here?'

'Pix.' Luke pulled a face.

'Pix? I thought he was ill.'

Mary Erskine said: 'He seemed a bit better, and the doctor thought he'd be happier at school, get back to normal. His mother asked me to do it, she had a meeting, so I brought him . . . But he went berserk and attacked this room as soon as I brought him in here.'

Luke groaned. 'Poor little beggar, he was quite beside himself. I had to carry him out. Tried to reason with him, of course.'

'Did you ask him why he did it? What did you say to him?' And more to the point what did he say to you?

'Oh, I only tried to quieten him. I didn't want to question him the state he was in. I put him in my room with a soothing drink of orange juice.'

'No, you didn't. He's legging it down the road.'

Mary said quickly: 'I'll go after him. Oh my God, what will his mother say?' She ran from the room, not closing the door behind her. They heard her feet pelting down the corridor.

Luke stood irresolute. 'I wonder if I ought to phone the police.'

'No, not yet,' advised Una. 'Mary will catch him.'

'I wish we could help the child.' Luke sounded both puzzled and anxious.

'Do you think it is a case of child schizophrenia, it does exist, I believe?' Una spoke as if she knew.

Luke shook his head. 'I wish I knew.' Suddenly, he seemed to take in Una's appearance.

'My dear, what about you? What's the matter?'

Una told him. Briefly and as calmly as she could she told him about Ted. Not so very calmly, after all.

Luke put his arms round her. 'Oh my dear, I am so very sorry. And I'm going on about my own worries, forgive me.'

'Nothing to forgive, Luke.' She hugged him back, then moved away gently. 'Of course, I am upset.'

'You're controlling yourself so marvellously.'

'Not really, not underneath. I made a bad show to the young policeman who wanted to talk to me. Bit ashamed of that now.'

'My dear, there is no such thing as a bad show. I howled and screamed when my bad time came. Do still sometimes when no one is about.'

'But, I wish I hadn't done it. Couldn't stop myself. I just ran.' She gave a small smile. 'A bit like poor disturbed, frightened Pix.'

She passed a hand across her forehead. 'Is it very hot in here? Are you keeping the heating too high?' She had been cold and now felt overhot.

He touched a radiator. No, barely warm. 'It's you, Una. Let me take you up to my sitting-room and give you a drink. It's shock, I expect . . . Come on.' He took her by the arm. He tried to lighten the mood, with a jokey comment. 'The way money is I couldn't waste it on heating.'

'I wish you'd let me help you there.'

'No, Una dear. We've had that out before.'

Up in his own flat, he offered tea or coffee or whatever she wanted. Whisky might be best.

'Not coffee,' said Una with a shudder, remembering MOLLY'S GARDEN. 'Perhaps whisky. A small one.'

'Poor little Una,' said Luke, handing her a glass. He took none himself.

'Yes.' Una sipped it. 'You know what this means, don't you . . . ? By killing himself Ted was confessing to murdering the girl.'

Silence.

'Is that what you think?'

'It's what the police think.'

'But you, Una, what about you.'

Una waited for a long while. 'Yes, that's what I think. Ted killed Louise Farmer.'

CHAPTER TWELVE

The same evening, April 17

Charmian took her troubles home with her. She had more than Ted Gray on her mind. Grosser, more painful problems rested there. Among the reports on her desk had been one indicating that a paedophile sex-ring had moved into the area. A highly confidential list of names was attached: she didn't like what she read. Some of the names were of prominent persons and one at least was known to her. The report from the special drug squad did not please, either. She got the whiff of trouble for SRADIC there and possibly for herself in particular. Witch hunts could start anywhere and she had her enemies.

However, although she took troubles home with her, she only let them travel in the car, and dismissed them at the front door. She got out her key, opened the door and that was that: work troubles stayed the other side. She was home.

Home smelt of lavender cleaning polish, the faint hint of gingerbread she had baked the night before and just a suggestion of her breakfast coffee. Young Mrs Beadle had been in to perform her usual miracles.

It was a cool, damp April day, and after the brief period of sun, a mist was thick over the town. The river brings mists to Windsor, capping the towers of the Castle with white strands and hanging over the trees of the Home Park and the Long Walk. But tonight, for the first time, there was a breath of spring. A sense of movement away from the chills of winter, a feeling that the wind was changing towards the west and would bring warmth with it.

'I can feel the spring.' She had brought in a bunch of freesias mixed with mimosa; she laid them on the kitchen table and looked for a suitable vase.

Vaases, her mother had called them, making a long *a* of it. It was an ugly word, but what other word was there? Receptacle was even uglier. Dish, bowl . . . but you couldn't put freesias and jasmine in a bowl, they would flop. Her flowers always flopped after a short while, she suspected Muff of going round chewing the leaves. Teethmarks had been discovered.

The jasmine mixed with the freesia produced a deliciously sweet yet spicy smell. It triggered memories. Emotions were stirring inside her that she had thought were dead.

Over the past few years, she had concentrated on her career, not exactly repressing sex and sentiment, but not giving much time or thought to them.

Not that sex needed thought, it happened to you sometimes whether you expected it or not. Sentiments, emotions, all right, love, that was different, you had to open the doors to those strangers, and she had kept the doors closed.

There might be historical reasons for it, she thought.

I was married too young really. Married my boss. A good man and a good copper. Wasn't a success. If I married too young, then he married too late. After he died I had a brief kind of affair with his son by his first marriage. Not proud about that, but at least it was real, some feeling there.

Then after that I was more or less celibate. On and off there were episodes.

So ran her internal monologue.

And now there was Humphrey and he was very real indeed. But she had not opened a door in her mind.

Commitment, they called it, didn't they? She had committed herself in no way at all.

And now she found that strangely painful, as if there was a hole inside her, a drain through which affection and desire poured away ungratified.

Suddenly, she was aware that she needed both to love and be loved. And she knew why this was so: it was because Humphrey had been making it clear that she must decide if their relationship should go forward or declare itself dead.

She looked round her kitchen where she spent a good deal of her life because it was so sunny and warm. The bowls of spring flowers on the window sill, the lemon-scented geranium which carried on bravely from year to year in spite of her unskilful prunings and waterings, these belonged to her.

Muff pushed in through her own private door, she too belonged.

I can't give all this up, she thought. I created it, helped by Kate and Anny. Upstairs in her sitting-room were her books, a few cherished pieces of furniture and several pictures which represented her more avant-garde taste as opposed to Humphrey's collection of Victoriana. She had nothing against Victorian painting, and it would have suited her little early nineteenth-century house, but Anny Cooper had educated her eyes to see a different beauty in Bacon and Lucien Freud. Not that she owned or could ever afford to own the work of such painters but she had chosen a few paintings by Thistlethwaite and Mary Benson and John McMaster to hang on her walls.

She made some tea, and gave Muff a dish of milk. She drank and Muff slurped as was her way when feeling particularly companionable.

Silence and peace descended and she began to feel better, she could look forward to a shower and a meal. She had tickets for a Mozart concert tonight and that too was a treat which she would share with Anny. Also, Anny was cooking their supper and Anny was a master cook, she would forget her diet tonight.

Then the telephone rang and a strange woman's voice asked if was Miss Daniels.

'Oh good, I was told it might be you . . . Do you own a large tabby cat with a white front and a smudge across the nose?'

Charmian looked across the room at the very smudge on the white nose. 'Yes.'

'Thank goodness, I was so worried she might be a lost cat . . . she's been coming here for breakfast every day lately and I wondered . . . But Miss Eagle said it sounded like your cat and to ask . . . I live just round the corner in Prince Albert Drive.'

'I am afraid it probably is my cat, I am sorry if she's a nuisance.'

'Oh no, we love her, I was just afraid she was lost, homeless, you know.' The voice was eager, friendly. 'She's been making herself so much at home.'

Charmian looked at Muff sorrowfully. 'I don't know how I can stop her.'

'Oh, please don't try. It's a pleasure. Besides, we feel flattered to be her second home.'

Second home. Charmian bent down to stroke Muff. Sensible cat. Perhaps that was the answer for her and Humphrey: two homes, one here, and the other in his house in Chapel Close. No one invading anyone else's territory and days and nights by arrangement.

Humphrey, she thought, when you get back I might have a message for you.

He was away on one of those trips about which he said very little but seemed connected with NATO. This last trip had seemed particularly hot, demanding a briefing about which he looked silently worried. She knew better than to question. It was a measure of his trust in her that he mentioned it at all.

In fact, he told her more about his work than she ever told him about hers. That would have to be remedied somehow.

She was laughing as she went upstairs to get ready for her evening of Mozart. She was halfway dressed, the black Jean Muir with matching suede slippers from Abby Fischer, when the telephone rang again. 'Damn.' She hopped over to the dressing table, one shoe on, one shoe off.

She listened; a voice spoke hoarsely. 'Damn you, Anny,' she said without rancour. 'Fancy getting flu on our evening out.' The telephone muttered that there was a lot of it about. 'Can I do anything for you, you poor invalid? Right, sleep and quiet is all you need. I get the message. And yes, I can use your ticket.'

As she finished dressing, she considered whom to approach. She had a network of friends, but not a large one. 'I ought to have more friends,' she told herself, 'it's been all work and not enough of anything else.' It seemed to be the evening for home truths, but oddly enough this was not being dispiriting, she felt stimulated as if she was a student again, and it was the New Year and she was making good resolutions.

Whom should she ask to enjoy an evening of Mozart and Purcell in the august chambers of Windsor Castle itself?

Her own secretary, Tess, was one such, but she was not

answering her telephone so must be out already. Well, good, the girl had looked tired and tense lately and needed to relax.

She tried Dolly Barstow, but Sergeant Dolly was entertaining and did not seem too pleased to be disturbed. Well, that was good too, it meant she had got over George Rewley.

She thought of Lady Mary. Yes, Mary would be fine if she would accept, but she was such a sociable girl that a gap in her diary was unlikely. Everyone liked Mary Erskine.

And as she told herself she wanted a look at Mary Erskine. A friendly look of course, but a necessary scrutiny. She was struggling to assess Lady Mary; they lived by different standards, their sophistications were wide apart, and what was shocking to her, might not seem so to Mary. It worked the other way too and what made Mary raise an eyebrow could fail to raise a quiver in Charmian. She suspected that Mary put loyalty to friends and family pretty high, but life had taught Charmian otherwise. They came from different worlds.

But worth a try. Mary answered promptly, sounding hurried and surprised. 'Yes, I'd adore it. Lovely. Had quite a day, a bit of Mozart will be just the thing.'

Charmian made a quick calculation. 'We'll get something to eat in the Wine Bar in Castle Street.'

It was a pleasant place, run by a pair of amateurs who were refugees from high-powered jobs in the City of London, allegedly seeking a quieter life in the country. Service was a bit hit and miss, but tonight the two women were lucky, and after standing at the bar for a few minutes fell heir to a table in the window, overlooking the cobbled walk, and were soon served. The soup was hot and good.

Over the mushroom quiche which was about up to its usual standard, she studied Lady Mary. She didn't look like a druggie, but you could never be sure. 'Glad you could come.'

'Glad to be asked.' Mary sighed. Her pretty face looked weary. 'Been a rough day.'

Charmian nodded in sympathy, but continued to eat her quiche, she wasn't going to prod. Let Mary do it all herself.

'Not been too good with me, either.'

'You know about Ted, of course?'

Charmian gave another nod, she chewed on a tough bit of

129

mushroom. Surely mushrooms should be tender, where did they get their veg?

'Poor Una, she's being very brave. I suppose she must have suspected him all the time.'

'Looks like it,' agreed Charmian. 'She came to see you, did she?'

'Went in to see Luke Mallet, I was there. She accepts it totally.' Mary was only toying with her quiche. 'Bit unnerving, the way she is. She can be like that, can Una. Kind of dead in your hand.' She looked straight into Charmian's face, as if seeking an answer. 'But I don't see why Ted killed the girl. One of those terrible things that happen to men, I suppose. Sex, at the bottom somewhere. I always wondered about him and Una that way.'

Charmian poured them both some wine. Mary did not know, as she did, that Ted might have had a deeper and more layered motive, in which the primary target might have been Una herself.

'I think Una might guess a bit more of his motive,' she said.

'Poor Ted. You have to pity him. I saw him praying. In St George's Chapel one day. I mean he was an agnostic. I was worried, thought he might be ill, or desperately miserable and asking for help. I suppose now he was praying because he was guilty. Poor Ted, that's what I thought.' She said, 'I felt as though I ought to be praying myself.'

'What have you got to pray about, Mary?'

'I have bad thoughts,' said Mary Erskine sadly.

'You wouldn't care to amplify that?' Charmian was amused.

'Private bad thoughts.'

'We all have them.' Then she said: 'Have you done anything about the drug user?'

Mary hesitated. 'It's not me, you know.'

'I never thought it was.'

'I expect you did . . . I'm trying to help Delphine but it's difficult.' Now she was not looking at Charmian but down at her plate. She raised her wine-glass to her lips.

'Was that what brought on your bad thoughts, as you call them?'

Mary finished drinking her wine before answering. 'Not really.'

A lie if I ever heard one, thought Charmian.

As they walked towards the Castle, Mary said: 'It's Pix I'm worried about most just now.'

She told Charmian what had happened that afternoon. 'Went absolutely crazy, violent. He's strong, you know . . . I caught up with him and took him home but it wasn't good. Bit of a scene there. I'm not sure his mother handles him well . . . But the doctor had thought he was so much better. Poor little soul.'

'Any history of episodes like this before?'

'He's always been unusual, but then we have the odd eccentric in our family. In-breeding, I suppose. Una wondered if he had infant schizophrenia. If there is such a thing; she seemed to think so.'

'Oh, she saw him, did she?'

'Came along after it happened, she noticed him running off. Just as well, really because we wouldn't have known where he was.'

In the Wellington Chamber, in which they had good seats, more people knew Lady Mary than knew Charmian, while those who knew them both looked surprised that they were together.

The music soothed and enchanted as usual. Charmian drove her companion back to Chapel Close which was now bathed in moonlight. Una's house was all dark, she noticed.

As they passed Humphrey Kent's house, Mary said: 'I suppose old Humphrey will be back from Brussels soon.'

'I suppose so.' She was surprised that she felt a sudden joy at the thought.

'Tuesday week, he said.'

Now Charmian was surprised at something else, a rush of jealousy that Mary should know more than she did, but she said nothing and hoped she showed nothing.

'I'm helping him with his rose garden,' went on Mary happily. 'He's starting one.'

'I thought he already had roses.'

'Oh a lot, but they're old stock, needed replacing. And I know about roses. I know what he likes too.'

Charmian stopped the car. 'Here we are. Thanks for coming.'

'Lovely concert. You must let me take you next time.'

'Wait a minute, something to say.' On the way home, the thoughts that had been boiling up inside Charmian during the

131

concert came to the surface. She could not hide from herself that she was full of apprehension.

'About the boy. Tell his parents to look after Pix. Send him away. Has he got any grandparents? Scotland? Send him to them.'

'Why?'

'I just have this feeling that it would be best. Wiser. Safer.'

'Safer? For whom? Pix?'

Charmian looked at Mary but without seeing her, instead seeing something in the distance and trying to recognise it. 'Pix, of course,' she said.

She started the car, but Mary put her hand on the door. 'Before you go . . . Why did you really ask me tonight?'

Charmian considered for a moment then gave an honest answer. 'Curiosity . . . Why did you come?'

'Since you ask . . . Curiosity.'

Charmian found she was laughing as she drove off. Round the Castle, through the town to Maid of Honour Row, there was not much traffic and a full moon in the sky. Mrs Mallet's lights were still burning, she was a bit of a night bird, an insomniac so she claimed. Or had something else happened at St Catherine's to worry her and keep her awake? Perhaps Luke was there with her, talking of the future of the school. It would be good to eavesdrop.

'I'll make time to call on the school,' Charmian promised herself. Outside her house there was a car.

For one wild, delicious moment, she thought it might be Humphrey, home before expected and coming to her, not Mary Erskine and her bloody roses.

But she saw almost at once that it was not Humphrey.

It was Rewley's car.

Then a figure got out and came towards her. Rewley put his head through the car window.

'Wanted to let you know early. The pathologist has made up his mind: Ted Gray did not kill himself. It was murder.'

Charmian closed the car door and stood on the pavement. The lights shone out of her house, there was never darkness in her house.

'I don't know if I'm surprised or not,' she said. 'Any idea who did it?'

132

'I suppose we shall be looking for Rivers and Farmer to question them.'

'Ah.' She had almost forgotten them.

Rewley said: 'One other thing. Interesting. The blood on the girl's jacket . . . Not from Ted Gray.'

Someone unknown had walked on to the scene.

CHAPTER THIRTEEN

April 17 continued

'Whoever killed Ted Gray knew how to find him and how to kill him,' Charmian had said, as they parted. 'Think about it: it's a chain. Someone tried to set up a contract to kill with young Rivers; because of that, he was killed. Because he was killed, Louise Farmer, who seemed to indicate to her friend Lily Paget that Ted Gray was the contractor, was herself killed, and because Louise was killed, Ted Gray is killed.

'Is that the end of it? Or are we seeing too simple a picture. Is that really the way of it? One must never trust what one thinks one sees.'

As she spoke, the shadow of an idea moved lazily at the back of her mind, that repository of half-developed thoughts, so that she wondered if she had enunciated a profound truth, or something remarkably facile. Either way, she guessed Pix, that sighter of phantoms, would have concurred. The true position of Pix in all this still worried her deeply.

Victim? Deluded dreamer? Innocent little boy? You never knew where you were with children. They performed and you couldn't read the performance. Not even parents could always do so and outsiders hardly ever.

Rewley saw something in her face of this conundrum, but had his own puzzle. Ted Gray was just a bit above average height. So what of his private theory that the murderer was short, very short, a dwarf killer. An idea born of that loop that had been put round Louise's neck to strangle her, by a killer before whom she might have knelt in the mud.

'Get hold of Farmer and Rivers, question them,' Charmian called over her shoulder as she drove off. 'Try Cheasey. And let me know,' leaving Rewley muttering, 'All right for her.'

But the idea of Cheasey attracted him.

There was a family of dwarfs in Cheasey, of course, the Cheasey little men as they were known. Cheasey, which had everything else, also had the Tippers.

Try Cheasey. Why not?

George Rewley drove home to the small house he shared with Kate, and as he drove he came to the reckoning that he had to sort out his relationship with Charmian Daniels; it was a complicated one.

He had known her for some time, he had worked with her on several cases (willy-nilly, there had been no choice, the fates had just handed him over to her), he liked and admired her very much, and was married to her goddaughter. (He would think about that relationship later; his Kate was proving no easy mate, but he'd not expected other and as a matter of fact, he found it exciting. No boring days with Kate.)

But about Charmian Daniels . . . ? I am her stalking horse. What was it the dictionary called it: a person put forward to deceive.

Perhaps he was not quite that, but she was using him to push forward an investigation in which she could now take no personal part.

She hates not being in the field. Success has promoted her out of the tasks she really enjoyed. I suppose she did not know how much she would miss it, so she is making me her instrument. Of course, her very position as head of SRADIC means she gets to know everything, but she wants to know it first, and she wants to initiate action.

I am to do this for her. He had known it for some time now but without allowing himself to put it into speech. Now he said it aloud as he drove down the road to Merrywick where he lived with Kate.

For him the relationship had some advantages: it placed him in close contact with a woman of great influence, whose position guaranteed that anyone to whom she extended patronage would get a firm footing on the promotion ladder.

Rewley was an ambitious officer who knew he was capable of rising high, perhaps very high.

But he had no illusions. He knew that patronage had its dangerous side, it was not all rewards, there was an adverse balance.

In particular he knew that his immediate superiors, Inspector Fred Elman and Chief Inspector Bert Father, would resent any notion that he was, in any way, 'working' for Charmian Daniels. There was a unit loyalty, as in the army, and he would be going against this, offering his services outside the group.

Men are institutional animals, feeling a strong loyalty to the gang, and possibly women are not. He doubted whether Charmian Daniels felt any group loyalty, she would say her loyalty was an impersonal one to Justice. Or, if she did not put it so grandly, she would say she was dedicated to the idea of getting the criminal. The victim came into it, of course, but what she really sought was a resolution.

All the same, he thought in this particular case she had some personal needs to satisfy. Somewhere in this case, was a problem for her.

She had a secret life, one he did not understand, one he suspected she might not understand herself. He knew about the relationship with Humphrey Kent, that was on the record.

But where did he stand? Elman and Father were men he had to work with daily and they must already be watching him.

Rewley drew into a quiet road to think about it. From where he sat in the car, he could see the lights of Windsor, smell the river, and feel a cool, fresh wind blowing down the Thames.

He faced the fact that he did feel uneasy about his ambiguous position. The more so, since he knew that although Elman and Father admired Charmian Daniels and respected her abilities ('sees further into the forest than most of us,' Father had said once, in grudging praise), they did not like her.

Or more positively, they felt jealous of a highly successful woman, who was now in charge of SRADIC, the central collating unit, to whom all records of all cases in the southern area came.

Just recently, it had begun to look as if some officers were trying out various tricks by which they delayed the transit of records to SRADIC. Rewley was not among such officers, not senior enough to have been able to do so even if he had wanted to, but he had an idea that CI Father was such a one and had even been able to initiate a few techniques. He was a wily beggar and hadn't got where he was without learning how to use his feet.

Rewley had no doubt that Charmian would soon circumvent any little devices of this sort. She was a powerful lady, he told himself, even if she did not speak, you felt it when she came into a room.

Of course, for someone with his skill, speech did not matter, he could read faces. What he read in her face was perplexity, but also a determination that he respected.

Suddenly his mind was made up: he was going to go on supplying her with information, even going out and getting it as asked, he wanted to be on her side.

But he was a prudent fellow, so he would also find a way of letting CI Father know what he was doing. Father was a worldly wise chap who could probably see as well as Rewley himself that a junior officer did not lightly ignore such as Charmian Daniels. Too many paths to power lay her way.

He started the car and drove home.

Home was Largo Lane, Merrywick. The builder of Largo Lane, a small precinct of pretty modern houses, had been a Scot from Upper Largo in Fife, home of Robinson Crusoe, so that next door to Largo Lane was Crusoe Court. Rewley had agreed with Kate that Merrywick was a pleasant place in which to live, but he had refused to move into the apartment she had owned in the village, because Sergeant Dolly Barstow was a neighbour and between Rewley and Dolly there had been passages that a newly married man had better forget. Nor was he willing to live in the apartment in Wellington Yard, freely offered by Kate's mother, Anny Cooper. He liked Anny, she had charm as well as a great deal of money, but she was a lady so volatile and explosive that he thought it better to keep his distance.

Kate and her mother were on good terms, but did better if kept apart. As for poor Jack (he was always called that lately, Poor Jack, or Poor Old Jack), Anny's husband and Kate's father, he had been banished by Anny after a particularly violent quarrel and had not been seen for some weeks now. It was an on-and-off marriage which Rewley thought a bad example of married life and one which he had no desire to emulate.

All the lights were on in his house as he drove up which might mean Kate was home or it might not; Kate, always having been rich had no economies, lights and heating burned all the time, regardless.

He let himself into the house, walking straight into the large sitting-room. He threw his coat over a chair.

'Kate?'

No answer, but there was a note for him on the low table by the fire, which was burning down. No pretend gas or electric fires for Kate: this was real coal, real logs.

'Thank you for letting me know you would be working late,' Kate had written in her large, carefully designed writing which stretched across the page.

Sarky madam, said Rewley to himself, smiling. I left a message on the fax, you should have checked. And where were you all the afternoon when I tried ringing?

'Gone to a late show at Le Jardinière with Dolly. Work for her. She's taking her new man as camouflage. And me as chaperone.'

He knew what Dolly Barstow was after at Le Jardinière, it was the new case, just being developed. The club in Pardow Place House on the road to Slough was smartish and with a rich clientèle; it was also suspected of being a venue where little boys were to be procured. Perhaps little girls as well, some of the customers of Le Jardinière were reputed to be omnivorous.

Dolly could look after herself and she would do her best to look after Kate too, but Kate still had the casual rashness of a girl who had always known the protection of riches. He hoped the new man was capable. As he drank he wondered who Dolly's new man was. He usually knew all the gossip of who was with whom and why, but this relationship had got past him. Must mean that the man was not in the Force, and for Dolly that must be good news.

He finished his drink, looked hopefully for some food in the refrigerator and found that Kate had left him a salmon *en croute* to be heated up in the microwave.

'And don't put the salad in the oven too,' said the note pinned to it.

Since Rewley had lived on his own all his adult working life and had cooked for himself for all of them (except for a period in the station house as a young constable), he regarded this as a bit more of Kate's arrogance.

He watched the late-night TV news, noted that he could continue to watch similar programmes at intervals through the night if he felt inclined, then sat listening for Kate to come home from Le Jardinière.

The clock struck the hour. Midnight. He was just deciding that he might drive out to Le Jardinière himself when he heard a car stopping. He went to the window to look.

Dolly and Kate had arrived together.

He moved back into the room. He liked his house, needed his home. He had to have bricks and mortar and he had to own it, which was why he had not allowed Kate to put a penny towards the mortgage. Crazy, of course, when she was rich and he was poor, and not male machismo either, it was just that there was a space in his life, because of the way he had grown up in a silent world, he was different. George Rewley needed to belong to a unit.

'Saw you looking,' said Kate; she came into the room, bright-eyed and cheerful, swinging a red silk coat over her shoulder. 'Worried, were you?'

'Not a bit. Just curious. On your own?'

Kate laughed. 'Only for now. We did have company but it's gone home alone.'

'Where's Dolly?'

'Using the phone in the kitchen.'

Rewley raised his eyebrow. 'Urgent, was it?'

'She thought so.'

The two young women were old friends and sometimes rivals but they maintained a strong, humorous relationship.

The call must have been a short one because Dolly came into the room, leaving the door open behind her.

'Thanks for coming tonight, Kate. I'll be off now.'

Dolly Barstow was a tall, fair-haired girl, better educated and probably cleverer than Kate but Kate was an artist and unpredictable and might do and become anything, while Dolly would run on more standard rails. She was ambitious, a very good police officer, who modelled herself on Charmian Daniels.

She might go as far, or further, because Charmian would have eased the way forward, fighting some of the battles for her.

'How was Le Jardinière?' Rewley went over to shut the door, through which a strong draught was blowing. 'Let me get you a drink.'

'About its usual self,' said Dolly, as if she had weighed the whole scene up and found no surprises. 'Nothing to drink, thank you.'

'Get what you wanted?'

'I did. That's what I was telephoning about. If you think I am smiling, then I am. In a short while, several suspects will be picked up and be on their way to a police cell and hopefully to a long sentence.'

'Congratulations.'

'And what about you?'

'Two or three things on the go at the moment.'

'Not all engaging you equally,' said Dolly drily.

So she knew about his assistance to Charmian Daniels? Or guessed, wouldn't take much acumen, especially to someone who knew him so well. He wasn't the only one who could read faces: he saw Kate watching him with bright eyes.

'Some cases get to you more, you know.'

'Certainly do. Would it be easier if we kept emotion out of it, or not? Rhetorical question.'

She's leading up to something, Rewley thought. He saw it in Kate's watchful face, too.

'Thinking of going into Cheasey myself tomorrow,' he said. 'Making a foray into bandit country.'

'Good luck to you.' Dolly eyed him meditatively, and then sat down as if she wouldn't go just yet, after all, but had something further to say. 'Interesting night at Le Jardinière. Picked up some oddments of information myself. Just in passing, you know.' She was being deliberately casual. 'Perhaps I will have that drink. Just tonic and lemon and ice.'

'Come on, Dolly, let's have it.' Rewley moved to get the drink with some impatience.

'It was wall-to-wall Cheasey tonight. Plenty of faces you'd have known. Celebrating something, I think.'

'A wedding or a death, I expect,' said Rewley sourly.

'You know what they're like. Gossip, hints . . . Our Friend'

– she hesitated – 'Charmian, they say the paddy wagon is out for her.'

'Oh they are a repository of antique slang,' said Rewley with irritation. The Cheaseyites put their own gloss on the jargon they picked up, they had their own patois, so it was never clear exactly what they meant.

Dolly said indulgently, 'It's a game they play. It's all those old films they watch.'

'And what do they mean this time?'

'A drugs scandal is blowing up, someone in her circle is involved, it will rub off on her. It's meant to. She has enemies. And they will try to get her. Friendly faces, you know, with a knife ready for the back. Cheasey likes that, good fun for them.'

'She's always had enemies,' said Rewley thoughtfully. 'She knows that, and knows that they put on a friendly face.'

Fred Elman and Bert Father were not straightforward in their relationship with Charmian, and especially so since she had shot ahead of the game.

'I'm just telling you,' said Dolly.

'So what am I to do?'

'Tell her, warn her.'

'I think she knows already,' said Rewley, suddenly sorting out one of the strands he had sensed in Charmian's anxiety.

Dolly finished her drink, then stood up. 'Thank you for the drink, this time I really am going.'

But Rewley still had his mind on Le Jardinière. 'Did you see any of the Rivers or Waters lot there?'

She thought about it. 'Yes, one or two. Usually are some. They're kind of universal hangers-on, aren't they?' Little parasites clinging to the bigger animals' backs.

'Who in particular?'

She knew what he was after, it was no secret that Ginger Rivers wanted revenge, if he could get it, for the death of his boy.

'I don't know all the Rivers-Waters-Seaman clan by sight,' she said carefully. 'But Ginger wasn't there, he's the one you want, isn't it?'

'Want to talk to.'

'I did see Frank Waters and the one they call the Deep Sea

Diver . . . Do you know why they call him that, by the way? It's because he can't swim.'

'Ge on with it,' said Rewley.

Dolly drew in a breath. 'Ginger Rivers was not there and the reason, so the word was going round, was that he had been picked up by the Met.'

'When?'

'Three days ago . . . held in custody, bail refused.'

'Damn,' said Rewley.

'Three days means he couldn't have killed Ted Gray, doesn't it.'

'Farmer could have done it on his own.'

'Unlikely, I'd say, wouldn't you?' said Dolly. 'I mean, I've met him and so have you, he doesn't strike me as someone who could kill. Not with his own hands. That's why he teamed up with Rivers.'

'I think he might do it because of his daughter,' said Kate suddenly.

Rewley nodded. 'There's strong emotion here, you've got to take that into account. He's the one with the motive. I shall concentrate on him for killing Gray.' He added thoughtfully, 'I'd like to know what Fred Elman and Bert Father make of Rivers being out of action, I think Fred had him down for Ted Gray for sure. He won't like the disappearing act.'

'He always likes a simple answer, doesn't he,' said Dolly.

And it would have been simple, thought Rewley, when he and Kate were at last on their own. Gray guilty of killing Louise Farmer, then Gray wiped out by the vengeful parents. A nice solution.

It left things out of course: such as why was there mud on Louise Farmer's knees, but there could be any number of answers to that. She might have fallen down. It didn't have to be crucial. Only to him, at that moment, it was so.

There were other thoughts as well: the threat to Charmian's position. Wheels within wheels in police politics. There were always politics. Rewley was a sensible and worldly wise young man, and he was well aware that he had to step with prudence.

Kate stroked his cheek gently. 'Thoughtful? Come on, come to bed.'

They were young, they were recently married, for the next period of time they forgot about murder and sudden death.

But in the small hours, after a dream of little people with murderous loops of twine in their hands, Rewley woke and knew that something was happening.

Somewhere.

He made a noise, a sharp muttering noise and sat up.

Kate stirred sleepily. 'What is it?'

He did not answer.

'The horrors again?'

He muttered: 'It's happening.'

She woke up fully and put her arms round him. 'Oh come on, you're not psychic. It's a panic attack.'

He had them too often, she thought. In a kind of way, it excited her, she turned his face towards her and kissed his cheek.

After a short while, she said: 'I love my godmother Charmian, but you will really have to stop thinking about her.'

She too could play the psychic.

Unlike Rewley, Charmian slept well. True, she had a muddled dream in which a faceless child tugged at her skirt while she observed Mary Erskine dancing with Humphrey in full evening dress even as the Queen looked on, but she woke up laughing. Humphrey was a very poor dancer and if the dance was really a suppressed symbol of some other relationship between him and Lady Mary (dreams always did that sort of thing, didn't they?), then somehow she felt able to laugh at that too. They really had looked so comic.

CHAPTER FOURTEEN

That same night and into the next day

For a child Pix was a poor sleeper, but he had learnt to mask this from his parents who seemed to think a child who did not sleep ten hours a night was a child at risk. From what he had never been sure.

He valued his night wakes, for in them he did some deep thinking. Huddled under the blankets he entered his own world.

Luke Mallet would have been surprised if he had known how Pix thought of his school. The picture in the boy's mind was of a dark, heavy building full of secret places which held terrors. Caverns in the mind.

Pix was aware that his removal to Scotland was being planned, his parents had loud, clear voices and used the telephone to his grandparents frequently.

So it was being fixed up, his deportation. But it was taking a time. Not today, not tomorrow, maybe not even next week. His grandparents were about to travel on business (Grandpa was in banking, not a phrase that meant a lot to Pix, except it seemed to mean money, Grandpa was rich) and so could not be at home to receive their dear Pix. He hoped he was their dear Pix because he certainly loved them both, especially Grandpa who was generous and sweet-natured, Grandma was a tougher nut.

He was much recovered from the state he had been in when plucked from the cycle shed by Mary Erskine and Charmian Daniels. A bit of that had been acting, as he admitted to himself. Likewise when he kicked the Play House, half real, half not. But he was still liable to attacks of terror when he visualised certain figures and took up some particular memories.

He was willing to do a little talking, just to make his mother look happier, but silence still seemed to him the wisest course.

He had not been returned to school again, for which he was truly grateful, although he occasionally entered it in his mind, probing around as the tongue will worry an aching tooth.

You could not be expelled from St Catherine's, it was too liberal an establishment and the fees too high, but Pix had an idea he would not be welcome back. He had infected too many of his friends and companions with a virus of fear. Sixteen the count was, some recovering, others still bad.

He knew this, although no one had told him so, he had his own sophistications: he knew how to read silences and omissions, how to note whom he did not see, whose name was not mentioned.

He did not see any of his friends. They had been mysteriously withdrawn from the company of Pix, the plague carrier. But the other side of this otherwise unpleasant situation was that he had freedom. Freedom of time, at least, and limited freedom of movement.

He could play in the garden, he could play in the house, but he must not remove himself beyond the observation of his parents when they were home or the woman who looked after his baby sister. Those authorities had to be able to hear him or see him.

This was the theory, but in fact he was able to be completely alone in his play room which, accordingly, was where he spent most of his time.

Since he had for so long been an only child, baby sister had made no inroads on the play room. All in it was his; toys, bricks, and books. Some toys he had outgrown, but he was a boy who treasured things and there they all were, neatly on the shelves. Little sister would soon alter all this no doubt, he had already observed with foreboding her strong, grabby hands.

He looked at his own hands, brown, scratched but strong. For his age, he was muscular if not tall.

A voice called out: 'You there, Pix?'

'Here, Jeanie,' he answered. Not his nanny, thank goodness, but hers, the baby princess, so he used the girl's name. Jean. But she preferred Jeanie. More friendly, she said, not knowing that was not how he rated friends.

'I couldn't hear you.'

He put a record on his player. A piece of music chosen by his mother to educate his ears: Schubert, she said. He didn't like it or dislike it, just noise, and now convenient as a shield.

After thinking for a moment, he got out his box of bricks, for long untouched. Each brick had pictures of animals or birds on three sides and a number or a letter of the alphabet on the other. They were in good condition.

He threw them all on the ground, then, a methodical and literate child, he got the alphabet marshalled in a long, straight line.

After which he carefully spelt out a word. Not a difficult word to spell and one well within his vocabulary although not one you would expect a child to turn to. It began with a D.

Should he lay it out near the door where everyone could see it? He very much wanted to confess, but he dare not. He reached out a hand to scatter the letters.

He started to draw with chalks on a board instead; you could wipe that out. He used his elbow for that purpose several times.

Jeanie brought in his lunch on a tray. Peanut-butter sandwiches and wedges of cheese with a glass of fresh orange juice. This he liked. The cheese was low calorie, his mother being into calorie counting and Pix being a sturdy lad inclined to put on weight, but he noticed that Jeanie had sneaked in a chocolate bar.

'Thanks, Jeanie.' He tucked the bar discreetly in his pocket.

She gave him a friendly conspiratorial wink, as from one victim to another. She too found little sister a burden. 'A bit of what you fancy . . . ' She was plumpish and adored chocolate, she had paid for the bar herself. 'You've got red chalk all over your arm, you naughty boy.'

'Sorry, Jeannie.' She wasn't cross, he could tell. And in any case, she didn't do the laundry, that great machine in the kitchen did it.

Pix took himself with his lunch tray to the rocking-chair by the nursery TV set. The chair was big and soft and shaped to look like a friendly Teddy Bear. Usually he avoided it, he hated the feel of being hugged to death by a bear, but today he sat on the edge and watched the news.

A war, people fighting. He didn't take much interest, nothing to do with him. Presently, his eyes closed. He was tired because at night he was keeping awake as long as he could, even beyond his usual wakefulness, not wanting to see the face he met in his sleep.

He woke up to the sound of a car door. His mother was coming home from her work; he heard her voice talking away to Jeanie. In a minute the door opened, she was looking in, he kept his eyes closed. She tiptoed across and turned off the television set. She also adjusted the record-player which he hadn't bothered with either.

When she had gone, he went to the window to look out. Sunlight on the front garden, a car passing. Someone coming into the gate. It was Lily Paget and her brother. Trouble.

Lily rang the bell, fidgeting on her feet until the front door opened. They were not, however, admitted. Only delivering a note.

After a pause, Jeanie put her head round the door. 'That was Lily Paget at the door. Invitation to tea for you. Tomorrow.'

Pix distrusted Lily and her invitation. He knew her of old, she asked questions.

'Your ma's considering whether to let you go. Do you want to?'

Pix weighed it up. Then he nodded gravely. 'And will you ask her if I can have Minka in the house?' Minka was his gerbil whom he loved beyond anything and anybody except his mother.

'See what I can do,' said Jeanie, disappearing.

He went back to his books, gradually becoming aware of fresh voices. His mother seemed to be entertaining some friends. He heard her welcoming them: Lady Mary, and Mrs Gray, whom his mother called, distastefully to his ears, Cousin Una. He didn't want any more in the family, he had been quite content with his mother and father and his big half-brother Alex. Now there was a little sister, to add a cousin was unnecessary. And what a cousin, a teacher at St Cath's.

He crept to the door of the living-room to listen. He couldn't hear it all, only bits. Lady Mary's high, clear voice spoke of Charmian.

He knew who that was, the woman who had held him in her

147

arms the day the deader nearly got him. There were so many unpleasant associations connected with that day that he could not bear to think about them. Either grown-ups were ignorant of many facts or they did not tell the truth. Either way, he felt dreadfully insecure.

Could dead people, or a piece of them, a pair of hands, a face, move around? It didn't seem to be a problem that worried grown-up people. Perhaps you had to be young and very guilty to attract them: he believed himself to be both. He knew that children of his age could kill and be killed, that the dead did not always lie down quietly, and if he had infected some of his fellows with this belief, he had done no more than was right.

From what he could pick up at the door, Charmian appeared either to be in trouble or to be a trouble, possibly both. He did not mind that, he felt pleased that trouble should be distributed around his universe, let her have her share.

He heard the word 'coke'. Was his mother offering them a drink? But she never drank that sort of thing. This being the afternoon, she would offer them tea in those thin, pretty cups that he was not allowed to touch. A mug for him and baby sister.

Be teatime soon. Chocolate biscuits, perhaps, that was a good thought. Toast, yes, Jeanie might do toast, she liked it herself.

Was that Lady Mary crying? No, he thought not, one non-cryer recognised another. His mother then? No, she did not cry either and not her way of doing it. Small angry shrieks were more her style, soon succeeded by gales of laughter. He wished she would laugh now. So the tears had to be Mrs Gray.

Pix by no means shaped all these thoughts into clear words and sentences but they accurately reflected the emotions churning inside him.

The guests seemed to be moving round the room so that now it was hard to hear, but suddenly he heard Mrs Gray's voice loud and clear saying how terrible it was that Ted could have killed a girl and been wanting to kill her, his own wife. She was calling his mother Dearest Phyllida.

'Is that what the police think?' he heard his mother ask.

'It's what I think,' was the answer.

'But why?'

'He must have hated me,' came that sad voice. 'Or fancied

148

someone else. Someone I don't know about but who must have been there for some time, ages probably. Yes, that'll be it. And of course, there is my money, not a lot but nice to have.'

Lady Mary was murmuring something about Ted not being like that, and she couldn't believe it, while Mrs Gray was saying that he had been neglected, beaten and abused as a child which changed how a person related to other people. People could become things, she said.

'Darling Cousin Una, please don't,' protested his mother. 'Good heavens, darling, this is Gothic stuff.'

Then his name came up, but to his fury, he could not hear what was said, except something about Lily and her invitation. He heard Minka's name too and was hopeful.

The voices came closer, they were leaving.

He ran back to his chair, sinking back into Teddy's arms, eyes closed.

Una pushed the door open to look in. She crept quietly towards the chair, giving it the push that set it rocking.

'Teddy Bear,' she said gently. 'Teddy Bear.'

Pix went into his nobody-at-home act. His mother (and possibly that Charmian Daniels) would have known he was putting it on a bit and have given him a soft slap and said: 'Come on now, Pix,' but Mrs Gray did not know so she stood for a little while, saying 'Good boy, Pix,' then left.

Little sister came crawling into the room, ready to wreck his possessions. He picked her up, all warm and soft, and deposited her outside the door.

'Jeanie,' he called out. 'Her.' Then he closed the door firmly, she could not, as yet, open it.

He went back to his bricks where he spelt out two words.

DEATH
HER

Rewley was half right. Something terrible was about to happen.

CHAPTER FIFTEEN

April 17–20

Over the next few days various people were the subject of police questioning. Una Gray, as might have been expected, was interviewed several times. Each time, as she left the police station, she was photographed by the press and TV reporters all of whom tried to get something out of her, but she said nothing. Lady Mary Erskine was interviewed and photographed, what she said was friendly and polite but low on information. Luke Mallet came in for a lesser share, as did Pix's parents, both of them. But their involvement, and that of Pix, was kept out of the press at the request of the police.

Needless to say, stories of 'some funny business with the boys in that school' went the rounds, but without anyone willing to back them up, nothing could be printed. Although repeated and grossly added to they remained word of mouth.

Also, over the period of the next few days there were various reports being prepared by different police technicians, which were then read by the police team investigating the double murders and in turn filtered through to Charmian.

To Chief Inspector Father and Inspector Elman it was becoming clear that they had no hard forensic evidence that linked Ted Gray with Louise Farmer.

'Except where the jacket was found,' said Fred Elman doggedly. He had indigestion and a headache, and anyway, always liked to hang on to the picture he had formed and the picture he had formed was that Ted Gray had killed Louise and then he had been killed by the two parents, Rivers and Farmer.

It now appeared that Ted Gray could not have been killed by Ginger Rivers of Cheasey. Cheasey had protected its own by getting its son arrested. Possibly on purpose to prevent him killing.

But Elman still had the rest of his picture. In this, Ted Gray was as guilty as hell, motive unknown but probably sexual, and although Ted Gray was not done in by Ginger Rivers, he had possibly been done away with by Farmer.

'But it was not his blood and nothing forensic really connects him with her death or the jacket,' Father said again, with Rewley silently concurring.

'Except for where it was.' That was Elman.

'We shall have to talk to Mrs Gray again.'

'Won't get much out of her,' said Elman dourly. He had spoken to Una after her talk with George Rewley and learnt little. He felt very much inclined to leave further detailed investigation to Rewley and Dolly Barstow and attend to the matter of the disappearance of a royal servant from the Castle that had just been reported.

He'd keep nominal control, of course, as at a greater distance would Chief Inspector Father who had been deputed to go to a management training course at Oxford Polytechnic.

Badly needed by him, in Elman's not so humble opinion. He took some aspirin, a beaker of police coffee and felt better. Life was looking up.

He had his secret thoughts about the involvement in drugs and dealing in drugs of that person close to Charmian Daniels and hoped some hard action would be possible soon. When the dust from the explosions cleared, possibly Daniels would disappear with it. Cases like that had spreading tentacles. He had little against Daniels personally (except that he did not like women as rivals), still she was nothing but trouble. To herself and others. Look at the time she nearly got herself killed, or worse. They did not mention it now, of course, yet it had happened and it was still there, imbedded in the police folk-memory. Such a memory was exceedingly tenacious as he knew well. He himself, for instance, did not forget that Bert Father had had a bit of a run-in with a woman police sergeant who had later been murdered. It wasn't on Father's official police record, but there was not a

151

serving officer who did not know it and remember. Life was like that.

'Where's Farmer now?' he asked Sergeant Rewley.

'At home. I asked him to stay there for the moment. I don't think he knows what's hit him.'

'Go and talk to him, see what you can get.'

George Rewley had already visited the Farmer house several times to talk to Louise's parents. Grace Farmer felt as if he came daily, and that it was part of the horrible pattern of life now. She wondered if he called on the Rivers family as often. But probably not. Louise's death had been special.

She was avoiding all her friends, except Elfrida Paget, partly because Elfrida would not be kept out, and partly because Lily Paget had been so close to Louise. She thought now that Lily had been closer to Louise than she had been herself.

She moved around her house, keeping it polished and tidy but not doing much food preparing because nobody wanted to eat. Just shove something in the microwave when needed, she told herself. Her mother had come to stay for a little at the beginning, but had now gone back to Dorset because her dogs needed her. (She had brought two Jack Russells with her and that was quite enough.) Ellen, they called her Ellen since she did not like to be called mother or grandmother, said she would return when needed. Grace Farmer, who loved her mother but was quite different from her, was determined she was not going to be needed.

'Get back to work,' Ellen had advised. But Grace's studio remained locked while her partner tended to their gallery unaided.

Her husband had not moved from his chair by the window for two days, even spending the night there. He said he could manage his office just as well by fax and telephone, what there was to be done in London could be done by someone else, he no longer cared. He seemed a bit surprised that she was still bothering with the housework, not having grasped that dusting was how she tried to hang on to her world. She needed to impose order on her disordered universe. The house itself had that empty look that an unhappy household can give even the prettiest curtains and the best-polished furniture.

She handed her husband a cup of black coffee and a vitamin pill. 'He's here again,' she said, looking out of the window. 'Our pet private policeman.'

'Don't be bitter, Grace.'

'I am bitter, and you'd better be . . . He's on his own today, usually he brings a pal.'

'It's the way police work, Grace, in twos.'

'Well, not today.' She went to open the door for the sergeant. 'Do drink that coffee and take the pill, it looks so untidy there on the floor.'

George Rewley picked up the newspaper from the step, left there because no one wanted to see it, let alone read it, and handed it over. 'Hello, Grace.' They had got on to Christian names, not out of friendliness but out of the terrible kind of intimacy the investigation of Louise's death had bound them into.

'Hello, go on in, you know the way.' She took the newspaper from his hand, only to drop it into the kitchen waste bin. Even so she caught a flash of Louise's photograph next to one of Ted Gray.

The hall smelt of lavender polish and dead flowers. She hadn't observed that the tulips in the pot had been dead for a week; it was odd how flowers could go on looking alive until the smell alerted one to their deadness. She dumped them in the kitchen too.

'He's in a rotten mood today,' she said to Rewley's back. 'I shouldn't bother with him, if I were you.'

Rewley halted at the door, he could see Farmer's head above the chair. 'Just a few questions.'

'Same old question,' she said with irony.

'A few more new facts, they're always coming in as we go on looking at things. Then I have to ask more questions.' Rewley looked towards the window where Farmer could certainly hear their voices but was not reacting. 'Been there all day, has he?'

'Yes, and yesterday.'

'And the day before that?' This was the day when Ted Gray had been killed.

She didn't answer. So, he was out that day, Rewley thought. He held the door for her.

'I'm not coming in, do it on your own.' As she went up the stairs, she called down: 'Give him an anaesthetic first.'

153

She sat on her bed, the linen fresh and neatly tucked in. Tomorrow she would need to do a wash. Good old washing, a prime drug, better than alcohol. Below she could hear the rumble of voices, the sergeant's voice striking deep notes, her husband's somewhat higher tones. Higher than normal which showed something.

Rewley was speaking: 'Suppose he wasn't guilty? Ted Gray did not murder your daughter. You killed him by mistake.'

'I didn't kill him.' Brian Farmer was almost in tears. 'There was a time when I might have done, that's all.'

'You wanted to, you planned to.'

'But I did not do it.' He admitted he had been out the day of Ted Gray's killing; but said he had come home early and not gone out again. 'My wife would confirm that.'

'Anyone else? Did you have a visitor? Make a telephone call or receive one?'

'No. I just sat. I think I watched the TV news. The war, you know . . . '

'Can I see the clothes you wore that day?'

There was a pause. 'I think my wife has washed them.'

I bet she has, thought Rewley.

'I'll take them all the same.' Even washed clothes could provide some answers. 'Don't forget the shoes.'

As he left the house soon after this, carrying a parcel of clothes, he looked up at the upper window. Grace Farmer was staring at him.

I wonder if that woman up there could have killed him? Killed Ted Gray? She has the strength and the anger. Wives are important people, he reminded himself, a wife is not just the other side of her husband.

Oh God, he thought, I like them both, they are likeable people and yet one of them might have been led to kill a perfectly innocent man.

Because he was coming to the belief that whoever killed Louise Farmer it was not Ted Gray. Ted Gray was innocent.

With that terrible feeling of a doom round the corner, he was impelled to call on Charmian Daniels.

'Who was the killer of Louise Farmer?' he asked her. 'I saw

the mud on Louise Farmer's knees. Supposing she knelt before her killer? Why?'

'I saw that too,' said Charmian. 'Someone she trusted, someone on the ground who looked as though they needed help, someone small.'

'If not Ted Gray, then a very small man or woman?'

Charmian hesitated. 'Or a child? A disturbed child?'

'Pix?' Rewley threw up his hands. 'But he's a child, not even an adolescent . . . Kids don't kill adults, they haven't the strength.'

A girl, though, not strong herself.

'Supposing he had help?' suggested Charmian.

'Who?'

'I don't know . . . someone a bit . . . crazy?'

CHAPTER SIXTEEN

April 20

Colds, sore throats and anxieties were floating around in Windsor and Merrywick, and certain people thought they all came to the same thing so that you only had a cold if you were not enjoying life, but it was hard to be sure, as even The Queen was said to be down with something feverish.

Perhaps to hide from Pix, whom he certainly did not wish to see again, especially in the close proximity of his own home, Lily Paget's brother, Eddie, developed a cold. The tea party was postponed. But only postponed, since Lily was determined it should take place. She had her reasons. However, she too developed a sort throat and remained indoors for a few days, playing her favourite tapes and thinking. Perhaps she was not sorry to be out of action for a bit.

Pix too was quietly at home. There was a lot of hiding going on, just then. Anxiety was in good supply and well distributed round the community from Luke Mallet and his Minette to Lady Mary and Una Gray. Old Mrs Mallet was immune but she had long since awarded herself a prize for a good life and thus could rise above small worries. She was a little concerned about the Celebration Day for St Catherine's, its Jubilee, now rushing up fast and at which Charmian Daniels was to be one of the speakers, but that was not a small worry like murder or sudden death, which belonged to other people and could not touch her.

Charmian and George Rewley were two of the anxious people. By nature, they were resilient and optimistic, so for both of them this was behaviour out of character. There was certainly something in the air just then.

It was the nature, size and shape of the killer of Louise Farmer that worried them. If not Ted Gray, then whom? A small person could have killed her. The pathologist's report indicated that no great strength had been required, but from the injuries on her throat it appeared that the process had been slow. Just a steady tightening of the ligature round her throat.

More like a garrotting than anything else, Rewley told himself savagely.

He was running through a list of the Tippers, the Cheasey little men. They were such respectable little men (although occasionally unlucky as any family might be), that he could not see any of them as killers. And no evidence that any one of them had ever known Louise.

Charmian's anxieties were associated with his, but different. She was thinking about Pix as she applied a modest amount of eyeliner and put on her lipstick. One way and another he was in danger. She was convinced of it.

Both Rewley and Charmian had other work problems to occupy them. Quite sharp ones in Charmian's case as she became aware of the drugs case looming over her unit at SRADIC. She had virtually created this outfit, had chosen and appointed the people to work with her, she could not avoid some of the dirt rubbing off on her if the allegations proved true.

For his part, Rewley was confronted with the need to go to the Central Criminal Court to bear witness to his part in a big fraud prosecution just coming to trial. He would have to face a hostile examination by the defending counsel. He had expected the case to come in a month's time but for reasons to suit itself, the Crown had brought it forward. He wasn't going to be able to get round to the Cheasey Tippers just yet.

He had received the call with a muttered curse, at the very moment he was reporting his interview with Farmer to Inspector Elman. 'Damn. Why couldn't they have left things as they were?'

Elman shrugged. 'Ours not to reason why. I'll see the clothes get off to forensics. Tell them to get on with it. I'd like to believe it was Farmer killed Gray, it would be nice and tidy. Or his wife, I'd settle for his missus.'

'Wouldn't solve who killed the girl,' said Rewley.

'Might do, I haven't given up Gray for that, don't be despondent, lad.' Elman, for reasons personal and private to himself, was in a good mood. 'Can't get over the man's change of behaviour. A change of pattern like that is a good indication. And he had the girl's jacket. Never admitted to having it, but there it was in his house.'

He was brisk and cheerful, walking around the Incident Room they had set up for the Farmer killing and into which an additional team had moved to deal with the death of Ted Gray.

'Don't let the Daniels woman worry you,' he said in a jovial way. 'She can get under the skin better than any woman I know. Oh yes, I knew you'd been talking to her last night, and shall I tell you how I know? Your lady wife told me when I rang up last night to have a word . . . Think on that, lad.'

His superior was always at his most unnerving worst, decided Rewley, when he was humorous and acting a part; this time as a friendly north-country copper. True, he claimed to have been born in Derbyshire, but he had long since been a southerner. I shall have to have a word with Kate not to be free with information, he told himself. Just say she doesn't know where I am, that ought to be her line. I shouldn't tell her about my movements too much, I suppose.

But he always kept in touch with his Kate, he couldn't bear not to know where she was herself, apart from anything else.

'A walking question mark, Daniels is,' Elman went on, sitting down to study his files, while at the same time picking up the telephone, his favoured instrument, all in one smooth motion. 'Accounts for her success, I suppose.'

If he can praise a woman's success then either he's had a success of his own or he sees a chance of downing her, thought Rewley, with cynical knowledge of his colleague. He can be a bastard.

'But I think she might have a problem on her hands,' Elman finished. 'Only don't tell her I said so.'

As if I would, thought George Rewley, and as if she didn't know. She's a fly one, she can read all the signals.

Charmian's main worry that morning was one she voiced to herself.

'I wish that child had been got out of the way with his

158

grandparents while this was cleared up,' she said aloud as she drove to work. She had a wailing cat in a basket beside her on the front seat, so that it was almost necessary to speak one's thoughts aloud to hear them. Muff's voice, raised in anger, could penetrate anything.

Muff was on a trip to the vet to have her nails trimmed and to be dewormed. She would remain all day and be collected in the evening. The double indignity was hard for both of them to bear.

'Better you than me,' said Charmian, as she handed Muff over to her surgeon and sped away.

But she switched off what she called her worry button and began to think about Humphrey. Good thoughts, because the morning post had brought a letter. He didn't write letters much, but he had written her this one. She smiled. In letters he seemed better able to express some feelings than in speech.

She debated. Would she answer the letter on the terms desired? She might. The option was open to her. She had put on some new bright lipstick, perhaps that said something. It said look to the future and enjoy what's coming. But that was private and personal, there was business to attend to first. Rewley doesn't like what I said about a child and murder, she acknowledged as she parked the car, and it is a tough thought. But children can kill.

It would not be the first case of homicide by a child in her experience. In the last five years she had met at least one other, and in the noble town of Windsor with Merrywick at that.

No, Rewley does not like the idea: he is looking for a little man. She wondered what he was going to do about it. He would take some action if she knew him as well as she thought she did.

As he did.

On that first day, before he took off for the Central Criminal Court where he was to be kept hanging about on and off for the next three days, the sergeant telephoned Dolly Barstow.

He was lucky to catch her, because she was just going out, she said. 'So what is it?'

'Have you got much on today?'

'Well,' began Dolly, gathering herself up to tell him that she had a child abuse case, a missing wife (who had also taken a large sum of stolen money with her), and a suspected arson in a row of little terrace houses beyond the railway station.

But before she got anything out, Rewley said: 'Will you go to Cheasey for me, and try to check on the Tippers? See if there is anything that could possibly connect one of them with the killing of Louise Farmer.'

He heard Dolly draw in her breath sharply. 'Is there anything positive behind this?'

'Say it's just an idea.'

Dolly knew his ideas and knew that there could often be something solid behind them. In other words, George Rewley was more often right than wrong.

'They've never had a murderer.' Although one or two of them had been murdered. Cheasey treated the Tippers with a mixture of affection and casual mockery descending sometimes into violence. They were the clowns of the district, suffering therefore the licence and abuse meted out to the medieval jester. 'They're not even into petty crime much.' Indeed the local Cheasey police generally held them to be among the more law-abiding elements in that lawless society.

'It can start anywhere.'

'Right. Sure. I'll prowl around. See what I can pick up.' It so happened that she had to go to Cheasey on another case. The missing wife had last been seen in Cheasey, in the offices of the Cheasey Building Society where she worked – and from whom she had abstracted the money now missing with her. 'What will you be doing?'

He told her, including the name of the judge and the defending counsel, whom he disliked, having had a brush with him before.

'Give my love to the judge.'

'You know a judge?' He was surprised.

'Well, I know that one, she's married to an uncle of mine. Older than he is, a second marriage. I believe she's as sharp as a needle, and against men, so watch your step. I'll see what I can do in Cheasey. I've got to be there anyway. But don't expect quick results.' Cheasey took time, you had to follow the rules there, Cheasey rules, or you got nowhere. Frequently you got nowhere in any case. No, Cheasey was not easy territory for the police, either to get into or to get out of, it could be like a bog,

160

one step forward and two down. Dolly had worked there when she was a young constable on probation and almost had resigned after the first week, but had not and was now glad of it. There was a sort of fascination to Cheasey, it got to you. If you stayed too long, you went native.

'Thanks Dolly. I owe you one.'

More than one, Dolly said silently to herself as she replaced the telephone. But she didn't hold it against him, and on the whole Rewley paid his debts.

The day passed quietly for all the principal actors. Una Gray got up, walked, felt ill, then slept away most of the day. Lady Mary Erskine polished the soft leather of the books in the Royal Library and thought her own thoughts, but smiled cheerfully so the world would not know too much. Luke Mallet discussed with the principal assistant the music for the Jubilee concert and wondered if he had been right to ask Charmian Daniels to be on the platform. She was a policewoman after all, what had the police to do with a school such as his? Not as if it was a state-run primary in Cheasey or even Merrywick. Minette was back at her job, looking thin and peaky, more like a fragile child herself than someone who taught children. She'd have to go home, poor little soul. Her attraction for him lessened every day. Una was right, Minette was not solid enough.

Grace Farmer had persuaded her husband to rise from his chair to take a bath. She poured in bath salts and warmed the towels, trying desperately to create for him the comfort she could not find for herself.

'They took my clothes,' he said. 'They'll be cutting them up, taking bits out, looking for stains.'

'They won't find any. You didn't kill Ted Gray, I know that. Don't worry, they won't find anything.'

'Might do,' he worried. 'I did trudge around. They might find mud, grass, bits of leaves, and think I was in the Great Park.'

'Where did you get to that time you were gone for hours?'

'Roamed here and there. Not sure. Went up the Long Walk to the Copper Horse. I remember that bit, it was so cold and I felt sorry for the old boy on the horse. George III, isn't it? Silly, he's metal and been dead for years anyway.'

That was in the Great Park, Grace reflected. But not where

161

Ted Gray was found, he was further in where the trees were thicker. You could drive there. The Park covered a great area, the last remnant of what had been one of the old hunting grounds of the medieval kings of England. No one hunted there now, although there were bridle tracks for riders, and over to the west, a polo ground or two. Grace and Brian Farmer walked that way sometimes, but they did not ride and were not interested in polo. Brian must have wanted to be on his own, but it was not the sort of place you walked alone, you needed a dog or a companion. She felt pity for him.

'But not the day he was killed,' she said.

'No, not that day,' he said in a dull voice. 'I was home then, wasn't I? Were you?'

'Yes, of course I was.'

'Oh God, look after me, Grace.' He held out his hand and she took it, holding it like a child's.

Life had taken away one child and now given her back another. But she needed him as a husband.

'If Gray didn't do it – kill Louise – then who did?' he whispered.

'Oh he did it all right, don't worry about that.' She clung to Ted Gray's guilt as her only certainty. He had to be guilty. 'That detective knew it really, you could tell, he was just trying to throw you.' So you'd confess to killing him, but she didn't say that aloud.

While she coaxed her husband back to a normal life, she felt her own grasp of it slipping away with the nightmare shadows closing in. She felt she had never truly known Louise, never been as close to her as a mother should be, or she would have been told about her sad little love affair with a Cheasey boy picked up in a wine bar.

'I didn't even know she went to wine bars, Lily Paget knew, probably Elfrida Paget knew, but I didn't know, hadn't any idea.'

She could still talk to Lily about her daughter, but she did nothing about it, putting it off from day to day.

'I'll do it tomorrow,' she said before scrubbing out the dustbin for the second time that week. Dirt was horrible, it touched you and crawled all over you so that your skin itched.

162

She considered having a shower herself, but she had done so once already that day and a second shower, so early in the morning, suggested its own abnormalities. 'The water is lovely and hot . . . But no,' she had to halt her own slide downhill. She was beginning to realise that you contributed to chaos by continually trying to clear it up.

She reached out a hand to the telephone and then drew back. Tomorrow she would ring Elfrida and ask to speak to Lily. Or she might walk round there, just call. Probably best to do it that way, rather than hide your face behind a telephone. It would be just before the weekend and perhaps a good time to choose. Saturdays and Sundays, once enjoyable, were now treacherous times.

The police had not been around them these last few days, which might mean anything or nothing, she had learnt not to trust the surface of life.

Later that day, as if rewarding herself for not having taken that second shower, she walked to where Louise's body had been found.

'You still have a body, Louise,' she whispered, 'resting in some cold place. Very soon you won't have even that, we shall have taken that away from you.' She believed in cremation, they had settled on that between them, she and her husband.

Then she walked on to the edge of the Great Park to stare to where Ted Gray had been killed. No one had told her the location, but she guessed she could make out the spot; she gazed from a distance, but that was enough for one day.

Perhaps better go home and not be out too late, walks under the trees could be dangerous.

She telephoned Elfrida the next day to learn that Lily had just left to take home a little friend of her son's after a party. Well, not really a party, just a tea. No, the tea had not been a success, her son having fallen into a crying fit after talking to his guest, and she had sent Pix home early.

It was April 20.

On that day, April 20, Charmian who had had several important meetings in London, Oxford and Birmingham in the same week, so that she spent more time travelling than in her own office, was due back from the Midlands. I am an itinerant policeman, she told herself, covering the country to keep the Queen's Peace. She had learnt enough of the history of the land she lived in to know that medieval justices had traversed the country to hear pleas in the royal courts and that it had been a long while before the Central Criminal Court had settled itself in London. In the beginning, Justice had been where the Sovereign was. She felt herself well in the tradition of those early upholders of the law.

She had chosen to go by train rather than to drive so that she could work or read on the journey. The trains were warm and reasonably punctual so that her progress about the country was pleasant. As she went through her folders and made her notes she began to understand why a famous crime writer of her acquaintance had told her that, aping Anthony Trollope, he did his best work on the train.

She had lunched by herself in a café bar overlooking the cathedral in Birmingham. Enough of crime for the moment, she would think about her own life and how she was managing it.

On the whole, well, she thought. Yes, well done, Charmian, pass yourself a vote of confidence. Her career was prospering; she had her enemies, of course, but she was aware of them. Aware too, of what they could do, but at this moment she felt confident she could deal with them. She knew more or less what they were up to, even if the details of their operations were yet to be revealed to her. Elman, Father, they were certainly among the conspirators, but she didn't hold it against them. It was all in the way of business and she might do the same thing herself, if necessary. Friends too, could be dangerous.

Lovers, of course, even more so.

She smiled to herself. A man across the way at another table smiled back. Middle aged, prosperous looking, dark, well-cut town clothes. A business man, or possibly a lawyer, there were a lot of law offices just near here. Without meaning to, Charmian smiled back. She left shortly after this brief encounter.

Her interview with a law group was short, they just wanted to know each other's faces, it was part of the secret side of her work. This finished, and certain documents safely handed over, she turned her face towards the station. She walked down a narrow, glassed-in arcade, lined with shops. Such arcades are a charming part of Victorian Birmingham, and on a previous visit she had noticed a smart patisserie and a hat shop. Not many of those left around in these hatless days, she had thought, but there had always been customers in it, and there was one now. A woman dressed in turquoise, trying on a turquoise hat. It did not become her, nor did the hat. She was trying another one, feathers and flowers this time. Mother of the bride, Charmian decided.

Next she stopped outside a jewellery shop; she had time to spare. In the window was a small brooch of garnets, pearls and diamonds. They might be rubies and not garnets, in which case its price would be beyond what she could afford.

Within ten minutes, she was out of the shop, with the brooch comfortably tucked away inside her handbag. The stones were rubies, and rubies might be thought to be a stone not suited to someone with her coloured hair (although the red had quietened into russet) and the price was certainly more than she should have spent, but she liked the brooch. She had liked it, she had wanted it, so had bought it.

Head down, she banged into a passer-by so that her bag and papers went flying. He picked them up with an apology.

'My fault, I wasn't looking where I was going.' Then he hesitated, and smiled. 'But we've met. Or sort of.' It was the man from the café bar. Then, as if one smile deserved something extra, he said: 'Please let me give you a drink, by way of apology.'

'I'm walking to the station.'

'My destination too. There's a place on the station.'

They sat opposite each other at a small white table on the station concourse drinking coffee, she had refused wine. He had talked quietly and gently. He was in business, he didn't say what, but he was very well dressed and his watch was a large gold Rolex. The initials on his case were PC.

'Philip Carteret,' he said, and held out his hand.

'Charmian Daniels.'

'I thought you might be a lawyer? You could be one.'

'No, not a lawyer.' She lowered her eyes, but did not amplify the statement. Older than he looks. Hands worn. A ring on the little finger of the left hand. Is he really called Carteret? she asked herself.

'Just a thought.'

The conversation moved on to what he liked and she liked, music, theatre, books. An easy beguiling man, she thought.

By the time they parted, they had exchanged telephone numbers. One of those little madnesses, she thought. Or perhaps not.

He saw her to the train which sat waiting on the platform.

On the way home from Birmingham, her train stopped for some minutes in open country which was waterlogged and dark. The evening was drawing in to a chill night. She took out the last folder of notes that had made the trip with her.

Amongst them were some further laboratory reports on the clothing worn by Louise Farmer.

She knew about the bloodstains, which would be useful when they had a firm suspect but had so far been of no help. But she turned the page, read a passage, and then read it again. Well, well.

She sat looking out at the blackness, lights began to appear, they were rolling into a station. She had always used all the tools that science gave her craft, and had been one of the first to welcome the investment in mass spectometry and electron microscopes.

Minute traces of some mineral material had ben found on Louise Farmer's throat, these traces appeared to have come from the ligature, which must have been in contact with it.

Traces had also been found on the back of her jacket. The blue wool was speckled with tiny scraps of something that were invisible except to the artificial eye of the electron microscope. When submitted to the spectrometer they had yielded up more of a character.

These particles had now been identified by the spectrometer as chalk. Faint indications of colour were suggested: blue and red. The report was initialled I. J. with a big flourish. She knew that signature. She had met the signer once, on going round his laboratory, and had retained a vivid impression of his personality. Brash but clever. Isaac Jermond knew what he was talking about.

As the train drew into one of the outlying surburban stations before London, Charmian saw a group of children on the station. They were wearing school uniform, carrying cases with what looked like musical instruments, violins, horns, and in one instance a girl was weighed down by her cello. They were accompanied by several adults who were anxiously checking numbers. Charmian guessed they were a school orchestra coming back from a performance. Possibly a competition because they sounded excited and pleased with themselves as if they had done well.

She sank back into her seat. Chalk on Louise's jacket, chalk on her neck, chalk on the cord that had strangled her. Minute traces which must have come from the killer.

To Charmian blue and red chalk spelt school.

When she got back she drove at once to her office. It was late but her secretary was still there, packing up to go home. The girl looked tired.

'Hello, Tess, still here?'

'I had to catch up with things. I took a late lunch as you weren't here and did some shopping. I hope that was all right?' She sounded dispirited.

'Yes, fine,' Charmian nodded. 'As you're here, get me the Tech Laboratory B2, will you? I want to speak to Dr Jermond.'

She had spoken to Isaac Jermond on the telephone several times before now, but they met rarely, he was also busy, never keen to leave his laboratory bench. He was said to have a wife, even children, but they must all meet but seldom. Ike the Beaver was his nickname on the Force owing to his legendary keenness.

'Isaac? Charmian Daniels here. I've read your report on the Farmer girl's clothes. Could you run a check for similar chalk traces on Ted Gray's clothes for me? I'll clear it with Inspector Elman myself.' If there was trouble for her interference she would deal with it. 'But get on with it.'

'As a matter of fact, I've done the check already,' said Jermond with the smug efficiency that was characteristic of him. 'And yes, there are such traces on Gray's clothes. But less than on the girl's. I might have missed them but for her. I finished about ten minutes ago.'

'That's splendid. Good work.'

'Glad to have helped.'

'Could you let me have a copy tonight? Send it round by hand.'

'I might manage.' He would drop it in himself. He knew the value of personal contact with a power base. He wished it was easier to make contact with Daniels but she always seemed to be rushing around. People said she didn't have a husband but might have a lover. 'To the office?'

'To my house, please. I expect the messenger will know where to go.'

'What do you think, lady?' said Jermond to himself, as Charmian put the receiver down without waiting for a reply. He always knew where to go.

Charmian collected herself together once again, gathering up such files as she wanted to study that night, and departed homeward. On the way, she collected a meal of fried fish and chips from her local fryer. Of all the take-away meals available to her, ranging from curry, pizzas (any number of those), hamburgers (yes, a good selection of those also, some more eccentric than others) as well as boxes of Korean and Mexican and the more domestic Chinese, this was the one she liked. Besides, Muff the cat liked fish, and did not spurn the odd chip if well cooked and crisp.

The house in Maid of Honour Row, newly cleaned by young Mrs Beadle, welcomed her with the kindness that houses and indeed all inanimate objects seem able to show on occasion, just as they can be awkward, clumsy and downright malevolent when it hurts most.

There was a brief note on her fax machine from Rewley. 'Cheasey no go. Dolly Barstow reports that on the night in question, and for several after, all the little men were having a Knees Up to celebrate the wedding of the Little 'Un.'

The Little 'Un, as Charmian knew, was the freak in the Tipper family, being the only male of average size. Indeed something above average, since he was six feet and over. She wondered whom he had married, there was always great pressure on the Tippers to marry within the clan.

'Over to you,' Rewley's message said.

Yes, it was over to her.

Nothing else of much interest on the fax, except the sort of stuff that came in constantly and had to be dealt with. Paper, reams of it, curling round her feet.

She ate her meal in the kitchen, but laying the table carefully with a linen mat and napkin, standards had to be kept up. After she had handed Muff her share, she opened a bottle of red wine. All the time she was avoiding her answering machine in the room above. It was amazing how messages could pour in on you unsought now, she looked back wistfully to the days when you had to pick up a telephone and open a letter. You could be private then.

There was a message on the answering machine, from Lady Mary. Amazing how the people you wanted (like Humphrey) never got through.

'Hello, this is Mary Erskine. I've got Una here. She's laid out with something. A migraine, I think, I found her stretched out on her kitchen floor . . . Can you come round, she's got a tale she wants to tell you.'

—Don't you mean you have? thought Charmian. I'll get to you later. Maybe. Lady Mary did not stand high in her list of favourites at the moment. She knew the legend: how everyone loved Mary, yes, she had charm, but there was a darker side. Nevertheless, she picked up the telephone and spoke to Mary Erskine. 'What is it with Una?'

'Something about the boy Pix, I don't know. Nothing in it perhaps but anyway, she can't talk now. I gave her a painkiller and she's asleep.'

'We'll leave it then. I'll get in touch later.'

Charmian stroked Muff and considered. Was this anything or nothing? Perhaps she should walk round?

Before she could do anything, the bell rang and there was Jermond, eager faced, just as she had remembered him, only fairer and younger. He handed over an envelope. 'Here's the stuff you wanted.'

'Thank you.'

He hovered on the doorstep, so that Muff advanced to stare at him curiously. 'You've heard the news?'

He knew she had not.

'I've heard nothing.'

'There's another body in the park.'

'Who?'

He shook his head. 'Don't know. That's all I've got. Just the flash news. Don't know if it's fish, fowl, girl or boy.' He could be very flip.

At once Charmian tried to telephone the Incident Room, but got no answer. The phone rang but no one picked it up.

In the Incident Room, the police war cabinet, headed by Elman and Rewley, had been summoned and was meeting. Telephones were ringing all round them too and lights were flashing on green screens.

'We shall have to tell that woman,' Elman said. 'Sooner or later.' When he said 'that woman', you knew whom he meant: Charmian.

The phone on Inspector Elman's desk lifted up its voice and rang, and rang.

'Don't answer it,' he said. 'Not yet.'

Being unable to make contact with the police team (although she had a pretty good idea that she was being deliberately ignored), she rang her god-daughter, Kate, at home.

'Hi,' said Kate, cheerily. She was in a transatlantic mood. 'How are you?'

'Fine.'

'You sound cross.'

'Not cross.' Anxious, puzzled, not cross.

'Still, you didn't ring just to say hello; I can tell. Is it me you want or my darling husband?'

'Your husband.'

'He isn't here, of course.'

'Take a message, will you, Kate? Ask him to search the records for any man called Philip Carteret. Or he may just call himself Carter. But initials PC. I think he may be a con man, and he may have a record.'

Or he might not. She might just have a slight case of paranoia.

On that same day, while the train carrying Charmian was still travelling across England, Lily Paget had seen Pix home after the aborted tea party. He had run on ahead of her, but she thought he was going straight home. She could see him at the gate before she turned away.

170

CHAPTER SEVENTEEN

April 20

On that same day, April 20, Grace Farmer had at last made a firm attempt to see Lily Paget. It was mid-afternoon on a warm but cloudy day when she telephoned.

'Hello Elfrida, it's Grace.'

'My dear, how are you?'

'Oh middling. You know . . . '

'I can guess.' And Elfrida could, she had more imagination than some of Grace's friends. 'Is there anything I can do?' She had made this offer several times only to be refused, but this time she thought Grace did want something from her. 'Shall I come round?'

But it turned out Grace wanted Lily.

The relationship between Lily Paget and her mother was a tricky one. The trickiness impinged on Elfrida's friendship with Grace Farmer, because Elfrida did not truly understand her daughter, nor had Grace understood Louise, and in Grace she saw a reflection of herself. Perhaps it was their generation: our mothers understood us only too well, so we do not want to understand our daughters. Let them keep their privacy and we will keep ours. Love them, of course, nature saw to that as a rule.

But she could guess that now Grace wished she had been closer to Louise; she herself had been making tentative approaches to her daughter — a pair of designer jeans with an oversized sweater, a bottle of Polo (that was what they wanted to smell of just now) but it hadn't got her anywhere. Oh, Lily did her stuff and was polite and friendly but it was thus far and no further. Couldn't blame her really and Elfrida did not, she could remember when her mother bought a lipstick when no one repeat no one was using lipstick except the very palest whitest stuff and she had thought: the Old Lady's got it all wrong. But she in her generation hadn't got it wrong, the fashion objects she had donated to Lily were the rightest possible and both parties knew it. So Lily ought to have melted rather more than she had done. Tough little Lily.

The murder of Louise Farmer had hit them both hard, it was their first contact with violent death.

Murder. It seemed incredible to Elfrida that a girl she knew could be murdered. For Lily the impact must be much worse. Not that Lily had said a lot, barely even warning her parents about her visit to the police. That had hurt.

The boy was distressed too, but this could be due to Pix who seemed to have stirred up all his friends. Eddie was settling down again now, although it had not been wise to invite Pix round to tea. But the kid wasn't a leper and it seemed a shame to treat him as if he was one.

But now he had been, eaten cake and gone, Elfrida thought she could understand why people were keeping him at arms' length. There was a sort of quiet frenzy inside him that you picked up whether you wanted to or not. Not, in most cases, she supposed.

So when Grace telephoned, Elfrida had to say: 'Lily's not home, she's walking Pix back.' It had been a bleak little tea party, with Pix suddenly saying he must go home, and her own son looking white. Definitely Pix had a way of casting a shadow. 'She won't be long, she didn't take a coat and it's turning colder, isn't it?'

Grace hadn't noticed the change of temperature, she was permanently cold herself these days.

'Why don't you come round, Grace?' Elfrida went on. 'Then you can talk to Lily if you want to.' And I can be there to see that things don't get out of hand. Yes, you want to talk to Lily about Louise, all right, I understand that, but I don't want Lily distressed. She's only a girl, after all. But this was not said aloud. Perhaps Grace picked it up, though.

'Thank you, I won't do that . . . I think I might go for a walk myself,' murmured Grace vaguely. 'It's such a nice afternoon.'

'No, it's getting colder,' persisted Elfrida. She's not taking anything in, that poor woman, she decided. 'Shall I come round to see you? I'd like to, Grace dear.'

Grace murmured that it was sweet of her, but the house was rather too miserable to be in at the moment.

'How's Brian?'

'He's gone back to the office. Honestly the best thing for him, even if he doesn't do much when he is there.' And she didn't think he did.

'But what about you? How are you really?' What does it feel like, she meant, to be the mother of a slaughtered child. Once said, she wished she hadn't said it, but Grace did not recoil, she was past that reaction.

'Oh you know. There's the house. I keep busy. I have the cleanest house for miles around, probably better polished than the Castle itself. But it's an empty house.' And emptied in the nastiest possible way.

This too feels an empty house at the moment, thought Elfrida, although Lily was only to be out for a little while and her son was sitting in the kitchen drawing pictures with his crayons. He was drawing a house. At least it looked like a house. The boys seemed to have houses on the brain, he and Pix had been talking about a house. Houses, houses, she thought, houses should be such a strong, protective symbol, not a symptom of disquiet.

'Shall I telephone when Lily gets back? Or send her round? She'd be glad to come, I know.' She knew no such thing, still she could persuade Lily if she tried hard enough. 'But she's got to go and collect her cycle from somewhere she left it.'

Lily had called out as she left: 'Mum, I've got to pick up my bike on the way back, but I won't be long.'

Grace murmured something vague and put the telephone down.

Lily had been surprised when she got the message. She had found the scrap of paper in the bag of her bicycle when she left it outside the library as she often did. Of course, anyone would know it was her bike because it had her name painted in large white letters on the mudguards. That was a school rule. Her bike, anyway, had character, was recognisable as hers because Lily, in a fit of exuberance, had painted it with yellow stripes like a zebra. She was a well-known figure cycling around the town on it. There goes

Lily, anyone could have said that, anyone heard, anyone known who owned the cycle.

The note was not signed and rain had softened the paper, blurring the writing:

I have something I can tell you about Louise. You will want to know. I know about her death. If you walk in the park by the Copper Horse, then I will meet you. Any day between 5 and 6. I will be looking.

Lily laughed and crumpled the message up.

'You'd be lucky, Mr Whoever you are. I'm not such an idiot as all that.'

She unlocked her bike, and continued her monologue.

'That's quite a walk to the Horse. Whoever you are, you can go on looking. Only a fool keeps that sort of appointment. No name, either. How would I know you?' She did not throw the message away, but put it in her pocket.

She pushed the cycle down the road, there was a suspect tyre with a slow puncture that had not been improved by a night out in the rain. Lily was obliged to pay for her own repairs, she got a generous amount of pocket money, but she had to budget. It was her parents' idea of training her for the future, a poor one in Lily's opinion. She was both tired and bored, a dangerous combination. She had engineered the invitation to Pix because she wanted to get more out of him about his fantasies or whatever they were. She thought there was something real, terribly real, and that it had some connection with the death of Louise. Common sense said you didn't have two mysteries going on at once in the same circle of people. (Common sense could be wrong, of course, Lily did not trust it, but it was worth a try with Pix.) But all that had happened was that her kid brother had got tearful (although making a good tea, five chocolate biscuits, was it?), and Pix had retired within himself.

Taking him home, they had walked in silence for a bit, and then Lily had said, after taking thought: 'Pix, I'm going to do something . . . about that business, you know what I mean. I think I can make a guess who is behind it.' She remembered a phrase of her father's which had struck her as interesting and weighty. 'I'm telling you because I think it's in your best interests.'

174

Pix gave her a wary look. He did not like his interests mentioned. Lily remembered that look now.

Poor little beggar, she felt sorry for him, and she thought he knew that, he was a sensitive boy and he had smiled at her, but she thought now she should have handled things better. They had walked on towards his home in silence on both sides, Lily holding his hand. Within sight of his house, Pix had suddenly said goodbye and started to run.

She had watched him to his gate, that being her duty, then turned round to walk away. Clever kid, no doubt of that, she was clever herself and recognised the quality in another, but loopy. Strong too, her hand still felt it where he had hung on to it as they walked.

Lily collected her cycle from outside the school library, her school was large, old and smart, she was a lucky girl to go there, everyone said so. Lily herself would have preferred an establishment where academic values rated higher than nice manners.

It was then she had found the note, read it, wondered how long it had been there, and checked her possessions in the saddle bag: spare shoes, some school books and a pair of white socks. All there, but a bit damp.

She began to move away, her thoughts troubling her. One way and another her involvement with Pix had brought some new ideas about Louise's death.

Perhaps she had not been right about Mr Gray? She pushed her bike onwards, head down.

She missed Loulou. They had been friends since they could walk, quarrelled sometimes, but always come back together. She had trusted Louise and Louise had trusted her. They had done silly things together, rash things and sometimes good and sensible things, but they had never let each other down. They had grown apart a little when Louise took up with the Rivers boy from Cheasey, but the bond had held. When Louise needed someone to talk to then it was Lily she talked to. Lily knew she was cleverer than Louise, but her friend had a marvellous sensitivity to people, she got things right about them. All the same, Lily felt that she herself would not get killed the way Louise had.

Louise as a dead person who had crossed that mysterious

channel between life and death was a hard concept for her. Especially hard because Louise had not died naturally. Illness would be bad, but you could understand it. An accident in a car or falling off a horse, that too was something you could fit into a believable scheme of things. But murder, violent death, that made you angry.

From across the street, some school friends hailed her. 'Come with us, we're going to Baskin-Robbins to have an ice-cream.'

'Sorry, can't. Got to get home. I promised.'

But she left her cycle to walk across the road to speak to them, Jancy and Alice and Oliver and Paul. They were a set, the best set in the school. Everyone said, 'Oh Jancy and Alice, that's the set to move with,' so that even the independent Lily was not above feeling their allure. She could see that Jancy had a hair-piece on, false hair cascading down her neck, and being Jancy it did not match the rest of her hair. Did not even match itself, being striped in several colours of which red was one.

'Jancy, your hair,' Lily said. 'I love.'

'Horse, dear, coloured horse. Makes Oliver sneeze, doesn't it, precious?'

At the kerb a small car was parked which she did not observe.

The group gossiped and laughed together for longer than Lily had meant to allow herself. 'I must go.' Reluctantly she said goodbye. 'Have an ice-cream for me,' she called over her shoulder. 'Chocolate and nuts, that's the one.'

When she got back to where she had left her cycle, it was gone. 'Damn, it's been nicked.' Cycles were always disappearing, she should have put the padlock on it.

She looked about for it, and walked to the corner. The ground sloped away to a site being developed into a group of expensive houses set in a small park with some trees left over from the days when a large private house had stood here. All the workmen had gone home.

She walked down the hill, looking hopefully for her property. 'Rotten kids,' she muttered to herself. No bike. She had been a rotten kid herself, not so long ago, and moved people's bikes, and then hidden in the trees to watch and giggle.

Still, no bike. She put her hands on her hips and looked around her.

176

Then she saw it, propped up against a tree. She thought she could see someone in the shadows. 'That's Linda Barnes, I bet, I recognise her size, little toad. I'll get you, sweetie pie,' she said vengefully and ran confidently, even aggressively down the slope towards the murderer.

A voice spoke softly: 'I said you'd come.'

Grace had felt very restless after she spoke to Elfrida. Her husband rang from London shortly afterwards.

'I'm a lot better,' he said. 'I think you were right, work does help. I shall stay late up here and finish a project. You won't mind?'

'No, of course not. I'm glad,' she said, and meant it. 'Don't be too late back, though.' She did not wish to admit it, but she was nervous in the house on her own now after dark.

'No. And I'll telephone when I'm setting out.'

Somehow she didn't like that, it was a touch too reminiscent of the way she had heard Ted Gray had gone on.

Her restlessness increased so that she found that she had put on a raincoat together with stout walking shoes and was striding along almost before she realised what she had done.

It was raining again and there were trees overhead, so she must be in the Great Park, having walked, as she now realised, at tremendous speed. Unconsciously she had taken several of the short cuts known only to locals and definitely frowned upon. The Park did not like you to use them, she herself had a key to one gate, but that she was allowed. A special privilege because her father had been who he was.

Grace stopped short, took a deep breath and tried to place herself. In the distance she could see the statue of the Copper Horse. But that was a landmark which stood out for miles, and she was well away from it. Still, the sight of it enabled her to work out where she was; she had travelled quite a way, and now stood in a belt of trees near to one of the roads that ran through the Park. It was deserted. In fact you rarely saw anyone walking here except in the summer, but the occasional car came through at all seasons. There was a small parking place over there to the west, supposedly reserved for those with special permits, but in fact, she had seen an ice-cream van parked there one hot day and

177

a coach-load of tourists busy buying cornets. Is nowhere sacred these days? an irate old friend had said, and Grace had had to conclude that privilege certainly was not.

She walked on more slowly now, she knew exactly what she was doing, she was trying to get in touch with her daughter who had loved these trees and paths. She might see Louise, or hear her voice. She knew it could not happen in reality, the universe as such did not work to those rules. It did not summon up those you wanted from the dark, one must not fall into the Faustian heresy. But she drew in deep breaths and felt that, yes, she was closer to Louise.

Grace turned to walk back, Brian would be coming home, he would need a meal, she would be glad to see him. There was hope in that emotion, by nature she was an affectionate and loyal person, so that the terrible deadness of all feeling that had descended fast after the death of Louise had been an added pain. She had been tough and aggressive with her husband and she knew it. Suspicious too, but she was certain now that he had not killed Ted Gray.

Her mood lightened even more as she hurried to get home. She was almost on the edge of the Great Park when she saw a young woman coming towards her. At first she thought the girl was coming to greet her but then she saw that she was moving blindly across Grace's path.

She almost walked into Grace, and then swayed. Grace held out her arm to steady her.

'Are you all right?' Silly question, of course the girl was not, she looked terrible. Grace thought she knew her, she had certainly seen her face before. Didn't she work at St Catherine's? 'What is it? Can I help?'

The girl stared at her, unseeing, looking at some other face, some other scene.

A name struggled to the surface of Grace's mind. 'It's Minette, isn't it?' Memories of last year's sports day at St Cath's, the carol service and the nativity play, awoke inside Grace. Yes, she had seen the girl there. 'Minette?' She didn't know her other name and she couldn't call her Miss or Mademoiselle. 'What is it, my dear?'

She looked more closely at the girl. There was mud on her

hands, scratches on her arms, a scattering of leaves in her hair. Had she been in some sort of accident? Been attacked?

Minette showed signs of wandering onwards but Grace held her back. 'You must let me help you. What is it? What has happened?'

Minette turned her head away, as if she did not want to look into Grace's eyes. 'Je suis folle.'

Grace frowned as she tried to follow what Minette had said.

'I think I am mad. Je suis folle.'

'I don't think you are,' said Grace doubtfully. But the girl was certainly very disturbed, she was trembling and straining as if pushing against something invisible.

'I have seen something that cannot be there,' said Minette. 'I am like the little boys. I have been infected. I see things.' She shivered. 'Or perhaps I do things.'

Grace controlled herself, she wanted to run, but that wouldn't do, must help. 'Let me take you home.' Where was home? The school? Luke Mallet would know what to do.

'There was a murder at home, where I came from in Toulouse. A girl. You know how these crimes go. It was very frightening. I was frightened.'

Grace felt a cold, sad feeling inside herself. 'Please don't go on,' she whispered. 'This is what you must not tell me.'

'So I came away,' said Minette. 'To be safe. But there has been a girl killed here. Did you know that?' Grace gave a soft sound, like a mew of pain. It said she did, of course she did know, she above all knew. 'And now I have seen another dead girl . . . Of course, she was not there, not really. A phantom. Only in my mind.' She put a hand to her forehead.

Grace was suddenly rough. 'Take your hand down. Look at me. Where did you see this dead girl?'

'In the dead wood where I was walking.'

She really is mad, thought Grace, but I must ask her: 'Did you touch her?'

Minette did not answer. 'I fell down,' she said. 'I have mud on me. Perhaps blood.' She looked at her hands. 'I want to confess, I must confess.'

Grace took a grip on herself. Some other hands must deal with this. She put her arm round the shoulder of the now weeping girl. 'Come on, I am going to take you back.' Back where? Back somewhere.

She led the girl out on to the road, towards the town where the lights were coming on in the dusk. This stretch of the road was deserted, but a car was driving towards them. It stopped and Luke got out.

'Minette, there you are. I have been driving round and round looking for you.'

Pointless activity, said a cold, hard little voice inside Grace's head, he's only found her now by chance.

'What have you been doing? You've been gone such a long time. You shouldn't go wandering off like this. Just a walk, you said. Some walk, dear . . . Now don't cry. Did I frighten you? I'm so sorry, but you're hysterical, you know. Did you get lost? And you're all muddy, what have you done to yourself?' He had his arms round Minette and was leading her to the car. 'Thank God, I've found you . . . Mrs Farmer, it is Mrs Farmer? Thank you so much for looking after her. I'd better get her home. Let me give you a lift too.'

'And then I think you had better telephone the police,' Grace heard herself say. 'I don't know what she's seen or what she hasn't seen, what she's done or what she hasn't done, but someone ought to listen to her and then go and look.'

Twenty minutes later, a police car drove into the Great Park, Minette sitting beside him. The driver followed her directions to a point where they must get out of the car and walk.

Not far, just towards the trees.

The third body had been found. A girl again. The policeman did not know her face, but she was soon identified as Lily who had been missing for several hours but only just reported to the police by her anxious mother.

FILOFACE

3

There were several additions to the profile at this point in the diary.

1 Relationship between first and second girl, they were close friends, victims, decreases the possibility of it being a random killer.
2 Slender possibility of a serial killer remains.
3 MOD the same in both cases. Skill but no great physical strength involved. Manual skill, strong hands?
4 Known to victim?
5 Girls at same school, killer knew and known at school?
6 Killer clever and persuasive.
7 Seems harmless to victim.
8 Killer smart and manipulative. Takes a chance?
9 Certain evidence connected to the attack on Paget suggests the killer imaginative. Well educated?
10 Almost certainly local to Windsor and Merrywick. Cheasey also.

An imaginative, wily person, well educated(?), not physically strong but with powerful hands who drives a car about an area known to him.

Or to an accomplice.

CHAPTER EIGHTEEN

April 21

A blanket of silence descended over the case in the next few days. For this the police were responsible, to the fury of the media. But they had their reasons.

It was known there was another victim, the journalists and TV newsmen could even provide a name, Lily Paget, but no name was officially confirmed. The Paget family was spirited away, and the Farmer house was closed. They had gone to stay with relatives, the press was told, but as with the Pagets, the how and why and where was withheld. The why, the newspapers could answer for themselves, even how (for cars had been seen leaving and evading pursuit), but where and for how long, that was another matter. There was speculation and rumour in plenty, but not much hard fact.

Was Brian Farmer under arrest for killing Ted Gray? No, the word was that nothing to incriminate him had been found on his clothes or in his house or car, and he was in the clear. A few people said that the way Mrs Farmer had cleansed the house and their possessions, this was not surprising, but this was regarded as a poor joke. The chap was innocent of murder.

Minette's name was not mentioned, but her existence was known. 'A compulsive confessor,' a police statement had said blandly. 'We do get them in such cases. Of course, we are checking, but no real evidence exists to connect this person.'

The media did not know whether to believe what they were fed or not.

Those in the know, like Charmian Daniels, understood and

respected what had been ordered. In fact, in a quiet way, she was responsible for it. She had her underground channels of communication and had suggested that, for the safety of all concerned and for one person in particular, it would be better if silence was preserved. For a short time at least. Silence could not last long and she had the feeling that it would not be necessary. The killer was ready to go off pop. So she had applied pressure.

She had reached this conclusion and used this pressure because of what happened to her on the morning of the 21st.

Several things in quick succession. The first and the best had appeared on her fax machine that morning while she ate her breakfast and she had not expected it. Not there. Not anywhere. Well, that might have been an exaggeration, perhaps somewhere, sometime. In the future.

The fax said:

What about getting on with that ceremony? If not St Margaret's Westminster or Westminster Abbey, why not St Giles', Oxford.

Letter follows, and telephone call later.

The fax sender did not identify himself but she could put a name.

Humphrey. She laughed quietly to herself so that Muff who was always watching jumped away in pretended alarm. Wasn't there a song: 'She didn't say Yes, and she didn't say No'? That was how she would play it.

Was he drunk, she asked herself? No, just supremely confident and happy. He had had a success on that half secret errand of his and wanted to share it. Just like a man, she thought, deciding that the way to share happiness was to share a bed. But she rather liked that, the happiness bit. For a moment or two it spread to her, and then the bad things started to happen.

As she left the house, the telephone was already ringing, but she was in a hurry and did not stop. Let them leave a message. Or him.

She could, of course, have telephoned Humphrey herself, she had several numbers she could ring that he had left behind hopefully, but she was not going to do so. She was playing by her own rules now.

When she got into the office, she took off her coat, tidied her hair, removed several tabby hairs from her tweed skirt, and

183

prepared to face the pile of papers on her desk. She had already observed that her secretary's eyes looked puffed and red but had decided not to notice. So she's been crying? It did happen.

'Coffee?'

'Oh yes, please, Tess.' She didn't look up as the cup was placed on her desk.

Presently, she became aware that the girl was hovering just behind her.

'All right,' she said, putting aside what she was reading. 'What is it? Let's have it.'

'My boyfriend has been picked up by the Drugs Squad. Dealing. Heroin, cocaine.' She didn't say he wasn't guilty of the charge or sound indignant. Just depressed.

'I wasn't with him, but they'll get round to me. I think they've been watching me.'

Yes, so have I, thought Charmian. And wondering, but I wasn't sure . . . I should have sent you packing before this, but I didn't want to destroy the career of what might have been a perfectly innocent person.

'It'll be my turn next.'

'I'm sure it will be.' I don't know why you haven't been arrested already. Unless they are giving us both a bit of rope. Hoping that I will somehow tie myself up in it.

'I am presuming you knew what he was up to?' she went on in a cold voice. Not a time to be friendly.

The girl nodded.

'And using? Are you?'

'Well . . . you know.'

'No, I don't.'

'Nothing important . . . '

There was a pause of significant silence.

'A bit more than that, I think.'

The girl burst into tears, not noisily, but with silent despair. Charmian let her go on for a bit, then she got up, and handed her a bunch of tissues. 'Here you are.' She walked to the window to stare out, her back tactfully turned.

There was silence again for a few minutes. Charmian considered. There was a rehashed kind of feeling to this conversation.

'Have you talked to anyone else about this?'

The girl fumbled for what to say. 'I didn't want to, but I think I was watched.'

I bet you have been, thought Charmian. 'So you said and that's no answer,' she said.

'Lady Mary,' began the girl. 'I told Lady Mary . . . '

Charmian swivelled her head round. 'Are you talking about Lady Mary Erskine?'

'Yes, Lady Mary. My gran worked for her parents . . . housekeeper, dad was in the same regiment as his lordship.'

'I see.' She was beginning to see.

'So you told Lady Mary you were in trouble, and why did you do that?'

The girl looked puzzled, but a long family tradition of always going to 'the gentry' with anything lay behind and was not to be gainsaid. 'I knew she'd understand.'

'Was your boyfriend supplying her too?'

'No!' But the cry, although indignant, did not quite carry conviction.

'Come on, out with it.'

'Well, to be honest, there's a bit of a problem there too. Oh, not Lady Mary, she wouldn't, but a sort of cousin of hers.'

'You trusted her. Didn't think she'd inform on you?'

'She wouldn't, you see, she's very loyal.'

Oh yes, sure, thought Charmian. But what about me? Aren't I a friend? What about a show of loyalty to me?

'So Lady Mary advised you to talk to me?'

'She thought it was about time . . . '

I shall have a word with you, my dear Mary, said Charmian to herself. But for now, she knew what to do.

'You can't go on working for me, I'm afraid.' In spite of her anger, her voice was sympathetic.

'I've packed up my things already,' said Tess humbly.

She knew she was trouble, thought Charmian, but she hung on all the same. Her sympathy edged away. She herself knew what was going to happen: her judgement was going to be questioned, her wisdom held up for comment, and if she was really unlucky she would be regarded as personally involved. She knew Lady Mary as a friend, in some circles, that might be enough. She had set up SRADIC so hers was all the responsibility.

But she knew how to fight if she had to and she would fight. But it might not come to a battle. She was a political animal, and knew that very often the best way to win a battle was not to fight it. You walked round it.

She put in a request for emergency secretarial aid and got back to her routine work. 'Get me Diana Farrell, if you can,' she said. 'She's helped me out before and we work together.' Diana was older and altogether a more substantial and solid presence. She felt the need of someone like that about her at the present.

So far that day, one good thing, one bad thing, but the bag of happiness inside her saw her through.

She had no more news of Lily Paget. As far as she knew, there was no more to know. Even Sergeant Rewley had gone quiet.

Unless the blackout had descended upon her as a person too, and he was keeping his distance because of what she might be embroiled in? But she didn't believe that treachery of Rewley.

'Things do happen, don't they?' said Diana as she bustled in. Diana did bustle, it was something Charmian remembered about her and was perhaps her only drawback. Tuned in to the local gossip, Charmian decided, but she thought Diana would not go beyond that somewhat oblique remark. 'I can only give you today, but I'll see you have the best we have tomorrow.'

Charmian nodded. 'See you do.'

Before leaving for lunch, which she meant to take defiantly and publicly in the main canteen, which would surprise them all and might put some off their food, she rang Lady Mary Erskine. At home. She would have pursued her to the Castle itself if she had had to, but Mary was there in the Chapel Close.

'Oh Charmian, it's you.' Mary Erskine sounded nervous.

'I think we have to talk.'

'Oh right.' Yes, she was nervous. Good, thought Charmian. I'll see she continues that way. 'Is it Una?' Mary began a sentence about Una looking ill, but Charmian broke in.

'Not Una. I've just had to sack my secretary.'

'Oh Tess?'

'Yes, Tess. You probably can guess why.'

Mary Erskine remained silent.

'There's some questions I ought to ask you.'

'Yes, right,' said Mary. 'Come and have a drink when you've

finished for the day. I'll see if I can get hold of Luke.' She sounded more cheerful.

'No. No Luke, no drink and not at your house. Not at the end of the day either. Two o'clock here.'

'Well, I don't know if I can manage . . . '

'See you do,' said Charmian. 'Two o'clock.'

She put the receiver down, conscious that she had nicely unbalanced the other woman.

Then she walked across the street to the main police buildings and marched into the canteen. It was a democratic place where everyone queued, but all the same, a group of tables by the windows which were slightly separated from the rest had fallen to the lot of senior officers. Very senior officers like Charmian were not really expected to appear. Or not without warning.

A slight hush fell on the room at the sight of her.

'You can go on eating,' she said under her breath. She chose what she wanted to eat, salad and cold meat, and sat herself next to a uniformed chief inspector whom she knew. He looked pleased and unsurprised, for which she gave him a good mark. He earned an even better mark by keeping up an easy stream of comment on a concert he had just taken his wife to at the Barbican.

The salad was good, the meat tough, but she ate with relish and returned to her office in good spirits.

But there, she took a telephone message from George Rewley which broke into the black silence.

'Thanks for telling me,' she said. Pix.

'Oh, you had to know. News blackout, of course, just in case he's been kidnapped, but we think not, he seems to have gone of his own accord. Whatever that means with a kid that age.'

Lady Mary arrived punctually at two o'clock. She was as beautifully dressed as always in a toffee-coloured tweed suit with an apricot and blue silk shirt. She looked down at her Gucci shoes but did not speak. She knew the value of forcing the other person to utter first as well as Charmian did.

Charmian decided to sit it out. They sat for some time in silence. Then Lady Mary raised her head. 'All right. Get on with it.'

Charmian said, as if reading it: 'You have a cousin, the girl Delphine, who is a user of hard drugs. Cocaine and heroin, I

187

am informed. Yes, the police do know about her, Mary. They have their methods . . . But they haven't heard about you yet. My guess is that you have been helping her procure the stuff.'

Lady Mary gave a sort of groan. 'No, not like that.'

'You have been in contact with the man passing it to her, and gave a testimonial to his girlfriend so that she got a position in my office. She knew of her contacts but did not mention them. Not to me, not to anyone.'

'You make it sound terrible.'

'What the hell have you been up to?'

Mary hung her head. 'I don't know if I can make you understand.'

'Try.'

'I wanted you involved; I wanted you in trouble.'

'You may have succeeded,' said Charmian grimly.

'I'm popular. People like me. But no one loves me. I don't know why but I never seem to call out that very special feeling . . . '

'Oh, come on, Mary.'

'No, try to understand . . . We're a set . . . Or we were. Una and Ted, Luke and his wife . . . of course, she's dead but her ghost still lives on, believe me. And then there was me and Humphrey.' She gave Charmian a direct look now. 'I love him. Of course, he's a lot older than me, been married before, but I loved him and I thought he might, just might, come to love me. And then you came into it.'

A set? Her words echoed thoughts that Charmian had long had; the relationships between this group of people were complex and went deep. She had recognised this before she realised it could touch her own life.

'I was jealous,' said Mary Erskine. 'Not a nice feeling.'

Charmian had had a touch of it herself but this was not the time to admit it. 'What about Luke and Minette, were you jealous of her? She's an outsider.'

'Mad Minette? We thought Luke was crazy to fall for her. No, I wasn't. I think she was jealous of us. I think that may have triggered off some of her confusions.'

'How is she?' Charmian had heard all about Minette and what she had found in the park, but the curtain of silence had fallen here too.

188

Mary shrugged. 'Better and worse at the same time. You don't get over these things quickly. Anyway, she's going home. I mean, when she can,' she said hastily.

When she was allowed to, the police had asked her not to leave.

'Well, there it is,' said Mary Erskine. 'I wanted you disgraced and out of the way. I thought it might happen. I was foolish, and selfish and now I am ashamed. I don't know why I did it.'

People always say that when they are found out, thought Charmian. 'I liked you, Mary, I still do, but I feel sad. And let down. Betrayed, if you like.'

'What will you do? Will you tell Humphrey?'

'Don't think I subscribe to any public school conceits that honour demands silence from me,' said Charmian savagely. 'But you can tell him yourself.'

Then she relented. 'It probably won't be necessary. He probably knows.'

All the cards were in her hands, and she knew it, but she wanted to go on living here amongst these people. 'I'm not saying I will forget this, it will be built in to what we know of each other, I'm not going to bury it, but I shan't hang on to it either.'

'I shall wake up in the middle of the night and remember,' said Lady Mary. In the long history of her family there had been saints and sinners, madmen and philosophers, traitors and men who had fought to the finish, she had the blood of all of them in her.

Lady Mary stood up. 'Unless there's anything else, I'd better move. There's a lot going on at the moment.'

Their eyes met, they both knew what they were thinking, and about which they were not speaking, it was part of the silence thing.

'It's the St Cath's celebration tomorrow. Shall you be going?'

'Yes,' said Charmian. 'I'm speaking.'

'So you are,' said Mary wearily. 'I'd forgotten for the moment with all this. I think it should have been put off. In the circumstances . . . '

189

Because as well as the body in the Park, they had someone missing . . .

Charmian recalled the conversation which had told her about the boy Pix.

'And the parents have only just reported it?' she had asked.

'Yes, they were out looking for him all night . . . Seems he came home from his tea party with mud all over him. Very late, although Mrs Paget, heaven help her, says the tea party ended early when Lily saw him home. Well, we know what happened to her, poor kid. The boy was put to bed, but was later found to be missing.'

'Was he questioned about Lily?'

'It seems not.'

He had been gone some hours before his parents, confused and anxious about they hardly knew what and dare not admit to, had told the police.

'Mary,' Charmian said, 'what did Una Gray want to tell me about Pix?'

'I don't know.' Mary shrugged. 'Something she had seen, but she was being sick on and off and I didn't encourage her. Didn't believe her.'

'Where is she now?'

'I don't know. Home, I suppose. She always bounces back quickly after one of those attacks.'

'Right.' Charmian made a note. 'I'll speak to her.' As Lady Mary left, the phone rang again, again it was Rewley.

'We now have news of the boy,' he announced.

'Good news?'

'Not good, not bad. But interesting. We think he knows the person he went off with.'

Charmian frowned.

'We have a witness.'

'A reliable one?'

'Who knows what's reliable? In this context, yes, we think so. At least, she's talking.' Talking was the thing, when people talked they opened up a world.

Una Gray. She had told Pix's mother, her eyes wide, puzzled and intent but speaking with sincerity. She had been for a walk the night of Pix's disappearance because she could not sleep and felt a headache coming on and she had seen Pix leaving his parents' house. No, she had not done anything about it then, because it had seemed all right. Afterwards, she had been worried, but her head had been so bad.

'Yes, he ran towards her and took her hand. Yes, a woman. No, I didn't recognise her, she was too far away.'

CHAPTER NINETEEN

The next few days in April

The police machine rolled on. Lines of investigation spread out, involving the uniformed branch more and more as further officers were involved. Teams and sub-teams formed themselves, worked together, reported their results, broke up and were re-formed into different groups. The forensic department found itself with plenty of work examining clothing from Lily Paget and comparing traces on it with those on Louise Farmer's and Ted Gray's. No chalk this time, but they were looking at body traces. They had developed a technique for identifying skin flakes from the killer. Similar traces had been found on all three victims. Likewise matching sweat marks. So they knew that they were looking for one attacker and one only.

If they could locate a suspect, they were well away.

There was a plan afoot to do a mass survey, this would be a street by street, house by house check. A lot of over-time was being worked already and there looked like being more.

All this time, there was a quiet, intensive search going on for Pix. 'We won't be able to keep silent on this for much longer,' Inspector Elman had said. Meanwhile the media was obediently holding its tongue. But rumours were flying around. No ransom demand, so it wasn't a kidnap, but there was this story of him going off with a woman.

The police diary, the record on the combined lines of investigation which was made up every day, took note of all these activities.

This diary, for the making up of which a small team of two men was responsible, was on the computer, hard copies were then printed and faxed out to recognised centres.

Charmian would get her copy in due course.

But sometimes her own sources were supplying her.

That day, the 21st, the day with its discoveries both good and bad was not yet over. As she got into her house, she heard the telephone ringing. It was Mary Erskine.

Somehow from her voice, Charmian could tell that she had been calling several times but had not wanted to leave a message on the machine. She tried to sound reasonably friendly but she herself was tired and hungry, the healthy salad lunch had left a large potato-sized hole inside her. 'Is it Una again . . ? I mean, I know her story now, what she's reported.'

'No, not that. Can I come round to see you and bring Pix's mother with me? She wants to talk to someone.'

'What about Inspector Elman?' said Charmian, although admitting to herself that Elman might not be the person she would ever choose to unburden herself to.

'No, please, not official like that, she needs someone like you. I know, after everything that was said today, you might not feel like it, but please do.'

More curious than she was willing to admit to herself, Charmian found herself agreeing.

'Very well. Come round this evening. Come together. But I can't promise to keep any secrets, mind. Anything relevant I shall have to pass on.'

'It won't be like that.'

'You can never tell.' Charmian considered her own position. 'I shall have to have someone with me.' Rewley, she thought, bringing Kate with him so that it looked like a casual social visit. And if Kate couldn't come (because who could ever tell about Kate), then Dolly Barstow, who had her own techniques for disappearing into the woodwork as if invisible, yet was always there when wanted.

There was a pause. Mary Erskine was obviously consulting someone, Pix's mother presumably. 'All right,' she said reluctantly. 'We see that.'

Charmian put down the receiver and set about organising what was left of her evening. A shower, a change of clothes, and a meal.

And then her visitors. George Rewley took some persuading but eventually agreed to come. And yes, Kate would come too, couldn't stop her.

Charmian thought she heard her god-daughter's voice in the background, and she was happy about it, but it was Rewley's calm, reflective voice that gave her most pleasure. He had intuition, that one.

It was at that moment, in retrospect, that she started to organise the campaign that was to give her and her office another dimension.

Kate and Rewley arrived together, within minutes afterwards Lady Mary drove up with Pix's mother in the back of the car.

'I'll make some coffee, shall I?' said Kate, disappearing tactfully into the kitchen. Clearly she was in one of her best and most cooperative of moods, almost docile if one had not observed the bright alertness of her eyes. She was willing and able to observe and reflect all signals that looks said.

Mary Erskine introduced Pix's mother. 'She's a sort of cousin,' she said nervously. Then she caught Charmian's gaze. 'Well, yes, there are a lot of us.'

'It's pretty remote,' said Pix's mother in a husky voice. 'And not really important.' She was twisting her hands in her lap. 'This is hard for me. My husband thought I shouldn't come.'

'But I told her she should,' said Mary Erskine.

'It's about Pix . . . You know, of course, that he's missing. I don't know how long it can be kept quiet. Not our idea, but the police. We went along with it . . . Had to.' She was taking a long time to get to the point. 'You know how it was with Pix?' She looked at Charmian with inquiry.

'Let me hear from you.'

'He came back from the tea party at the Pagets' on his own. He was pretty late, later than I had thought he would be. I telephoned Mrs Paget and she said he'd gone off with Lily. Some time earlier, she said, and Lily ought to be back soon.' She stopped.

'Go on.'

'I didn't know about Lily then, no one did. But Pix came in

194

late and on his own and said Lily had sent him to walk home by
himself . . . That was a lie, I think . . . He had mud and leaves
on him, so I knew that wasn't all the story. He wasn't telling the
truth. He didn't always. Not lies exactly, just his way of looking
at things.'

Charmian heard Rewley give what sounded like a sceptical
snort.

Pix's mother went on, almost as if she was confessing: 'He was
late back, he was very late back, and I didn't know where he had
been, or what he had been doing. I still don't know, but I think
something bad happened to him then, something he would not
talk about, and that it was connected with his disappearance.
He ran away. Or was taken. I don't know which. It's almost as
if he was summoned away.'

The room was silent. Charmian could hear her own breath.

'He's only a child,' said Pix's mother. 'One knows he couldn't
do anything wrong . . . ' Her eyes pleaded for absolution from
Charmian. 'Nothing really wrong, nothing cruel or violent.'

'And what about now?' asked Charmian, avoiding a direct
answer. 'Have you any idea where he is?'

'We put him to bed, then when I went in later to check, he
was gone . . . We spent the night looking for him.'

Rewley met Charmian's eyes, but he said nothing. He gave a
small shrug: Why did they not go straight to the police? the shrug
was asking. What is it they know or fear?

Pix's mother answered his tacit question: 'We were so frightened, we didn't know what he might have done. We wanted to find
him . . . He has been in such a very strange state lately . . . We
still didn't know about Lily.'

'You think Pix knew about Lily?'

'I think he must have done . . . Known something.' She lifted
her head. 'It's an ugly thought but I'm trying to handle it.'

Mary Erskine put a protective arm around her.

'He is only a child, and he is my child . . . I know he couldn't
have done . . . anything really wrong.'

'We know that,' said Mary Erskine, putting in a protective
comment. 'All of us here know that.'

'Is that all you wanted to say to me,' said Charmian. Kate had
arrived with a tray of coffee and biscuits which she had managed

to find somewhere. Chocolate biscuits and interesting looking. Didn't know I had those, thought Charmian.

She took a cup and handed it to Pix's mother. 'There's more, isn't there?'

'Yes . . . Una Gray said she saw Pix going off.' Her voice held doubt.

'You don't believe her?'

'I believe she saw him, yes. But she said she did not recognise who he was with. I do not believe that . . . I just don't. There is something there I cannot believe. I think she did recognise that person.' Her voice fell away. 'Or something,' she muttered.

'I'll speak to Mrs Gray myself,' said Charmian. 'I can promise you that. But I'll have to choose my moment.'

'Thank you.'

'And do you have any idea who Mrs Gray might have recognised?'

'No.'

'Or why she chooses to lie?'

'No.' A shake of the head. 'I can't say.'

Or won't say, thought Charmian. I'm not sure if I believe all this.

Charmian said: 'Why did you ask to speak to me? To me, specially?'

'I didn't think the other police officers would understand.'

'But you thought I would?'

'I wanted to speak to a woman.'

'I see.'

'I feel we are surrounded by a dark sea of misunderstanding and lies.'

Three reasons when one would have been enough, thought Charmian. Which was the real one?

At the door, as the two women left, Mary Erskine said: 'It's the St Catherine's Jubilee tomorrow. So I shall see you.' The thought seemed to worry her.

'I shall be there,' Charmian said.

After the two women had gone, Charmian said to Rewley: 'What did you make of that?'

'Not telling much.'

196

'She's brought to the surface something that we've been thinking all along. And very brave of her, too. She is frightened that Pix might be the killer.'

'You've been thinking that way, I don't know that I have. It's hard to see a kid of his age as doing those particular murders.'

'I've known some vicious child killers,' said Charmian. 'Not all of whom were caught. People like you couldn't believe it then either. So some of them got away with it. Not all, but some.'

'Is this such a case?'

'I'm thinking about it.'

'You're too much for me sometimes,' said Rewley, allowing himself the ease of approach of almost a son-in-law.

Kate tucked her feet underneath her. 'You two were so busy looking at Pix's mother that you didn't notice the other one.' There was not much love lost between Lady Mary and Kate, they were two of a kind and not disposed to see virtue in each other. 'She's tearing herself to bits. I don't like the lady, although I know the rest of the world loves her, but I felt sorry for her.'

'She's got her troubles,' said Charmian.

'You sound smug.'

'Not really.' Just on the winning side.

'Yes, but look at it. Why did she bring Pix's mother round here? It seems to have been her idea. She came as a kind of chaperone. I think she knows something about these murders and wants to know what you know.'

Clever Kate. 'And do you think she found out?'

'I know I haven't.' Kate got up to pour some more coffee.

Charmian looked at Rewley. 'What's to know?'

He shrugged. 'You've got the diary. No sign of the boy, and no progress on the other cases. It's gone dead.'

'It could revive at any moment,' said Charmian.

'Oh yes. And we have our secret card to play. I think Elman is relying on that.'

They looked at each other. Both knew what this secret card was.

'I just hope it doesn't let him down,' said Rewley.

'What's the prognosis?'

'Touch and go. It could go either way.'

Kate poured some more coffee for them both. 'Here, drink

this, it's bitter and strong . . . I hate it when you two talk in riddles.'

On the doorstep, when Kate had gone ahead to the car, Rewley said to Charmian: 'Oh, by the way, that query you wanted put through on a Philip Carteret . . . No record under that name, but he matches the description of Adrian Caithness who sometimes calls himself Philip or Peter. A record of clever cons. Did time for one.'

'So I got that right.'

Rewley did not meet her eyes. 'Specialises in lonely ladies,' he said.

'Really?' Charmian was cross. She didn't look like a lonely lady. Or did she?

'And there is a rumour that he might have done away with his wife.'

CHAPTER TWENTY

The rains stopped for St Catherine's celebratory day, which started with a gathering in a marquee erected for the occasion on the big front lawn, this was for all Old Boys (and girls, who felt they were regarded more as honorary boys which annoyed some and pleased others), together with the parents of present pupils and local dignitaries. The current pupils were herded into the school hall under the eye of the deputy head to await the arrival of those superior beings who would grace the platform. The less important guests were seated in an annexe where they would see and hear by means of a TV screen. In spite of the stern eyes of Miss Coalshanks, the deputy head, there was a subdued din in the hall. But being a fair woman, she recognised that her charges were bored, and she would only inflict punishments if the noise got out of hand.

She reckoned that she was about ten minutes off this necessity. She looked at her watch, Luke had better got on with it.

In the marquee, which together with the TV equipment had been donated by a rich former pupil, Luke cast an eye over the platform contingent which he had gathered together like a sheepdog and which showed signs of slipping away.

He wanted to get this day over in peace. Police activities were continuing and he knew it. There had been an unobtrusive but intensive search of the school buildings for Pix or traces of him. No sign. Like Inspector Elman he knew that they could not keep the lid on this affair much longer.

At the moment he wished passionately that the Board had not asked Charmian Daniels to be one of the principal speakers. You can have too much of the police. As it was he could hardly bear to meet her eye.

As a matter of fact, it had been his mother who had issued the invitation to Charmian, and he could not bear to meet her eyes either. She was having an animated and apparently happy conversation with Charmian Daniels at this very moment. How could she? They could be bankrupt and the school closed any minute. It didn't bear thinking about. Of course, Ma had her little nest egg, which was probably quite a big nest egg, as she was clever with money, but he did not count on that for himself. She held on to the money bags, did Mamma.

He was not in the know about the police diary, but if he had known he would have been pretty sure that he figured in it.

As he did: the headmaster of St Catherine's, Lucas Mallet, had no significant information. School said to be in debt. Bills are paid but slowly. Said to be something of a womaniser. A few names were listed here.

His mother had her hand on Charmian Daniels' arm and was leading her forward towards the hall.

Oh bugger, he said inside himself, he hated days when his mother took the bit between her teeth and was in charge. He was head now, she had retired, she forgot that and only remembered it when it suited her.

As Mrs Mallet made her regal entrance on Charmian's arm, the assembled school stood up, the choir-mistress waved her baton and the school anthem arose to the ceiling. Whether Luke liked or not, the celebration was under way.

One and a half hours later, the proceedings drew to an end. Luke had spoken, the distinguished Old Boy had spoken, the Mayor had addressed the gathering and Charmian, observing Una Gray seated among the teaching staff, was winding the morning up with a crisp, neat speech.

She was still speaking.

Luke, from his vantage point on the platform, surveyed the room. They looked a harmless lot, but he knew from bitter experience that his parents numbered among them several powerful organisers with access to the media in all its forms, nor did he forget cable television, although heaven forbid that the troubles of St Catherine's should be flashed around the globe. Money and influence sat there. He had to hope they were still on his side. Too much to hope that a rumour, several rumours, were not roaring around them.

Charmian was drawing to an end, she was on her last sentence, she was asking for the day's holiday as arranged beforehand between her and Luke and as eagerly expected by the pupils and more morosely by their fee-paying parents.

But it was done and an appreciative hum arose from the body of the school. She was a good speaker, Luke admitted. Brisk and not boring. Who could ask for more?

It would have been a happy day if it wasn't for this terrible cloud hanging over them. The money didn't matter, he'd manage, he always had, but murder did matter.

There was a buffet lunch for all in the marquee, pupils included, with champagne for the platform party and decent white wine for the lesser mortals. Both wine and food were excellent, provided by a former pupil who had gone in for catering and was doing very well.

The waitresses had been recruited locally but some had come from Cheasey, so there would be a bit of pilfering, but that had been allowed for in the price.

Charmian ate her lunch, then detached herself from Mrs Mallet and the Distinguished Old Boy, both of whom showed a desire to hang on to her and ask questions, and made herself a free agent.

She looked over the crowd. Neither the Pagets nor Pix's family were present but she had not expected they would be. Lady Mary was in one corner of the tent, wearing a smart silk suit and several rows of pearls, drinking champagne while talking with animation to a group of parents. Private unhappiness was not going to wear a public face, the Erskines did not behave like cowards. Una Gray was by the entrance, on her own. Charmian started to move towards her.

Luke saw what Charmian was doing and cut across her path. 'Wanted to say thank you. You did us proud.'

'I was glad to do it.'

'As you can imagine, this isn't a very happy time for us here. I don't suppose you have any news for us?'

Charmian shook her head.

'Of course, the only good news would be to find the boy,' said Luke heavily. 'No, that would be the best news. Good news would be finding the killer.'

He hesitated before going on: 'The police don't think that Minette . . . ? No, I can't ask you and you couldn't say anyway . . . '

'How is Minette?' Charmian said.

'Much calmer, more herself every day. The police have interviewed her, you know, questions about what she saw and that sort of thing. A couple of them, Inspector Elman and a woman sergeant. Rather nice to her. Didn't act as if they thought she was guilty of killing anyone. Took some of her clothes away and asked if she'd mind providing specimens. She didn't mind, poor girl. They had a doctor to look at her. Asked permission, of course. I think he might have been a police psychiatrist . . . He didn't say much. She ought to go home, but they asked her to stay until . . . ' he hesitated. 'Until the inquests are over.'

The inquest on Louise Farmer and that on Ted Gray had both been adjourned with minimal publicity. Luke did not know what was going on about Lily.

'I'm looking after Minette,' he said. 'And of course, we are all doing what we can for Una. I feel so sorry for her, her misery seems to drag on and on.' He looked across the room. 'There she is, all by herself, just moping. And I can't seem to help her. She's one of my closest and dearest friends.'

'Friendship is a lot but it isn't everything,' said Charmian. 'Sometimes you need something stronger.'

'You don't sound like a police officer when you say that.'

'I'm a woman too.'

Una saw them looking at her, she gave a bleak smile.

'I'd like to talk to her,' said Charmian.

'Don't say too much about the boy then,' warned Luke. 'Last straw for her, the lad going, God help him.'

'There's been a search here, I suppose?' In fact, she knew there had been and no result.

'We had a trio of plain-clothes police here yesterday,' said Luke, still looking at Una. 'Didn't find anything. This secrecy thing seems pointless. The kids here all know. Not supposed to know but they do. Especially when one of them asked the Head of Day School (who's as bright as they come, I may say), if the boys had any special place.'

'And have they?'

'Of course. Staff aren't supposed to know but we do know. So we showed them the boys' hiding place and the girls' hiding place. Not the same, you know, gender operates there. The girls like the Play House. Clean, dry, you can draw the curtains.'

'And the boys?'

'The old bicycle shed, muddy, dirty and cold, but that's it,' he said briefly. 'No sign there, of course.'

Across the room, he saw Mrs Mallet addressing a small, plump man with white hair, she appeared to be about to beat him with her hand. 'Oh there's mother attacking the MP about the poll tax. He isn't even our member, I must go and stop her. Do excuse me.' And he hurried off.

Charmian walked across to Una Gray, just catching her as Una tried to escape through the door. But she stopped politely for Charmian.

'I ought to say to you what a splendid speech you made, but the truth is I didn't hear a word of it. I couldn't concentrate.'

'I've been more or less warned off talking to you by Luke Mallet, but on the other hand, Pix's mother thinks I ought to talk to you.'

'I don't know why.'

'You did see the boy going off with someone. She thinks you know who it was.'

Una was silent.

'Supposing I made a guess, and that if pressed, you would say it was Minette you saw.'

Una took a deep breath and turned her head away. 'Yes, it was Minette,' she said. 'And I wish you didn't know. How did you?'

'Just a good guess,' said Charmian. 'You ought to tell Luke.'

'How can I?'

'But you'll have to,' said Charmian firmly. 'And the police. I know it means coming into the open, but it'll have to be done.'

'I was probably wrong. How could it be Minette? I wish I hadn't let you say that. I shall deny it,' muttered Una. 'I'm going home now.'

'Yes, you'll be better there. Shall I get Mary Erskine to go with you?'

'I don't think she wants to be too near me, she thinks I'm bad luck and I suppose I am.'

The small in-group was breaking up, driven apart by murder and suspicion. They might still be kin but soon they would not be friends.

'I'll drive you home, I'm just on the way,' said Charmian.

'I'll walk, thank you.'

Charmian let her go, and then departed herself, saying a few polite goodbyes as she went. Forget Ted and Una and their neuroses and psychoses, she thought as she drove. Don't bother about them. Think what really happened and who died.

Luke Mallet watched both of them leave, and saw Charmian talk to a boy on the way to the car.

Damn, he thought, somehow I smell trouble there. I wonder if I ought to follow her?'

FILOFACE

4

Speculative but probable that the disappearance of the boy Peter Prescott can be linked to attack on Lily Paget.

1 Killer known to the boy.
2 If this is so, then equally the boy is known to the killer.
3 Suggests killer part of the circle which links Farmer, Paget and Prescott families.
4 Focus on schools.
5 Sex of killer: no clear indication. Is there a third sex?

CHAPTER TWENTY-ONE

On the way out, Charmian saw one of the older boys. He had a charming, intelligent face. The sort of face she was looking for. You could talk to a face like that and you might get something back. She had learned in her career to watch for such faces.

'Can you show me the way to the car park?' she asked.

'Yes, it's over this way.' He pointed across the cross to the belt of trees. He looked down at her shoes, expensive and pale. His mother had trained him about shoes. 'It's jolly wet on the grass though, I'll show you the path.'

'Thank you.' She let him show her along the gravelled path. A helpful, polite boy, anxious to be obliging. 'You were leading the choir, weren't you?'

'Yes.' He bounced along beside her cheerfully. 'I'd like to have gone to the St George's Chapel choir school, I auditioned for it, but I haven't really got that good a voice. I can sight-read though.' He pointed. 'Here we are.'

It was still early to leave, no one around, which suited Charmian.

'That looks like an old bicycle shed,' she said, as if she had not seen it before. 'I remember one like that at my school.'

'That's right.' He gave her an alert, wary look. 'Course, we don't use it now, we've got a better one over the other side where the bikes can be locked up. Most people get collected by car, anyway.'

Sign of the times, thought Charmian.

'Does look a rundown old shed. I heard you had a tramp living in it.'

'Yes.' Another careful look at her face. 'The police came and took him away. They knew him. They would, wouldn't they?' He drew away a step, as if Charmian was in dangerous territory.

'Doesn't seem too comfortable, I'm surprised he chose the place. And didn't he get hungry?'

206

The lad looked at her with bright eyes. 'I expect he brought food with him. Or he could go out at night and get some. He must have been used to managing, mustn't he?'

For some reason, I am amusing him, Charmian reacted. 'You'd better get back. Thank you for showing me the way.'

He nodded, gave her a shy smile and sped away, and she thought he seemed glad to go.

She waited until he was out of sight, then inspected the old cycle shed. She had been in it once before and it remained now what it had been then, a gloomy, cold and muddy spot. An unlikely resting place for any knowledgeable tramp. She had to assume the tramp was a sensible fellow.

She considered making a closer inspection, but she was wearing a good silk suit from Caroline Charles, which she was not prepared to sacrifice, not to mention those pale kid shoes of which the boy had been so protective. This was a jeans and boots job.

Also there was an inquiry to be made first.

But her immediate need was to go straight back to her office where her new stand-in secretary was already at work.

She was followed, at a discreet distance, by another car but she was too abstracted to notice this because she was wondering about the shed. It had possibilities, she thought.

She hung up the jacket of her silk suit, looked at her face in the glass, a bit flushed, and turned to where her new secretary sat.

He was a stocky young man with ambitions that were still ranging wide and free so that they might take him anywhere. He knew the background to his temporary secondment here and was not hitching his wagon to Charmian's star in case she did not survive. But meanwhile, he greeted her politely and with a smile. He meant to work hard.

Charmian smiled back as she settled herself at her desk. 'Any messages?' Hard-working and knows where he's going, but might run into the wall before he gets there, had been the unofficial comment passed on to her with his arrival. Not by Diana whose nominee he was, but by George Rewley.

'Nothing important.'

She dictated several letters, wrote a memorandum for the benefit of a colleague, made an appointment to see one of her most powerful backers and patrons (this might be important and she wanted to state her case first if it came to a fight), then settled down to read some reports.

She read them with her customary concentration and attention to detail but underneath she was thinking: events had happened with such speed and complexity that it was hard to form a picture. Sort out the elements, she told herself. Make a catalogue of who and why and where.

Ted Gray, the man who wasn't there, who sent messages and indicated meeting places but never kept the promise to be there. Ted Gray who was thought to have put out a contract on his wife with a Cheasey boy and then killed the boy by running him down in a car when he refused the contract.

Ted Gray who was thought to have killed Louise Farmer but who did not, because he was dead himself. Ted Gray who had bought a shotgun, and had left his London office carrying it in a sports bag but had not killed himself with it, appearances to the contrary.

Ted Gray, who was central to the whole train of events, but by his absence more than anything else. Ted, whom I never got to know, she thought, because he was dead before I came on the scene. Know thy victim.

Where had Ted Gray been at all the crucial times? He was a missing man in more ways than one.

And Una, what about Una Gray whom Ted had wanted to have killed? The wife who received the messages from her husband, who met the trains he was never on, but who found the jacket of a murdered girl in a kitchen cupboard.

Associated with all this was the story of the boy Pix, who saw people where they were not, who feared the walking dead, and who had now disappeared after being in the company of the second girl to be attacked. Lily Paget, the close friend of Louise.

And what about Minette? Just one of the hysterics who are known to hang about the edges of any major crime investigation, sometimes confessing to what they are not guilty of, was this her part? If so, poor girl, but she had certainly muddied the waters. The forensic tests on her clothes might clarify the position of Minette.

Ted and Una Gray, Lady Mary Erskine, cousins and kindred,

Luke Mallet and Minette, that group of intimates, all related one way and another, well born if you could still use that phrase certainly well connected and with some money. But each with their secrets. Una, the child whose very existence was hidden, and Ted who had been brought up as an orphan. Drawn together by what they had had done to them.

She tried again: she began to let a picture form in her mind. Imagine a man, on bad terms with his wife. A man called Gray whom a girl, Louise Farmer, thought was responsible for the death of the boy she loved. A man whose address she had discovered and for which knowledge she might have been killed herself.

That was the true beginning to it all: with Ted Gray, the enigma.

Ted, whatever did you do, except plan to kill your wife, that got you killed yourself?

Did the plan go wrong? Was the wrong person killed?

She sat looking at her hands, flexing the fingers as if they ached. She remembered how she had got into trouble once for telling a childish lie and her mother had rapped her fingers. What was the nursery precept: Oh what a tangled web you weave when first you practise to deceive. With luck, and they had had one piece of luck, it might be possible to unravel the tangle. Pix was in that maze somewhere and had to be found.

She was interrupted by a phone call.

'Hello, Rewley?'

What she got was a bombshell. 'The newsmen have got into the hospital. A TV reporter and cameraman. Don't know how they did it or how they knew to but it's happened.'

Charmian was calm about it, more Elman's problem than hers, and anyway she had expected it. 'It was bound to happen sooner or later.'

'Doesn't really help,' said Rewley. 'We're holding them, of course, but we'll have to let them out soon.' And all the news channels would be buzzing. Fred Elman might have been too clever by half with his blanket of silence.

'I think things are breaking in any case. I've been at St Catherine's. You know the school was searched for the boy. What can you tell me?'

209

'I wasn't one of the search team but I know about it. They didn't find anything.'

'Did they ask if any food was missing from the school kitchens?'

There was a pause before he answered. 'I see what you are getting at, but if food had gone it would have alerted the school at once.'

'Possibly. Possibly not. The tramp who was living in the shed there for a bit may have lifted food. And the boys may have known. They may know now. They know something.' She had a quiet conviction on that point. 'I'd like to talk to that tramp. Any ideas where to find him?'

'None,' said Rewley promptly. 'But if he was taken in, try the Albert Road station, they cover that area. They'll probably know him if he's a local, you know how it is. Mind you, they move around these chaps. But the Albert Road mob are your best bet. They may not have him, but they will know where to ask.'

'Thanks.'

'What are you on to?' He knew her, she had something on the boil.

'Just trying something on for size.'

He wished he could read her voice, but he could not. If he could have seen her face, now that would have been different, he could read faces and lips. 'There's a lot of neuroses floating around,' he said. 'Nothing quite straight.'

'Perhaps we've been looking at events the wrong way round. Seeing what wasn't there. Or seeing it upside down.'

'Like the kid with his fantasies? They need a psychiatrist that lot, as I said.'

Forget the talk of neuroses and psychiatrists, Charmian told herself as she drove away. Ask yourself what really took place.

Wearing jeans and a sweater, Charmian presented herself at the Albert Road station; even thus attired, they recognised her. There was mild surprise at her arrival, but she was greeted with polite helpfulness. They knew how to behave at Albert Road.

The desk sergeant identified whom she wanted at once. 'Oh, that was Arthur. We all know Arthur. He turns up everywhere.'

'I'd like to speak to him, if I co ld.'

'You're in luck: we've got Arthur in a cell. He's got a bad chest, has Arthur, and he always tries to be inside when the weather's wet and windy. Broke several windows yesterday, Arthur did, and the magistrate took pity on him and gave him a week.' He got up. 'Come this way, ma'am, and mind your feet. The stairs are a mite uneven. We had a lady fall down them last week.'

Arthur, a small, grey-haired man who claimed to be a 'Fifth Army man and was at Alamein with Monty', seemed pleased to see Charmian. He liked company and never minded answering questions. It was a lonely life on the road, and although he would have no other, he was partial to a bit of conversation when it offered.

He remembered his sojourn in the cycle shed.

'Not a very comfortable hole,' suggested Charmian.

He shrugged. 'It suited. I had my dog with me then,' he said. 'He's dead now. Bad chest like me. We ought to have gone together.'

'You'll be around for ages yet, Arthur,' said the local sergeant heartily. 'We're feeding you up.'

'Didn't you find food a bit difficult there?' asked Charmian.

'There was always food about,' said Arthur vaguely.

'It's a cold, muddy, damp hole,' said Charmian. 'Come on, Arthur. Tell, I want to know where you really were.'

'Ah.' Arthur gave a sly smile. 'That's my secret . . . But I might want to go back, see.'

Charmian looked at the sergeant.

'I'll just get us all a cup of tea,' he said tactfully.

As soon as he'd closed the door, Charmian produced a five-pound note. 'I think it's worth ten,' said Arthur judicially.

She had been followed from her office to her home, and then on to Albert Road, and she was followed now.

This time, Charmian had a consciousness of someone behind her and considered it, but there was no one as she got out of the car so she shrugged it off. Ahead of her she could see the school buildings of St Catherine's with the marquee so recently the scene of the party still visible to one side. It was getting dark and there were no lights in the school building. Even Luke's flat was blind.

She walked across the grass to the old cycle shed; she was on a voyage of discovery. She could have asked Rewley to come, she could have brought her dog, but it might all be a mistake, there might be nothing here to find.

She took a torch out of her pocket and entered the shed. It was long and low and the roof seemed to close in upon you as you went in, making it difficult for an adult to stand upright. A child, of course, would have had no difficulty.

She bent her head and walked forward. There were the old wooden racks meant to hold the cycles in place, one or two had fallen to bits. One even held the remains of an ancient rusted object that had once had wheels. Behind the racks was the wall, and you could see that this hut had originally been meant for something, storage perhaps.

At the rear a bit of sacking hung on the wall. Charmian drew the sacking away and behind it was a wooden door. Small but stout.

This was the real entrance to the 'boys' place', their hidy-hole. Here was where Arthur had tucked himself away.

She put her hand on the door and pushed. She had the impression that a light was doused as the door moved. It had opened slightly but there was resistance. Inside there was blackness and the strong old smell of potatoes. So that was what had been stored there once. It had been a storage place for winter root vegetables. The boys probably ate frozen peas now.

'Pix? Are you there?'

I may be making a fool of myself, a complete and utter fool, she thought.

A figure came up behind her.

'What are you doing here?'

She turned the torch on his face. 'Luke!'

'You shouldn't be here on your own,' he said.

'I did think of bringing my dog, but I decided against it . . . Has this place ever been a gardener's shed?'

He didn't answer, but put up a hand and turned the torch away from his face. 'Don't point at me . . . What's that door?'

'You ought to know, Luke, it's your school.' She turned towards the door, wondering if it was safe to turn her back on him. 'Did you follow me here?'

'Follow? No. I saw the light and came to see.'

Charmian said: 'I think Pix is in here. He may be dead, but I believe he is alive.'

She pushed the door wide open and moved the torch slowly round. It shone on a sack spread out on the floor, a blanket and a small figure huddled against the wall.

'Come on out, Pix, I saw your eyes move.' There was no movement. 'I am Charmian Daniels, I am a police officer. Behind me is Luke Mallet, your headmaster. Come on, Pix, we want you.'

The figure detached itself from the shadows and moved forward. Pix came out of the door and Charmian got her arms round him and together they came out of the shed to where Luke was standing outside.

'My God, Pix,' he said. 'What have you been up to? You've certainly put us through it.'

There was someone else there behind him, a dark shape which started to run into the shadows.

Luke turned round: 'Who's there?'

'I think you'd better catch her.'

'Catch her? Who is it?'

'You'll know when you see her face,' said Charmian drily.

CHAPTER TWENTY-TWO

Pix put his hand inside hers in a tentative, shy gesture. She held it firmly, giving it a reassuring squeeze. 'Come on, you villain. No one's going to hurt you. It's time to put all your ghosts to rest.'

They walked out on to the grass. The rain had stopped, the air felt fresh and clean.

On the gravelled path there were two figures. 'It's all right,' called Luke. 'It's only Una.'

'That's right,' said Charmian. 'Only Una.'

Luke had his arm round Una in a protective way. 'Poor old thing,' he was saying. 'Don't cry.'

'Face her, Pix,' said Charmian.

Pix tried to move behind Charmian. 'No, no, don't want to.'

She steadied him. 'She can't hurt you, Pix. It's all over.'

'What's this? What do you mean?' Luke held on to Una. 'This is Una.'

'Yes, Una. It takes a woman to understand a deviousness so horrible.' She held Pix firmly against her, sheltering him with her body, she could feel him tremble. She had never had a child, but she knew now what it was to love a child, to protect and comfort it. It was like sex, press the right parts of the body and the feelings swept over you. In this moment and for this moment, perhaps only for this moment, she loved Pix. 'You can never be forgiven for what you did to this child. If there is a hell, you are in it now.'

'What are you saying?' said Luke.

'Tell us what she did, Pix, when you saw her going towards where her car was parked when she was supposed to be in the Play House letting you all have that freedom time Luke liked you to have.' The wind blew a mist of rain across her

214

face, unconsciously her voice rose. 'Free, but keeping an eye on you from where she sat behind drawn curtains. Only she wasn't there, was she, she'd crept through the door behind the Play House and away, as you knew, Pix, because you saw her in the distance.'

Louise Farmer had been strangled in the car in the car park. Charmian didn't know on what pretext Una had got her there, but it might not have been difficult. Possibly just a simple invitation to meet her there.

'Una!' said Luke. 'Answer her, of course you were in school. This is all part of Pix's fantasy, this woman has caught it too. Pix, this is rubbish, speak up.'

'I thought I saw her in the Play House, I saw her head and the green overall.'

'There you are,' said Luke, 'let's stop this game.'

'A papier-mâché head,' said Charmian. 'A broomstick figure, Pix.'

'No deaders walking? I dream about deaders. No double people?'

Something real and pitiful in the boy's voice got through to Luke and his arm dropped away from Una's shoulders. 'Una . . . No, you couldn't have . . . ' He turned to Pix as if he didn't know what to say. 'Child . . . ' he began.

'Oh we can use the words murder and death and deception in front of this child,' said Charmian harshly. 'Because she has taught him all about them.'

Luke faced Una. 'For God's sake, say something Una.'

Una found her voice. 'A deranged child and a stupid woman. They are making me their victim.'

'Pix is your victim, the boy Rivers was your victim, Ted was your victim, Lily Paget was your victim.'

'Prove it.'

'Oh we will prove it, we have a witness . . . No, Lily Paget is not dead and she will be able to talk.'

Una stood still for a moment, then she swung round and began to run. Away into the rain and the night.

'Don't go after her, Luke. She'll be caught.' Dead or alive, thought Charmian. There was always the river. In the distance, she heard a car start up.

215

'Why, why?' said Luke. 'What did she do it for? What did she want?'

'You, Luke, you were the prize.'

And the school, and the status it would give her, but most of all you, Luke, with your beautiful face.

She put her arms round Pix. 'Come on, I'm going to take you home. Cheer up, you did well.'

'What about . . . ' he hesitated. 'You know, the people who walk about . . . ' He lowered his voice to a whisper. 'Dead and alive.'

'The person you saw was not dead, Pix.'

'But if someone could be in two – one part of them would be dead, she said so.'

She said so, she said so, thought Charmian vindictively. Una deserved whatever she got.

'No, no ghosts, Pix,' she said gently. 'Trust me. No bad dreams.' She thought he did relax his guard, but it would take a long, long while, perhaps for ever.

That was almost the worst of Una's crimes.

Only Una rushing through the night, pushing against the wind, stumbling in the mud, knew that death was in her blood. That blood which would not mix with Ted's so that no child could be born of their union. Her unknown father's gift to her, she thought as she ran, that rhesus factor.

'His fault and Ted's,' she said to herself between gasps as she ran. Ted had to die since he would not divorce and then she could have lovely, loving Luke and all those children to love and punish and to train. It was in the blood.

Blood group AB, rhesus factor e.

Before Charmian could take Pix home, she made a brief call to the Incident Room where she spoke to Fred Elman. A prickly call since he resented her interference while being grateful for what she had achieved. But he minded his words, because Charmian was winning all her battles and he knew it.

'Yes,' he said, 'yes, ma'am. Thank you. We'll put an alert out for her.'

'I think she will go home,' said Charmian, 'and try to bluff it out. I'm warning you.' Later, having delivered Pix to his parents and sent Luke back to tell his mother, she crawled round to the sane company of Rewley and Kate. It was well after midnight and Rewley had only just got home before her.

'Restore me.'

Over a drink, they did their best, Kate even removing the mud which Pix had distributed over her face. She must have embraced him, but she didn't remember.

'He was hiding, poor little beast. Terrified, thought Una would kill him . . . some of the other boys knew where he was, I believe, and helped him. He's respected as a thinker, is Pix.'

'I think he's brave,' said Kate.

'I think we're all brave, just to go on living.' It could be a horrible, dangerous world.

'So it was Luke she wanted.'

'Money too,' Charmian said sipping her drink. 'She could have divorced Ted if she'd waited, but she wanted his money now so that she could buy her way into Luke's heart and school. She knew he needed liquid cash.' Always would, she suspected, and would always find it. And Luke was not one to wait around, someone would snap him up.

'Thank God I'm poor,' said Rewley, but he gave his Kate a confident smile. 'But I'm glad it's over. It was giving me nightmares.'

'You thought it was the boy.'

'Not really, he wasn't a freak, but I did think he might have been in there somewhere.'

'Thank God, not,' said Charmian, who had had her own dark fears. 'But he was used, as others were. Ted Gray himself for instance. It was not by chance he found Louise's body, I bet Una half confessed and dispatched him to find her . . . What a marriage. She was a monster. Made one, if not born one. No wonder her husband became frightened of her and tried to buy a gun. And he was right to be frightened.'

The picture of the victims kneeling . . . Suddenly it was vivid and horrible. Lily Paget had described how she had run to help Una, who appeared to have fallen down, only to find herself on her knees and being strangled. Una must have used the same technique with both the others. Ted she shot with his own gun, Lily she did not quite succeed in strangling, Lily was unconscious, and while unconscious was driven to be dumped in the Great Park, but she did not die.

'I wonder how much Una contributed to Minette's state of mind,' said Charmian. 'I think she may have fed stuff into that girl.'

Pix had added his mite of information. 'He started to talk a bit, once he got home, which was good,' Charmian told them. 'There's a lot still to come out from him. He said he watched Lily, followed her instead of going straight home. He wanted to know what she was going to do. She had said she was going to do something. Talk to Una, she now says, she didn't exactly suspect her, but she remembered that Louise only had the name and address in Chapel Close and had not actually said it was Ted Gray. They had both assumed it was Ted who had taken out the contract to kill, but Lily started to wonder. Pix followed, saw Lily claim her bike and meet her friends. Then he says he saw Una move the bike and hide it. He was frightened she had seen him, and ran home.'

'But he didn't stay there,' said Rewley.

'No, in the middle of the night he decided that what he had seen meant something bad for Lily and he'd be safer in hiding.'

'I don't think I've come across a more cold-blooded killer,' said Rewley. 'She used everyone.'

'Me included,' said Charmian. 'Or she tried to. Una would rather not have got her own hands dirty, but when the Rivers boy failed her, she mowed him down in her car. Pure fury, I suppose.'

'Self-protection,' said Rewley.

'That too, but mad, bad and dangerous to know, our Una. That first death started a chain of others. But it was Ted who was the primary victim.'

'Funny business about meeting at the station,' said Rewley.

'There were no such messages, Una invented all that. To understand all that you had to invert it: the trips to the station . . . we speculated that they got her out of the house, so that Ted could get up to whatever he wanted in the house after murdering the girl. Hide the jacket for instance. But what they really did was to give Una the chance to say yes, that was what he did, the house was empty, he hid Louise's jacket, he was guilty. It worked both ways.'

218

'What put you on to her?'

'It began to get clearer and clearer.'

'Not to Elman, he was still putting his beef on Minette for the girls and Brian Farmer for Ted Gray. But the forensics wouldn't help him. They will now, of course. The blood alone will tell.'

'He'd have got there in the end,' said Charmian tolerantly. She had won and she knew it.

'I doubt it, I bet he's really miserable now.'

'All he had to ask himself was who was the most important victim, and once you saw it was Ted Gray himself, you saw the whole thing.'

'I don't know if I did,' said Rewley. 'And Elman certainly didn't.'

'I was always worried by Una, but I was confused by the behaviour of the girl Minette. Not to mention Pix himself. He was terrified of Una. But Una kept wanting to talk to me. That worried me. I think she wanted to incriminate Minette . . . Later, of course, she was desperate to lay hands on Pix himself, that's why she followed me. She saw me talking to one of his friends and guessed I might have a clue where he was.'

'That kid was out of his mind . . . He needs help to get over this.'

'He will tell his mother, I expect. He trusts her. Not many people he trusts, but he does trust her.'

'If Gray had kept quiet, then she might have got away with it. Elman liked her, you know, didn't think she was in it.'

'I don't think she was a compulsive confessor,' said Charmian, 'not like Minette. But there is always a tremendous need to unburden yourself, even by telling a lie.'

'Why did Ted Gray come back?' asked Kate. 'He wanted to run away, that was why he went to London.'

'It is hard to understand,' said Charmian. 'But I think he loved her and so when she summoned him, as I think she must have done, he came back, she met him in the car, then drove him to the park where she shot him.'

'Where is she now?' asked Rewley. 'I take it you've got that in hand?'

'Elman's in charge of all that. She'll be picked up. There was a police car in Chapel Close, I drove round that way to get a look.'

'Do you think she'll try suicide?'

'Not her. Hire a good lawyer, that's her style,' said Charmian crisply. 'But the forensics will get her . . . blood match with luck, the skin traces on the jacket. The chalk and the cord she used, they can be traced. I expect she wore gloves at all times but gloves can leave prints too.'

'What about Luke?' It was Rewley's question. 'Will he hang on to Minette?' He himself had found Minette very appealing. He could see her with Pix. Pure jealousy as well as expediency would have been enough.

'He's in a state of shock,' said Charmian. 'Sex is the last thing on his mind.' Although that would not last for long.

'He's quite a dish,' said Kate thoughtfully.

Rewley shook his head. 'Now, now.' He got up to pour Charmian some more coffee. He could see she was more shaken than she wanted to admit. Not like her, either. Something to do with the boy, he could read that far.

'They'll all cling together, that group,' said Kate. 'Lady Mary and Luke Mallet and the Prescotts.' Being herself the daughter of new money and bohemian ways, she had some scorn for what was left of the scions of the old nobility.

'I don't know about Mary Erskine,' said Charmian. 'She's got her own troubles.'

Even as she spoke those words, Mary Stuart Dalmeny Erskine was refusing an offer of marriage from Alexander Prescott.

'No, it's no good, Alex, you're a marvellous man but it wouldn't do. I'm older than you and there might be a court case coming up . . . Delphine Gillon . . . No, drugs, Alex. It wouldn't do your career the least bit of good, the army wouldn't like it.' Alex was murmuring about giving up the army. 'No, no, it wouldn't work. You love it, it's your life, and we haven't more than tuppence ha'penny between us.'

He took her hand.

'You were great to stay with me while I was with Una tonight.'

'Mary . . . '

'No, Alex, I'm trouble and probably always will be. You're better without me.'

But she let a tear drop down as he kissed him goodbye and

closed her front door behind her. He wasn't a prince but she could have settled for him.

Neither of them had mentioned Una, although they both knew what had happened. Mary had stayed with Una until the police took her away and Alex had supported her, although his face was white when he picked up the details about his step-brother Pix.

Mary let thoughts and pictures form. The bruises on Una's arm, not from an attack by Ted, but given by Ted in self-defence. Poor Ted, who had prayed because he knew his wife had killed Louise Farmer. No one had told Mary but she understood that Ted had not found the girl's body by chance or coincidence. No, he had come home from London and Una had confessed to the killing and sent him down to find the body.

She always meant to involve Ted, get him some way, Mary thought, and Ted knew it which is why he tried to run away and hide. Una followed him there to his office, I bet. It was a lie that she didn't know where he was. And then he came back because she asked him to, spun some yarn.

I ought to have guessed when she told me how young Louise was. She had seen that girl when dead.

We're bad blood, she thought, and then, Una was terribly damaged by the way she was brought up, you've got to remember that. She's damned, though, and so is Delphine. I hope I am not.

She would have liked to drag Charmian Daniels into the ring of damnation too, but she could not quite bring herself to do so, because she recognised a heart of goodness there.

She had one last terrible thought: had Una killed Netta too?

Charmian stirred her coffee, and considered Rewley. Should she tell him now? Should she say: I have spoken to the Powers That Be and I have told them that I need an investigating unit of my own. There may be cases when I will want to initiate my own independent inquiries. This has been accepted. I am asking for you to be transferred and one other person, possibly Dolly Barstow. You will get promotion to Inspector . . . He would like that. But she'd have to sell it to him. He was independent. She put down her coffee-cup. 'I'd better be off. Thanks for your support, you two . . . I'd like to have a word with you some time, Rewley. There's something I want to tell you.'

She kissed Kate and drove where her cat Muff awaited her with anxious pacing tread. You are too late out, said her walk.

She fed the cat, took a shower and went to bed. Her bedside book was an anthology of Victorian poetry, she was into Browning at the moment and thought she might be working up for a go at Gerard Manley Hopkins, fascinating rhyme schemes, but tonight she ignored it and listened to the radio instead. One war was over, it seemed. But there was probably another one on the make.

Her encounter with the boy had stirred her more than she wanted to admit. Could it be she was a motherly person after all? A nice lad, clever and brave. In his way, he was wise.

She awoke next day feeling alert and cheerful. She would deal with the drugs problem: Lady Mary could stand up and say her piece there. Especially as in Charmian's opinion she had guessed that Una was guilty. No, Lady Mary could expect a tough time from the drug squad.

And as for the letters (another one yesterday, saying the same things) from Humphrey, she would answer when and how it pleased her. It was her game.

Later that evening, as she relaxed with a cat and a drink, the telephone rang.

'Hello.'

A charming male voice. 'Charmian? May I call you Charmian? Philip Carteret here. I am in Windsor, can we meet?'

'Right, Mr Carteret,' she said. 'Why not?'

MYSTERY   Melville, Jennie.
Melville
          Dead set.

$17.95

DATE			

ept